Award-winning, bestselling novelist Gianrico Carofiglio
was born in Bari in 1961 and worked for many years as
a prosecutor specializing in organized crime. He was
appointed advisor of the anti-Mafia committee in the
Italian parliament in 2007 and served as a senator from
2008 to 2013. Carofiglio is best known for the Guido
Guerrieri crime series: *Involuntary Witness, A Walk in the
Dark, Reasonable Doubts, Temporary Perfections* and *A Fine
Line,* all published by Bitter Lemon Press. His other
novels include *The Silence of the Wave.* Carofiglio's books
have sold more than five million copies in Italy and have
been translated into twenty-seven languages worldwide.

ALSO AVAILABLE
FROM BITTER LEMON PRESS
BY GIANRICO CAROFIGLIO

*Involuntary Witness*

*A Walk in the Dark*

*Reasonable Doubts*

*Temporary Perfections*

*The Silence of the Wave*

*A Fine Line*

# THE COLD SUMMER

## Gianrico Carofiglio

Translated by Howard Curtis

**BITTER LEMON PRESS**
**LONDON**

BITTER LEMON PRESS

First published in the United Kingdom in 2018 by
Bitter Lemon Press, 47 Wilmington Square, London WC1X 0ET

www.bitterlemonpress.com

First published in Italian as *L'estate fredda*
by Giulio Einaudi editore, 2016
© Gianrico Carofiglio, 2016

English translation © Howard Curtis, 2018

This edition published by arrangement with
Rosaria Carpinelli Consulenze Editoriali srl.

A CIP record for this book is available from the British Library.

ISBN 978-1912242-030
eBook ISBN: 978-1912242-047

Typeset by Tetragon
Printed and bound in Great Britain by Clays Ltd, St Ives plc

Bitter Lemon Press gratefully acknowledges
the support of the Arts Council of England.

Supported using public funding by

ARTS COUNCIL
ENGLAND

LOTTERY FUNDED

# THE COLD SUMMER

# HISTORICAL NOTE

*The summer of 1992 was exceptionally cold in southern Italy. But that is not the reason why it is still remembered. On 23 May 1992, Giovanni Falcone, his wife Francesca Morvillo and three members of their police escort were killed by a massive bomb placed in a culvert under the A29 highway between Palermo and the international airport, near the town of Capaci. Then, on 19 July 1992, Paolo Borsellino and five members of his police escort were killed by a car bomb in Via D'Amelio in Palermo.*

*Falcone and Borsellino were the two most prominent anti-Mafia prosecutors in Sicily. Their investigations posed a major threat to the Sicilian underworld, especially to the most powerful and feared of the Mafia clans, the Corleonesi. Both murders aroused a massive public outcry throughout Italy and resulted in a major crackdown on the Mafia. Those responsible for the killings, both the bosses and the actual hitmen, were identified, tried and sentenced, with no possibility of parole. Many are still serving their sentences in maximum-security facilities, while others have died in prison. The summer of 1992 would turn out to be the beginning of the end for the Corleonesi clan.*

*At the same time, furious wars were going on in Apulia among the local criminal Mafia gangs, different from the Sicilian ones but equally ferocious.*

*This book is about the Apulian Mafia war.*

# ACT ONE

## Days of Fire

# 1

Fenoglio walked into the Caffè Bohème with the newspaper he'd just bought in his jacket pocket and sat down
at the table by the window. He liked the place because the
owner was a music lover and every day chose a soundtrack
of famous romantic arias and orchestral pieces. That morning, the background was the Intermezzo from *Cavalleria
Rusticana*, and given what was happening in the city,
Fenoglio wondered if it was just coincidence.

The barman made him his usual extra-strong cappuccino and brought it to him together with a pastry filled
with custard and black cherry jam.

Everything was the same as ever. The music was discreet
but quite audible to those who wanted to listen to it. The
regular customers came in and out. Fenoglio ate his pastry,
sipped at his cappuccino and skimmed through the newspaper. The main focus of the local pages was the Mafia war
that had suddenly broken out in the northern districts of
the city and the unfortunate fact that nobody – not the
police, not the Carabinieri, not the judges – had any idea
what was going on.

He started reading an article in which the editor himself, with a profusion of helpful advice, informed the
law enforcement agencies how to tackle and solve the

phenomenon. Finding the article engrossing and irritating in equal measure, he did not notice the young man with the syringe until the latter was already standing in front of the cashier and yelling, in almost incomprehensible dialect, "Give me all the money, bitch!"

The woman didn't move, as if paralysed. The young man held out the hand with the syringe until it was close to her face. In an impressively hoarse voice, he told her he had AIDS and yelled at her again to give him everything there was in the till. She moved slowly, her eyes wide with terror. She opened the till and started taking out the money, while the young man kept telling her to be quick about it.

Fenoglio's hand closed over the robber's wrist just as the woman was passing over the money. The young man tried to jerk round, but Fenoglio made an almost delicate movement – a half turn – twisting his arm and pinning it behind his back. With the other hand, he grabbed him by the hair and pulled his head back.

"Throw away the syringe."

The young man gave a muffled growl and tried to wriggle free. Fenoglio increased the pressure on his arm and pulled his head back even further. "I'm a carabiniere." The syringe fell to the floor with a small, sharp sound.

The cashier began crying. The other customers started to move, slowly at first, then at a normal speed, as if waking from a spell.

"Nicola, call 112," Fenoglio said to the barman, having ruled out the idea that the cashier might be in a fit state to use the telephone.

"Down on your knees," he said to the robber. From the polite tone he used, he might have been expected to add: "Please."

As the young man knelt, Fenoglio let go of his hair but kept hold of his arm, although not roughly, almost as if it were a procedural formality.

"Now lie face down and put your hands together behind your head."

"Don't beat me up," the young man said.

"Don't talk nonsense. Lie down, I don't want to stay like this until the car arrives."

The young man heaved a big sigh, a kind of lament for his misfortune, and obeyed. He stretched out, placing one cheek on the floor, and put his hands on the back of his neck with almost comical resignation.

In the meantime, a small crowd had gathered outside. Some of the customers had gone out and told them what had happened. People seemed excited, as if the moment had come to fight back against the current crime wave. Some were yelling. Two young men walked into the café and made to approach the robber.

"Where are you going?" Fenoglio asked.

"Give him to us," said the more agitated of the two, a skinny, spotty-faced fellow with glasses.

"I'd be glad to," Fenoglio said. "What do you plan to do with him?"

"We'll make sure he doesn't do it again," the skinny fellow said, taking a step forward.

"Have we ever had you down at the station?" Fenoglio asked them, with a smile that seemed friendly.

Taken aback, the man did not reply immediately. "No, why?"

"Because I'll make sure you spend all day there, and maybe all night, too, if you don't get out of here right now."

The two men looked at each other. The spotty-faced young man stammered something, trying not to lose face;

the other shrugged and gave a grimace of superiority, also trying not to lose face. Then they left the café together. The little crowd dispersed spontaneously.

A few minutes later, the Carabinieri cars pulled up outside and two uniformed corporals and a sergeant came into the café and saluted Fenoglio with a mixture of deference and unconscious wariness. They handcuffed the robber and pulled him bodily to his feet.

"I'm coming with you," Fenoglio said, after paying the cashier for the cappuccino and the pastry, heedless of the barman's attempts to stop him.

# 2

"I've seen you somewhere before," Fenoglio said, turning to the back seat and addressing the young man he had just arrested.

"I used to stand near the Petruzzelli in the evening when there was a show on. I parked people's cars. You must have seen me there."

Of course – that was it. Up until a few months earlier he had been an unlicensed car park attendant near the Teatro Petruzzelli. Then the theatre had been destroyed in a fire and he had lost his job. That was how the young man put it: "I lost my job," as if he had been working for a company and they'd dismissed him or closed down. So he'd started selling cigarettes and stealing car radios.

"But you make hardly anything at that. I'm not up to doing burglaries, so I thought I could rob places with the syringe."

"Congratulations, a brilliant idea. And how many robberies have you committed?"

"I haven't committed any, corporal, would you fucking believe it? This was my first one and I had to run into you, for fuck's sake."

"He isn't a corporal, he's a marshal," the carabiniere at the wheel corrected him.

"Sorry, marshal. You aren't in uniform, so I had no idea. I swear it was my first time."

"I don't believe you," Fenoglio said. But it wasn't true. He did believe him, he even liked him. He was funny: his timing when he spoke was almost comical. Maybe in another life he might have been an actor or a stand-up, instead of a petty criminal.

"I swear it. And besides, I'm not a junkie and I don't have AIDS. That was all bullshit. I can't stand needles. If talking bullshit is a crime, then they should give me a life sentence, because I talk a lot of it. But I'm just an idiot. Put in a good word for me in your report, write that I came quietly."

"Yes, you did."

"The syringe was new, you know, I just put a bit of iodine in it to look like blood and to scare people."

"You do talk a lot, don't you?"

"Sorry, marshal. I'm shitting my pants here. I've never been to prison."

Fenoglio had a strong desire to let him go. He would have liked to tell the carabiniere at the wheel: stop and give me the keys to the handcuffs. Free the boy – he still didn't know his name – and throw him out of the car. He had never liked arresting people, and he found the very idea of prison quite disturbing. But that's not something you broadcast when you're a marshal in the Carabinieri. Of course, there were exceptions, for certain crimes, certain people. Like the fellow they'd arrested a few months earlier, who'd been raping his nine-year-old granddaughter – his daughter's daughter – for months.

In that case, it had been hard for him to stop his men from dispensing a bit of advance justice, by way of slaps, punches and kicks. It's tough sometimes to stick to your principles.

It was obvious he couldn't free this young man. That would be an offence – several offences in fact. But similarly absurd ideas went through his head increasingly often. He made a decisive gesture with his hand, as if to dismiss these troublesome thoughts, almost as if they were entities hovering in front of him.

"What's your name?"

"Francesco Albanese."

"And you say you've never been inside?"

"Never, I swear."

"You were obviously good at not getting caught."

The young man smiled. "Not that I ever did anything special. Like I said, a few cigarettes, a few cars, spare parts."

"And I guess you sell a bit of dope, too, am I right?"

"Okay, just a bit, where's the harm in that? You're not arresting me for these things as well now, are you?"

Fenoglio turned away to look at the road, without replying. They got to the offices of the patrol car unit and Fenoglio quickly wrote out an arrest report. He told the sergeant who had come on the scene to complete the papers for the Prosecutors' Department and the prison authorities, and to inform the assistant prosecutor. Then he turned to the robber. "I'm going now. You'll appear before the judge later this morning. When you talk to your lawyer, tell him you want to plea-bargain. You'll get a suspended sentence and you won't have to go to prison."

The young man looked at him with eyes like those of a dog grateful to its master for removing a thorn from its paw. "Thank you, marshal. If you ever need anything, I hang out between Madonnella and the Petruzzelli – you can find me at the Bar del Marinaio. Anything you want, I'm at your disposal."

This second reference to the Teatro Petruzzelli put Fenoglio in a bad mood. A few months earlier someone had burned it down, and he still couldn't get over it. How could anyone even think of such an act? To burn down a theatre. And then there was the absurd, almost unbearable fact – God alone knew if it was a coincidence or if the arsonists had wanted to add a touch of macabre irony – of burning it down after a performance of *Norma*, an opera that actually ends with a funeral pyre.

The Petruzzelli was one of the reasons he liked – had liked? – living in Bari.

That huge theatre which could hold two thousand people, just ten minutes on foot from the station where he worked. Often, if there was a concert or an opera, Fenoglio would stay in the office until evening and then go straight there and up to the third tier, among the friezes and the stucco. When he was there, he could almost believe in reincarnation. He felt the music so intensely – that of some composers, above all baroque ones, especially Handel – that he imagined that in another life he must have been a kapellmeister in some provincial German town.

And now that the theatre was gone? God alone knew if they would ever rebuild it, and God alone knew if those responsible would ever be tracked down, tried and sentenced. The Prosecutor's Department had opened a case file to investigate "arson by persons unknown". A good way of saying that they hadn't the slightest idea what had happened. Fenoglio would have liked to handle the investigation, but it had been entrusted to others, and he couldn't do anything about it.

"All right, Albanese. Don't do anything stupid. Not too stupid, anyway." He gave him a slap on the shoulder and walked off in the direction of his own office.

At the door he found a young carabiniere waiting for him.

"The captain wants to speak to you. He'd like you to go to his office."

Captain Valente was the new commanding officer of the Criminal Investigation Unit. Fenoglio hadn't yet decided if he liked the man or was made uncomfortable by him. Perhaps both. He was certainly different from the other officers he'd had to deal with during his twenty years in the Carabinieri.

He had arrived only a few days earlier, bang in the middle of this criminal war that didn't yet make sense to anyone. He came from Headquarters in Rome, and nobody knew why he had been sent to Bari.

"Come in, Marshal Fenoglio," the captain said as soon as he saw him at the door.

That was one of the things that puzzled him: Captain Valente addressed everyone formally, always using rank and surname. The unnamed rule of behaviour for officers is that you use rank and surname towards your superiors and call your subordinates by their surnames, or even their first names. And of course, among those of the same rank, first-name terms are the rule. Among non-commissioned officers, things are less clear, but in general it's rare to find the commanding officer of a unit being so formal with all his men.

Why did he behave in that way? Did he prefer to keep a distance between himself and his subordinates? Was he a particularly formal man? Or particularly shy?

"Good morning, sir," Fenoglio said.

"Please sit down," Valente said, motioning him to a chair. That combination of formality and cordiality was hard to make sense of. Then there was the decor of the room: no pennants, no crests, no military calendars; nothing to suggest that this was the office of a captain in the Carabinieri. There was a TV set, a good-quality stereo, a sofa and some armchairs; a small refrigerator and some pictures in an expressionistic style, somewhat in the manner of Egon Schiele. There was a slight perfume in the air, coming, in all probability, from an incense burner. Not exactly a martial kind of accessory.

"I've been wanting to talk to you for the past two days. I'm afraid I've come to Bari at a bad time."

"That's true, sir. And with the lieutenant's accident, you don't even have a second-in-command."

The lieutenant had broken a leg playing football and would be out of action for three months. So the unit had found itself with a new captain who had no knowledge of the city and its criminal geography and was without a second-in-command, all in the middle of a Mafia war.

"Can you explain what's going on in this city?" Valente said.

# 3

"It all started on 12 April, with the murder of Gaetano D'Agostino, known as Shorty. He was shot dead in the Libertà district, where he'd gone to see his mother. He lived in Enziteto – a rather complicated area, to use a euphemism – and belonged to the organization of Nicola Grimaldi, known as Blondie, also known as Three Cylinders."

"Why Three Cylinders?"

"Grimaldi has a heart defect, some kind of arrhythmia. I don't know the exact medical definition. Anyway, the idea is that his heart functions on three cylinders instead of four. Although nobody would ever dare use that nickname to his face."

"He doesn't like it."

"No, he doesn't like it."

"You were saying: D'Agostino was one of Grimaldi's men. So the murder was committed by a rival gang?"

"Unfortunately, it's not as simple as that. I should say in advance that the investigation into this murder is being conducted by the police flying squad, as they were first on the scene, although we also have a file on the case. The problem is that there doesn't seem to be any conflict at present between Grimaldi and other criminal groups in the city or the surrounding areas. If there were, we'd have seen losses on the other side, too, in places like San Paolo, or Bitonto, or Giovinazzo. But there haven't been any. All the victims owed allegiance to Three Cylinders, and the rest of the city's quiet."

"So what's going on?"

"The hypothesis is that there's a conflict inside the organization. Since the 23rd of April there's been no news of the whereabouts of Michele Capocchiani, known as the Pig, who's one of Grimaldi's lieutenants and a highly dangerous criminal. His wife reported him missing and a few days later we found his car burnt out, but with no body in it. On the 29th of April, there was the murder of Gennaro Carbone, known as the Cue —"

"The Cue?"

"Apparently, Carbone was a really good pool player. He was found dead outside the amusement arcade he ran on behalf of Grimaldi in Santo Spirito. A particularly violent attack, using automatic weapons. The hitmen had a sub-machine gun and a .44 magnum – the cartridges are unmistakable, even when they're twisted. One bullet from the sub-machine gun ricocheted and wounded a passer-by. A few days ago, on the 9th of May, there was an attack with a similar MO on a man named Andriani – I can't remember his first name right now, but anyway, another of Grimaldi's associates. He had a miraculous escape. A further element, which we were tipped off about and have been able to corroborate, is the disappearance of Simone Losurdo, known as the Mosquito. Nobody reported the disappearance, but he was being kept under special surveillance and hasn't reported to police headquarters since 21 April, in other words, two days before Capocchiani was reported missing."

"What do his family say?"

"Losurdo's wife comes from an old underworld family. People accustomed to not talking to us. We asked her where her husband was and she replied that he never tells her what he does, he comes and goes as he pleases. But she was very agitated: my guess is that Losurdo is dead. But the most significant element in this business is the disappearance of Vito Lopez, known as the Butcher."

"Why the Butcher?"

Fenoglio smiled and shook his head. "The nickname has nothing to do with the murders he's almost certainly committed. His father had a well-established butcher's shop. Lopez is someone who didn't really need to become a criminal."

"You say his disappearance is the most significant element?"

"Like Capocchiani, Lopez is one of Grimaldi's lieutenants, probably the most respected and certainly the most intelligent. There's been no trace of him for several days now. The difference between him and the others is that we don't have an exact date for his disappearance – all we know is that nobody has seen him since the end of April. Above all, his wife and son have also disappeared. That's why I don't think Lopez is dead. I think he's gone away with his family. This would fit in with what we've heard from our informants: that there's a rift within Grimaldi's group. The killings and the disappearances could well be a consequence of this rift."

The captain placed a hand on the desk and ran it across the wood, as if examining the texture. He opened a drawer, took out a cigarette case and held it out to Fenoglio.

"Do you smoke, marshal?"

"No, thank you, sir."

"Do you mind if I do?"

"No, of course not."

"Let's open the window anyway."

Fenoglio made to stand up, but the captain got there first. He opened the window wide, returned to his seat and lit his cigarette.

"What are you doing at the moment?"

"We've questioned a whole lot of people, without success. We've tapped a number of phones, but nothing has emerged. They're mainly using mobile phones now, which, as you know, are difficult to tap. We should bug Grimaldi's house, but it's very difficult to get into. One possibility is to ask the telephone company to cooperate with us. We simulate a breakdown and when the residents call maintenance, we send our men in, disguised as engineers; they pretend to check on the nature of the problem and place a few bugs. If you agree, we could request authorization from the Prosecutor's Department in the next few days."

The captain made a sweeping gesture with his hands, as if to say: of course, whatever you need. It was a slightly over-the-top gesture, an unsuccessful attempt to play the part expected of him.

"Who's the prosecutor involved?"

"There are a number of files: the absurd thing is how fragmented the investigations are. The Carbone murder, which we're handling, has been assigned to Assistant Prosecutor D'Angelo, who in my opinion is the best, although she's not always easy to deal with. In terms of character, I mean. But she's hard-working and well prepared, and she's been involved with this kind of case for a while now: I think her previous posting was in Calabria." Fenoglio broke off, thinking that the captain was about to say something. When he realized that he wasn't, he continued, "Maybe one of these days we'll go and see her and I'll introduce you."

"Yes, of course, we'll go together." Valente looked like someone pretending to take an interest in a conversation while actually wanting to be somewhere else.

"I can also put together a memo summarizing the things I've told you today," Fenoglio added.

"Thank you, there's no need. You've been very clear and exhaustive. In the next few days we'll go and see Dottoressa D'Angelo and talk about bugging the house and all the rest." As he said these last words he got to his feet, with a slight smile on his face, as if apologizing for something.

# 4

At 1.30, Fenoglio shut the file he had been looking through, closed his notepad, took a book from the small library he kept in his office, and went to lunch.

The trattoria was in Corso Sonnino, five minutes' walk from the Carabinieri station. It was busiest in the evening, which was what Fenoglio liked about it: there weren't usually many people there at lunchtime, and he could always sit at the same table and linger as long as he liked, reading and listening to music on his Walkman.

He'd been having lunch in this little restaurant almost every day since Serena had left; that was two months ago now. I need to take a break, she had said, immediately apologizing for the clichéd words. They had taken too many things for granted, which is never a good idea, and after a while she had become aware of her resentment, like a stain on the skin: the day before, you didn't know it was there, but it couldn't have formed in a single night. She felt guilty about that resentment, she felt ashamed, she had tried to rationalize it, had tried to tell herself that it was an unfair reaction, but rationalizing is pointless in such cases. He had never asked her the reasons for that feeling, of which he himself had been aware in the last few months, although he had tried not to take any notice of it, tried to ignore it. Not the best strategy. He hadn't asked her for the reasons because he guessed what they were, and at the same time because he was afraid of hearing them spelt out. Work, of course. The fact that he was always out, day and night, on Sundays and public holidays, didn't make married life easy. But work hadn't been the main problem, the sore point, the insoluble dilemma.

The main problem was simple and merciless, anything else was a side issue: he couldn't have children and she could. The doctors had been clear and unanimous on the matter. That unexpressed biological window, getting smaller from year to year and about to disappear, was the crux of it, the source of the anger, the reason for a decision that, although meant to be temporary, already felt like a sentence for which there is no acquittal.

As she spoke, Fenoglio had felt a very strong urge to take her in his arms and tell her how much he loved her, to make promises, to beg her not to leave, but he hadn't found the courage, and he hadn't found anything to promise, and he hadn't found the words. He had never been capable of showing his feelings, tending instead to withdraw into a pained silence, a reserve that might seem like coldness. Come to think of it, that might have been the most serious problem, even more than the inability to have children. She had said it herself: you mustn't take things for granted. She meant: you mustn't take emotions and feelings for granted. They should be shared, they should be expressed, made tangible. You mustn't take love for granted.

So he had simply replied: all right, they would do what she wanted, he would leave as soon as possible. Serena had replied, in a tone that was a mixture of guilt, gentle sadness and unconscious relief, that she was the one who had to leave. The problem was hers: she had created it and she had to solve it, including from a practical point of view. She would stay in the apartment of a friend who was moving to Rome for work. Then in July there were the school leaving exams, and she was due to chair the examination board somewhere in Central Italy. Summer would pass, a few months would have gone by: enough time to figure things out and hopefully come to a final decision.

Do you have someone else? Will you have a child with another man and will the pain of it drive me crazy?

The same words that had appeared in his head, like a silent caption, that afternoon at home with Serena, now surfaced on his lips as he sat there at the trattoria table, the climax to this eruption of memories.

The waiter had materialized by his table: today's special was mussels with rice and potatoes. Fenoglio hadn't seen him coming, so in his embarrassment he said that mussels with rice and potatoes would be fine, without listening to the rest of the menu. Had he been talking to himself, and had the waiter noticed? Had he looked like a lunatic on day release from an asylum?

He recalled an episode a few years earlier. He had been in a bookshop, there weren't many people about, and after a while he had noticed a woman in her fifties. She was alone and she was talking in a voice that, although low, was perfectly audible at close quarters.

"So, I'm a bitch, am I? I'm not a bitch, you're a bastard. I look in your pockets because I have good reason. Aren't you going to tell me why you had a receipt from that restaurant? Oh, I broke our pact of mutual respect, did I? Wasn't it you who fucked that student? Oh, no, you can't just tell me you're walking out and leave it at that, it's too easy after you've stolen almost twenty years of my life, all thrown away. Don't you even realize what bullshit you're talking? A man has needs a woman doesn't understand? I should be happy to stay at home waiting for you while you fuck your colleagues and your students because you have *needs*? All that love, all that devotion, all that desire for beauty turned into a urological problem. You make me sick. You make me sick."

This went on for a few minutes, with the word "sick" becoming ever more frequent. Fenoglio had stood there hypnotized by that soliloquy, that sudden, impressive insight into a desolate soul. He had gone to get a coffee, and while he stood at the counter had thought about what he had seen and heard and, commenting on it mentally, had looked for interpretations and alternatives. A habit that was almost a neurosis. Maybe the man wasn't such a bastard after all. Maybe that receipt was for a business lunch and he had simply rebelled against an intrusion into his private domain and had considered it beneath his dignity to respond to the accusations. Maybe she was crazy – after all, she was talking to herself. God alone knew what the truth was, assuming there was just one truth.

In the midst of these reflections, which assumed the form of a genuine debate, with questions and answers and punctuation, Fenoglio was struck by a thought, like a stone on a window pane. He, too, was talking to himself, something which he did quite often. Perhaps on this particular occasion, he hadn't moved his lips to accompany his inner dialogue, but in other cases he definitely had. Serena would point it out to him: you're talking to yourself. Really? Oh, yes, you even change expressions, you gesticulate.

Just like the woman in the bookshop.

The border separating the mad from the normal seems clear, substantial, hard to cross. But in fact, it's very thin and at some points – at some moments – it vanishes without our realizing it. We find ourselves in the territory of the insane without understanding how it happened – and besides, do even the insane know they're in it?

He thought about reading a few pages of his book, but the waiter arrived with the plate of mussels and the usual beer. The food restored him to a reassuring material dimension, and by the time he left the trattoria the unease had subsided until it had almost vanished.

It had been a momentary thing, of course. But aren't they all?

# 5

Getting back to the office, in a perfect reproduction of the scene a few hours earlier, he found outside his door the same young carabiniere, who said more or less the same sentence to him. The captain wanted to speak to him and asked him to join him in his office.

"Do you know Marshal Fornaro?" Valente asked.

"The commanding officer at the Santo Spirito station?"

"Yes."

"Of course."

"What do you think of him?"

"A good man, a very sound officer. A bit old-school, but he's always done his job responsibly."

"He phoned me a little while ago and reported a strange story."

"What kind of story?"

"An informant of his told him that someone has kidnapped Grimaldi's son. There's already been a ransom demand."

Fenoglio shook his head in an instinctive gesture of incredulity. "To be honest, I find that extremely unlikely. Who would do something as crazy as that, even with a war on? Is Fornaro sure?"

"He says the source is highly reliable."

"Maybe we should go to Santo Spirito and find out more."

Ten minutes later, they were on the road in the captain's Alfetta.

At the wheel was Carabiniere Montemurro; beside him, in the seat reserved for the highest-ranking officer, the captain; Fenoglio sat in the back.

"Who could have done something like that?" the captain asked, turning to the back seat as they drove out of the city and onto the ramp leading to the northern ring road.

"Before taking it as read that there was a kidnapping, I'd like to speak to Fornaro and see how reliable the information is. Because – I repeat – it strikes me as highly unlikely. Kidnapping the son of someone like Grimaldi would be madness. It would be a declaration of total war."

There was no traffic on the ring road and they got to Santo Spirito in ten minutes. They drove along the seafront with its two-storey turn-of-the-century houses and stopped for a coffee in the little harbour used by fishermen and yachtsmen. It was a fine, bright if unsettled afternoon, the sky furrowed with large white cumulus clouds, the air cool and dry.

They were driving back up from the sea towards the Carabinieri station when they had to stop because of a small tailback of three cars. The first one – the one blocking the traffic – was a black BMW, stationary in the middle of the street. The driver was talking to a man standing next to the window. There were no other cars in front.

Montemurro let about ten seconds go by, then sounded his horn, to no avail. Usually at this point, once one impatient driver has sounded his horn, the others follow suit. In this case, it didn't happen. The drivers of the other two cars seemed to be in no hurry.

Montemurro hooted again, for longer this time. The man outside the BMW stopped speaking and walked to the second car in the line. There was a rapid exchange. The driver raised his arms, showing his palms: he wasn't the one who had disturbed the conversation with that ill-timed use of the horn.

"Should I sound the siren?" Montemurro asked, as the man – a bald man in his forties without a neck – came towards them.

"No," Fenoglio replied. He opened the door, got out of the car and walked over to the bald man. This action was followed by an almost rhythmical sequence of other movements. The man at the wheel of the BMW got out; the captain and Montemurro got out of the Alfetta; the bald man slowed down and his face – until then decidedly resolute and aggressive – seemed to change. The driver, walking quickly, reached him and pushed him aside. He was a thin-lipped, bespectacled man in a jacket and tie, and addressed Fenoglio in a tone midway between excitement and obsequiousness.

"Good afternoon, marshal. I'm sorry, we didn't recognize you. We'll get out of here right away."

"You should have got out of here before. It's too late now. Move your car over to the corner and clear the road."

The man assumed a crestfallen, imploring expression. "Can't you just drop it? Please, this is a difficult time. We didn't see you."

"I thought you were smart, Cavallo. Maybe I was wrong. Tell your friend to clear the road and stay in the car, and then join him there. Don't make me repeat myself."

The bald man seemed on the verge of objecting but Cavallo looked at him, a look that told him not to make the situation worse.

"Who are they?" the captain asked when the two men had walked away.

"The bald guy without a neck I don't know. The other man is called Cavallo. He works for Grimaldi, without being a member of his organization as far as I know. He puts him in contact with businessmen and politicians and is also believed to launder money for him through loan sharking. His nickname is the Accountant."

"Actually, he looks like one."

"I think he did in fact qualify as an accountant. While we're about it, let's question him and see if he knows something. Cavallo, come here."

The Accountant approached, a contrite expression on his face.

"I'm surprised. I wouldn't have expected nonsense like this from you. Thinking you could just hold up traffic like this."

"You're right, marshal, it was stupid. We were talking about something important and I got distracted. You know me, I don't usually do dumb things like this."

Fenoglio didn't reply. He glanced over at the BMW. "Who's that fellow without a neck?"

"A good man, only not very bright. He's a porter at Villa Bianca."

"And who got him the job at Villa Bianca?"

"You know, marshal, I have contacts, so whenever I can help out ..."

"Yes, why not? What's all this about Grimaldi's son?"

Cavallo seemed to involuntarily swallow a morsel of food he hadn't yet finished chewing. "What ... What do you mean?"

"I was right. You aren't as smart as I thought. I think we should all go to the station."

"Why to the station, marshal?"

"Because you were deliberately holding up the traffic, which counts as coercion. You might like to know that coercion is punishable by up to four years in prison. What we have to decide is whether or not to arrest you. With your record, I'm afraid we may have to."

"Marshal, please don't joke."

"Do I look like the kind of person who jokes?"

With a mechanical gesture, Cavallo adjusted the knot of his tie, even though it was perfectly straight. He took out a packet of Dunhill and a gold cigarette lighter that looked for all the world like a Dupont. He smoked, holding the cigarette right in the middle of his lips and not so much breathing it in as sucking on it.

"What's going on, Cavallo?"

Cavallo looked around, as if to make sure nobody was watching them. "Marshal, don't make things difficult for me. The orders are not to say a word."

"Just tell me what's going on, and nobody will have to know."

"Marshal ..." Cavallo's voice was almost a moan now.

"How long has the boy been gone?"

Cavallo threw down the half-smoked cigarette and stubbed it out with the tip of his shoe: he was wearing shiny new moccasins with tassels. "Since the day before yesterday. He left for school in the morning but never got there."

"Is it true there's been a ransom demand?"

Cavallo nodded.

"And has the ransom been paid?"

"I don't know. I know they were getting the money together. Now please let me go. We're in the middle of the street, everyone can see us. If Grimaldi finds out I told you these things, he'll break my legs."

"Go," Fenoglio said.

Cavallo hesitated for a moment, as if he wasn't sure he had quite understood. Then he turned and walked quickly away.

# 6

"So it's true," the captain said when they were back in the car.

"We have a huge problem," Fenoglio said. "Let's go and hear what Fornaro has to tell us."

Fornaro was standing waiting for them at the front door of the station. He looked like a character actor playing a marshal of the Carabinieri in a 1950s comedy: thick salt-and-pepper moustache, uniform made rounder by a prominent paunch, a stern expression but with a good-natured undercurrent. He saluted the captain, shook hands with Fenoglio and nodded in Montemurro's direction.

There was an unpleasant smell in the office, a mixture of mustiness, dust and rotting food, as if poor-quality dishes were frequently consumed there, the barred windows were never opened and a change of air only ever came from the corridor.

"Can I get you anything, captain? A coffee, a drink?"

"No, thanks, marshal. We've just had something. Could you repeat what you told me on the phone?"

"Yes, sir. A source who has proved reliable in the past, close to the circles around Nicola Grimaldi alias Blondie, informed me this morning that Grimaldi's younger son has been kidnapped by persons unknown and that in order to restore him a considerable sum has been demanded."

There were a few moments' silence. Fornaro had spoken as if reading a report.

"When is this kidnapping supposed to have taken place?" Fenoglio asked.

Fornaro hesitated for a few seconds, perhaps made uncomfortable by the fact that the question had been asked, not by the captain, but by someone of the same rank as himself. When he replied, the tone was less bureaucratic.

"The day before yesterday, but I didn't speak to the source until today."

"Did he tell you if the ransom has been paid?"

Fornaro shook his head. "He didn't know. All he knew was that the kidnappers had asked for a very large sum and that the family was getting the money together."

"Did you do anything to corroborate the tip-off after you'd received it?" the captain asked.

"Yes, sir. Immediately after obtaining the information, my subordinates and myself proceeded to the school attended by the child, where, having been received by the principal, we were informed that the child had not attended yesterday. That same morning, the child's mother had come to the school and requested to see him and had also been told that the child had not come to class."

"Have you talked to the boy's family?"

"No, sir. Having first verified the reliability of the information I judged it wise to inform you without carrying out any further investigative actions."

Fenoglio reflected. The kidnapping had taken place, there was no doubt about it. Two converging sources and the statements from the principal couldn't be a coincidence. It was unprecedented, something far from the usual patterns of criminal behaviour.

"Does your informant have any idea who it might have been? Are there any hypotheses, anyone suspected?"

"He hasn't said anything. But the rumour that's going around is that it's connected with a rift between Grimaldi and Vito Lopez."

"Meaning what?"

"Meaning that if there's a war between those loyal to Grimaldi and a group of rebels linked to Lopez, it's possible the boy was taken by Lopez's people. But that's only a theory of mine."

Once again Fenoglio noticed the different ways Fornaro spoke, depending on whether he was addressing him or the captain.

"Do you think your source can give us any other information?"

"I don't think so, he doesn't play an important role in the group. He reported to me the things that everyone in those circles knows, but Grimaldi certainly won't confide in him."

The captain took out his cigarette case, asked permission to smoke, lit a cigarette and seemed to reflect. "What do we do now?"

"We summon the boys' parents here to the station," Fenoglio suggested. "Obviously, they won't want to cooperate, but they'll have to tell us something to justify their son's absence."

"All right. Marshal Fornaro, send a car to pick up Grimaldi and his wife. We'll wait here."

A strange expression appeared on Fornaro's face: something like embarrassment, as if he wanted to object but couldn't find the right words to make the nature of the problem clear to the others. When you're the commanding officer of a station on the outskirts of town, you have to find a balance between asserting your own authority and showing cautious respect for people who are prepared to do anything. When you live and work round the corner from the homes and territories of highly dangerous criminals, you have to find a modus vivendi, accept boundaries and limitations that it's hard for those who come in from outside to grasp. Theoretical authority is one thing; the real world, where different rules apply, is another. Grimaldi wasn't the kind of man you could just drag to the station with his wife, like any common bag snatcher. You had to find a *way*. Fornaro didn't say any of this, but for Fenoglio it was as if he had recited these considerations out loud. He was about to say, "Montemurro and I will go and fetch Grimaldi and his wife, maybe with a couple of carabinieri from the station but only as backup, just so he sees who's involved and that the orders came from higher up," when a uniformed sergeant came into the room. He was breathless, and had the excited expression of someone with an urgent announcement to make.

"Begging your pardon, but a call has just come in. There's a shoot-out in the street in Enziteto between the occupants of two cars."

"How far is that from here?" the captain asked, with unexpected promptness and determination.

"Five minutes if we're quick," Fornaro replied.

"Let's take the M12s and the bulletproof vests and go straight there."

# 7

The two cars set off with sirens blaring, lights flashing and tyres screeching. Fenoglio checked the time and cocked his pistol. The captain had a sub-machine gun in his hand, already loaded, while Montemurro drove with a Beretta 92 between his legs. Nobody spoke. Ahead of them, the car from the station, with Marshal Fornaro and two corporals in it, sped on, jumping intersections and angrily running red lights. They drove through Santo Spirito, heading south, and turned onto the main road.

As they covered the mile or so separating them from the turn-off for Enziteto at a speed of over ninety miles an hour, Fenoglio found himself inevitably thinking of a very similar situation many years earlier, in Milan. He and two colleagues had been in a patrol car when they'd received a report of an armed robbery in progress, just a few hundred yards from where they were. They got there just as the robbers, still holding their guns, were coming out of the post office. There was a furious exchange of fire, at the end of which one of the robbers – a twenty-one-year-old – was dead and one of the carabinieri seriously wounded. A few weeks later, it emerged from the ballistics examination that the fatal shots hadn't come from Fenoglio's gun. Technically, he hadn't been the one who'd caused the young man's death, and the news had given him a sense of liberation. That had been short-lived. He had begun wondering if there was really any difference between himself and the colleague from whose gun the fatal bullet had been fired. If that other carabiniere had been the only one there, would things have ended up the same way? Dozens of bullets – in the end, they had counted thirty-two cartridges on the ground – had been fired almost simultaneously at the robbers, like a hard-edged mass of lethal metal. A web in which you couldn't help but become entangled. The question wasn't who had fired the shot that had reached its target; the question was who had participated in weaving that web. This had nothing to do with the legitimacy of the carabinieri's conduct on that occasion. Shooting at those robbers had been legitimate and inevitable, the young man's death the legitimate and inevitable result of a collective act. Fenoglio had wondered what he would reply if he was asked if he had ever killed anyone.

He would reply yes.

When they got to the scene of the shoot-out at Enziteto, there was nobody there. Fenoglio looked at his watch before getting out of the car: five minutes and a few seconds had passed. In emergencies, establishing the time is vital. It helps to counter the inevitable distortion of memories, their lack of consistency, the way they can be contaminated by imagination.

They turned off the sirens and the lights. The street was deserted, the windows barred as if the neighbourhood were uninhabited. There were many cartridges, concentrated in two spots, some twenty yards apart. Two groups had opened fire on each other with rifles and pistols, and if anyone had been hit, he hadn't left any immediately visible bloodstains.

The silence was unsettling. This, too, gave the impression

that the place had been abandoned. Which in a way was true, Fenoglio thought. Enziteto was a part of the city abandoned by everyone, although less than two miles from the sea, the restaurants, the bathing beaches, the airport. You take the little turn-off that leads to the neighbourhood from the highway, and from one moment to the next you find yourself somewhere unknowable. Somewhere abstract.

Yes, that was the right adjective. Abstract.

Enziteto, like so many strange marginal areas in the world, was an abstract place. He recalled a phrase by his fellow Piedmontese, the painter Casorati, which had struck him and seemed to him to contain a basic truth: "Painting is *always* abstract."

God knows who had called 112. There really was nobody there: not a single car passed, not a little boy by chance, not a moped, not a bicycle.

A mangy dog crossed the road, slowly, as if to underline the concept. Then the silence was broken by sirens. More Carabinieri cars arrived, along with police patrol cars, even the head of the flying squad. The world regained a modicum of precarious concreteness.

They did the rounds of the apartment blocks, in search of anyone who had seen something. Many doors remained closed. Some people opened and said they had seen nothing; others, with the promise of anonymity, recounted a shoot-out between the occupants of two cars, armed to the teeth with pistols, rifles and light machine guns.

They left a few hours later. In the meantime, everyone in the unit had been recalled to duty. Some were sent to do the rounds of the hospitals; others busied themselves with a blitz on the homes of the local criminals; three of them were brought into the station to be tested to see if there was any gunshot residue on their bodies.

Grimaldi and his wife were brought into the station in Bari to be questioned about the disappearance of their son. The report drawn up the following day by the Prosecutor's Department, in which they were accused of being accessories, described the session in this way: "The two spouses denied the existence of any problem, and in particular that their son had been kidnapped. Asked as to the child's whereabouts, they claimed that he was staying for a few days with an uncle and an aunt resident in Lombardy. They refused to provide telephone numbers for these relatives and were unable to provide any explanation as to why the child should have gone to stay with said relatives in term time. Grimaldi and his wife were urged to cooperate, and it was pointed out to them that such cooperation could be important in leading to the recovery of the child. But they refused any cooperation, denying the evidence, withdrawing into a hostile silence and refusing to sign the statement."

Late that afternoon, in the countryside near San Ferdinando di Puglia, some forty miles north of the scene of the shoot-out, a burnt-out Peugeot 205 was found. Despite its condition, bullet holes were still visible on it. The car had been stolen in Pescara, so the search was extended to that area.

More or less at the same time, three hooded men went to the house of Vito Lopez's sister-in-law, beat up her husband, who had nothing to do with criminal circles, and smashed up the place. They wanted to know where Lopez was. In the end they shot him in the legs and left after telling him that if he was left crippled he could thank that piece of shit, the Butcher.

Fenoglio went to bed at three in the morning. He didn't get to sleep until dawn, and by seven he was awake again.

# 8

It was mid-morning when Corporal Pellecchia shuffled into Fenoglio's office.

"What's up, chief, seen a ghost?"

"No, why?"

"You're not looking good."

"It was a tough day yesterday."

"Yes, it was."

"Where did you go last night?"

"They sent me on a few pointless searches. Waste of time."

"What do you think of this story about Grimaldi's son?"

"I always thought Lopez was a smart guy – a son of a bitch, but smart. Clearly I was wrong. Anyone doing a thing like that is crazy."

"Are you convinced it was him?"

"Who else could it have been?"

Fenoglio didn't reply. Who else, indeed, could it have been?

"This morning, before coming here, I talked to a friend," Pellecchia went on, sniffing. It was a tic, the result of having been headbutted during an arrest. "He told me something interesting."

"What?"

"Grimaldi's wife has an appointment with a medium."

"A what?"

"A medium, a clairvoyant, someone who talks to dead people. To find out where the boy is."

"Do you know when she's going?"

"This afternoon, at the amusement park on Largo Due Giugno. The medium sees people in her caravan. She says she has the power to leave her body and locate missing persons, bullshit like that. I don't know if this information is of any use."

Fenoglio clicked his fingers, stood up, grabbed his jacket and headed for the door. "Let's go. We need to get there before Grimaldi's wife. Call Montemurro, he can take us."

The traffic was overwhelming and the car advanced a few feet at a time, with long pauses in between. A journey that would usually have required less than ten minutes took them nearly half an hour. They stopped a couple of blocks from the amusement park and Fenoglio told Montemurro to wait for them in the car.

The sky was grey, the weather very cool, promising rain. It didn't feel like May, and not just because of the temperature. There was an unpleasant electricity in the air, like an omen or a threat.

"What's her name?"

"Madame Urania."

"Urania?"

"Urania, yes. These charlatans always have stupid nicknames. What do we say to her?"

"I don't know yet. We have to find a way to get her to help us."

The place – like all amusement parks by day – felt desolate and sad, with the merry-go-rounds stationary and the shutters of the booths down. Grey, solitary figures moved between the old caravans. Fenoglio remembered reading somewhere that walking in a closed amusement park is a perfect metaphor for senselessness. At the time, he hadn't quite understood what that meant, but now it struck him as clear and perceptive.

As they walked, they came across a very thin woman with a feverish look in her eyes.

"Excuse me, signora," Fenoglio said, "could you point us in the direction of Madame Urania's caravan?"

The woman looked at them, first one and then the other. She must have been thinking that there was a contrast between the kindness of the question and the appearance of the two men; she must also have been thinking that they didn't look much like Urania's usual clients. She decided it was none of her business.

"The last caravan on the left, right at the end. But I don't know if she's there."

Urania's caravan had a large owl painted on the door. Fenoglio looked around and knocked on the owl's beak. Some ten seconds later, from inside, a resolute voice asked who it was.

"Good morning. We'd like to talk to Madame Urania."

The door opened with a creak that sounded fake, like a special effect to create atmosphere.

"Who are you?" The woman was nondescript-looking, with the kind of face you can't even remember a few hours after seeing it. The interior was dark and there was a slight smell of incense.

"We're carabinieri. Can I come in?"

"I haven't done anything."

"We know, we just want to ask you a few questions," Fenoglio said, gently pushing open the door, trying to accustom his eyes to the semi-darkness.

"I'm expecting clients," the woman said, but the two carabinieri were already inside.

Fenoglio sat down on a chair, while Pellecchia leaned on a small table in the centre of which was a crystal ball. From a shelf, a stuffed owl stared down at them.

Fenoglio cleared his throat and got straight to the point. "We know you have rather a special appointment today," he said.

"What do you mean?"

"We mean a woman's coming here to find her missing son," Pellecchia said, abruptly accelerating the rhythm, as he tended to do. "Don't make us waste our time. I get pissed off when I have to waste my time."

The woman sat down with her legs together and her hands on her knees, looking unexpectedly composed. "What do you want?"

"Who called you to make the appointment?" Fenoglio asked, also adopting a less formal tone. He didn't like that assumption of familiarity common to police officers and carabinieri, but in many cases being formal simply complicated the work.

"A woman I know came here. She told me that a boy had disappeared and that I had to help them find him."

"What's your real name?"

"Rita."

"All right, Rita. Now listen carefully. It's very important for us to know what the woman who's coming here today tells you. Someone kidnapped her son. The family aren't cooperating, and we're worried about the boy. You have to get his mother to tell you everything and also ask her a few questions, explaining that in order to *see* the boy you need more information. Then you'll pretend to concentrate and say that you can't see him, that you'll need to try again when you're alone. Tell her you'll call her. Then we come back and you tell us everything."

Fenoglio hadn't finished speaking when the woman started shaking her head. "You want to get me killed. These people are dangerous. If they find out I tricked them to help you —"

"You'd be tricking them anyway, you know that as well as I do. We won't write anything down, and they'll never know you helped us."

"You can't force me."

Fenoglio let his shoulders droop wearily. "Maybe not. But do you have any idea how many offences you're committing every day in here? Fraud, misappropriation, abuse of public credulity. If I decide to cause you trouble, I just have to place a patrol car outside. Every time someone comes in, the carabinieri will come in, too, check on you, then take your client to the station to get his statement and ask him if he wants to file a complaint against you. How long do you think it'll be before word spreads and people start going to another medium? Plus, we may well need to confiscate the caravan as evidence. Shall I go on?"

A few minutes' silence followed. "You swear to me they'll never find out?" the woman said at last.

"They never will," Fenoglio replied.

"And you won't write my name down anywhere?"

"You have my word."

The woman sighed, resigned. "What do I have to ask?"

"We need to know if they've paid a ransom, if they have any suspicions as to who it was, and above all, how they communicated with the kidnappers: if they spoke by phone, if there was a go-between …"

"What if she gets suspicious?"

"I'm sure you don't have any problems asking questions without making your clients suspicious."

Urania didn't reply.

"Let's go over what we need to know."

"When the boy disappeared; what contact they've had with the people who took him; if they've paid and if they suspect anyone. After we've talked, what do I have to do?"

"Nothing. We come back, you tell us everything and it's over. Your name won't appear on any document."

She seemed to ponder Fenoglio's last words, as if they contained a hidden meaning. At last, she took a deep breath. "All right. Now go, I have to get ready."

# 9

On their way out, they passed a huge fellow with a white handlebar moustache and hands like frying pans. He might have been about seventy, but looked as if he could easily slap down three or four twenty-year-olds. He waved at Pellecchia, who waved back.

"Remember him?" Pellecchia said once they had left the amusement park.

"Who?"

"Whiskers. Don't you remember?"

"Who is he?"

Pellecchia rubbed his face. "Oh, of course. I'm going soft in the head. It happened about ten years ago, before you came to Bari. We arrested him after this incredible brawl." He continued speaking but Fenoglio stopped listening. About ten years ago. When he'd been on the verge of being transferred to Bari because he had met Serena and they would be married in a few months. The happiest part of his life had been about to begin; and now it was probably over.

"Hey, are you all right?" Pellecchia asked.

"Why wouldn't I be?" The question surprised him: Pellecchia wasn't the kind to notice subtle signals.

"I don't know, you're acting strange."

"Is it that obvious?"

"Yes, it is."

"I'm going through a rough patch. My wife's left home and I keep thinking about her." Even before he finished the sentence, he was surprised that he had uttered it. He had never been especially inclined to confide in anyone, and the last person he would have thought of telling his problems to was Corporal Antonio Pellecchia, known as Tonino. It was hard to imagine two more different people. They had been working together for years and had never had a conversation that wasn't about the job in hand.

"So these things happen to superheroes, too."

"Excuse me?"

"You know what the boys call you?"

"What boys?"

"The boys in the unit."

"What do they call me?"

"Mr Perfect. Some also: Mr Uptight. No offence. I don't think there's any need for explanations."

Indeed, there was no need, and Fenoglio didn't say anything. They walked for a while in silence, both looking straight ahead.

"Shall we have a coffee, chief?"

"Sure, it'll only be the sixth one today."

They went into an anonymous café. Behind the counter was a thin girl with a long, rather equine face and a look of quiet desperation. Pellecchia greeted her by name – Liliana – and she replied with an infinitesimal nod.

"Two coffees. We'll sit in the back."

Fenoglio felt an inexplicable sense of relief as they took their seats in that bare back room. They were the only ones there, and it seemed like a refuge. Pellecchia lit his cigar butt, took two puffs and put it down on the ashtray to let it burn itself out, as usual.

"Have you separated?"

"I don't know." And after a hesitation: "She told me she has to sort out a few issues. She added that she was sorry it sounded like such a cliché, but unfortunately that's the way it was."

"Does she have someone else?"

"She didn't say. But it's possible."

Liliana arrived with the two coffees, along with two pastries and two chocolates. Pellecchia waited until she had put it all down and gone back to the counter.

"My wife left me ten years ago. It's not hard to figure out why a woman would want to leave someone like me. At the time I was really pissed off, but although it bugs me to admit it, she had every reason in the world. But why would a woman want to leave someone like you? The only reason, in my opinion, is if she has someone else. Pardon my frankness."

Fenoglio ate the pastry and the chocolate. Pellecchia did the same. Then they drank the coffee. The scene resembled a ritual with specific rules, almost like a tea ceremony.

"You're surprised you confided in me, aren't you?"

Fenoglio had the impulse to deny it – no, why should he be surprised? – but realized it would have denoted a lack of respect. "Yes."

Pellecchia sniffed. If it's possible to convey different emotions by sniffing, then Pellecchia's sniff now was different from his usual one. Usually, his sniffing communicated annoyance, arrogance, boredom, insolence. This time, it seemed to Fenoglio that there was a hint of melancholy in it.

"You don't like me, I know. But I haven't liked myself for some time now, so I can't blame you."

Again Fenoglio had the impulse to lie and suppressed it. "Maybe you've never liked me much either."

"That's not completely true. Let's be clear about this: you've often been a pain in the arse, for the reasons already mentioned. It's annoying having someone who always goes by the book as your immediate superior. But at the same time ..." Pellecchia seemed embarrassed. "Well, I've always admired you but never had the courage to admit it to myself – and for a reason you may not imagine."

"What's that?"

"There's a scene in that film with Robert De Niro, *New York, New York* ... what's her name, the actress who also sings?"

"Liza Minnelli."

"That's the one. Anyway, Liza Minnelli has nothing to do with what I meant to say. When I was younger, some dickhead told me I looked just like Robert De Niro. As I was an idiot, I started watching all his films over and over, just to see how much like him I was and feel smug about it. A real idiot."

"You want to know something?"

"Go on."

"I feel like an idiot most of the time. In normal circumstances, let alone at a time like this."

"Half an hour ago, I'd have thought that was absurd. Not now. Life is fucking strange. Anyway, in one scene, when De Niro has already become famous, a guy asks him for advice. He answers something like: You want my advice? Okay, stay away from the shit." He broke off and seemed to ponder for a few moments. "I've always thought that was the best advice I've ever heard. Stay away from the shit. It's what I should have done in my life. But I never managed it."

"It's hard in our line of work."

"True, it's hard. You're too close to it. I've got myself dirty a few times, and after a while I didn't feel like getting clean any more. I didn't even want to think about it." He sniffed. Without meaning to, Fenoglio also sniffed. "You're close to the shit, too, like all of us. But you never get it on you. I don't know how else to put it. It's like you had some kind of power, like all those fucking superheroes. It annoys me, and I admire you for it. Maybe it annoys me because I admire you, or vice versa. Am I talking crap?"

"No, you're making perfect sense."

"Like hell I am. All right, anyway. In all these years we've worked together, I've never seen you slap someone who was handcuffed, I've never seen you write anything false in a report, and I've never seen some arsehole of an officer or some arsehole of a judge step on you. You know something I'll never forget?"

"What?"

"It was five or six years ago. We brought in a young guy who was peddling dope on Piazza Umberto. We were slapping him around a bit to get him to tell us who he'd got it from. There was that idiot of a lieutenant who was always tanned and toned from the gym."

"I remember him."

"He enjoyed beating people up. After a few slaps he took a cloth and wrapped it around his hand. He was going to punch the guy in the face. Not that he gave a fuck about what the guy had done, he just wanted to have a bit of fun. You know I've never had any problem beating up these sons of bitches. But I don't do it for the hell of it, only if there's a good reason. You said something like: 'Can I talk to you for a moment, lieutenant?' and you left the room together. After five minutes you came back in without him.

Just like that. You piss me off, but you were great that time. I'd have liked to know what you said to get rid of him."

Fenoglio shrugged, but was unable to suppress a smile. That lieutenant was a coward, and it had been a real pleasure threatening him with a charge of coercion and assaulting a suspect.

"I've done lots of things I'm ashamed of," Pellecchia went on. "I've justified them up to a point by telling myself there was no other way of doing this job. If you want to nail these bastards, you have to be more of a bastard than they are. I always told myself there was no other choice if you wanted to help this fucking society a little. But then, for many reasons, I had the feeling I'd lost control."

Fenoglio understood that well. Throughout his career in the Carabinieri, he had heard these arguments; he had heard that there was no other way. The rules are important, but they can't always be respected. Sometimes they can – sometimes they *must* – be broken for the greater good. For the greater good, he had seen things that disgusted him, and he had decided that he didn't care about the greater good.

"I'm sorry about your wife," Pellecchia concluded. "Maybe she really does only need to sort out a few issues."

"Maybe. Now let's go, Montemurro's waiting for us."

# 10

They parked the car about a hundred yards from the entrance to the amusement park, in a position to see who was going in and out. Grimaldi's wife arrived about an hour later, accompanied by a short-haired, broad-shouldered woman with a resolute demeanour.

They came out again after about forty minutes.

"You two follow the women and try to find out who the other one is," Fenoglio said, getting out of the car.

In the caravan, the smell of incense was much more pungent than before. On the table lay a pile of tarot cards, a fabric egg with lots of pins stuck in it, a book of occult symbols, the crystal ball and the stuffed owl that had previously been on the shelf.

"Why the owl?" Fenoglio asked.

"It's a symbol of clairvoyance." They were silent for a few seconds, then Rita Urania broke into an almost conspiratorial smile. "It impresses the customers. Complete baloney. Like all of it," she added, indicating the other objects on the table. "Would you like a coffee?"

Fenoglio was about to say, no thanks, I've already had too much. Then it struck him that, given the circumstances, considering how they had interfered in the woman's life and forced her to cooperate, it would have been impolite to refuse, so he accepted. She told him to sit down, moved into the kitchen area of the caravan and made coffee.

"How did it go, Rita?" Fenoglio asked after taking a sip.

The woman opened two of the caravan's windows, lit an MS and sucked in the smoke.

"The boy's dead, isn't he?"

"It's quite likely."

Urania took another few drags. Fenoglio waited.

"I didn't want to say anything at first. She brought something of the boy's" – Rita pointed towards the sofa bed, on which lay a football kit in the colours of the Bari team – "and wanted me to find out where he was by touching his things."

"What did you do?"

"I told her I needed to know everything if I was going to try and see the boy, that touching the objects wouldn't be enough. Then she looked at the other woman, and the other woman told her I was right."

"Who was the other woman?"

"I don't know. She didn't introduce herself, not even when she gave me her hand."

"All right, go on."

"She says she was alone in the house. The boy had gone to school an hour before, more or less. The telephone rang and when she answered it a man asked to speak to her husband, but he wasn't there."

"Did she say anything about this man's voice? Did she recognize it? Did he have an accent of any kind?"

"I didn't ask her anything about the voice, it might have seemed strange. It's one thing to ask —"

"You're right," Fenoglio cut in. "You did the right thing."

"He said he was a friend and that he wanted to help them get their son back. That was when she got scared. The man repeated: I'm a friend of your husband's, you'd better get hold of him if you want to see the boy alive. He said he'd call back after an hour, and hung up. That's when she got all paranoid and called her husband on his mobile. He was really pissed off, he told her she was a fool, instead of calling him she should have gone straight to the school to see if the boy was there."

"And that's where she went."

Urania nodded and lit herself another cigarette. Fenoglio wondered how old she was. The face and the body suggested different ages. From the face, you would have said she was about fifty, but the body seemed that of a much younger woman.

"She went to the school and asked the caretaker if she could see her son. The woman went to the classroom to call him and they discovered he wasn't there. So she called her husband again. He was out on business, but he came home and called all the men who work for him, who are in his gang, as far as I could tell, and sent them out to look for the boy and ask questions to find out what had happened. Then those people phoned again."

"Why do you say 'those people'? Was there more than one of them? Was it a different voice on the phone this time?"

"No, I mean, she didn't know. It was the husband who answered the phone, but she kept saying 'the people who've taken Damiano', which is the boy's name."

"All right, I've got it. What did they tell her husband?"

"That they'd taken his son and that if he wanted him back he had to get the money together."

"Did she tell you how much?"

She hesitated for a few seconds, as if afraid she wouldn't be believed. "Two hundred million lire."

Fenoglio realized he had thrown his head back in an involuntary gesture of astonishment.

"The money had to be ready by the evening," Urania went on.

"What did Grimaldi say to this?"

"He said he wanted to talk to the boy, and the man on the phone replied that if he asked one more time he'd find him in a rubbish bag, cut up into pieces."

"Carry on."

"They started getting the money together, because they didn't have the two hundred million. They had a lot, but not that much."

"How did they manage to make up the full amount?"

"They started asking her husband's friends, and by the time these other people called again, they had everything. The man on the phone said the money had to be delivered by a woman on her own. If they saw anyone else around, they'd make themselves scarce and the boy would die. If they did as they were told, two hours later the boy would be returned."

"Who made the delivery?"

"The other woman, the one who came here with the wife."

"Where?"

"I don't know."

"Then what happened?"

"Two hours went by, it got dark and the boy didn't come back. So the husband sent his men out again, but they didn't find anything."

"Did she tell you if they suspected anyone?"

"She said it was a man named Lopez, along with some others, who used to be friends with her husband but had then betrayed him." She hesitated a few seconds, then added: "He said these pieces of shit would all be killed, that when they caught them they'd quarter them alive."

"How did it go?" Pellecchia asked in the office an hour later.

"Better than bugging his house. She got the wife to tell her everything, and at least we now know what happened on the day of the kidnapping." Fenoglio told him about his conversation with Urania, then asked: "What did the wife and the woman who was with her do? Have you identified her?"

"They went back together to Grimaldi's house. The other woman left straight away. We followed her to the hospital. Her name's Maria Pia Scaringella, she's a nurse in the orthopaedics department. We checked, she's on duty tonight."

"Is she from a criminal family?"

"No, and she doesn't have a record either. She's just a friend of Grimaldi's wife."

Fenoglio scratched his head. He was very tired, and Pellecchia looked even more so.

"All right, arrange for someone to pick her up at the end of her shift tomorrow morning. We'll bring her in and see if we can get her to cooperate. Maybe she'll tell us something useful about the way the ransom was paid."

"It has to have been that son of a bitch Lopez and his friends. There's no doubt about it."

"Quite likely. But when we find them – if we find them alive – we'll still need evidence if we're going to make them pay for what they've done. It won't be much use knowing it was them if we can't prove it."

# 11

When Fenoglio got to the station the following morning, the nurse was already there. They had left her waiting in one of the interview rooms.

"Not the quiet type," Pellecchia said. "At first she refused to go with the uniformed men I'd sent to pick her up. She raised her voice, even managed a few shoves. If she'd been a man, she'd have got a beating. She wanted a lawyer. It took them half an hour to persuade her. They had to threaten to charge her with resisting arrest. Now she's here, and really pissed off."

"The morning's off to a good start."

"Right. Shall we go?"

"Let's go."

They entered the room, which contained only an old desk and some equally old chairs. No windows, no natural light. The Scaringella woman had turned abruptly on hearing the door opening. From close up, she looked even more massive; her face was broad and flat (like a focaccia, Serena would have said), her nose small, her brutal eyes blazing with hostility.

"Good morning, signora, I'm Marshal Fenoglio," he said, holding out his hand to her. She took it after a moment's hesitation, trying not to lose her resentful demeanour. "I'm sorry we brought you here straight after your shift, but unfortunately we're dealing with an urgent matter and it wasn't possible to put it off. You know why we've summoned you, don't you?"

"I don't know anything. All I know is that I've just finished the night shift, I'm exhausted and you're keeping me here. I want a lawyer."

"Why do you want a lawyer, signora? We're not accusing you of anything."

"You arrested me."

"No, signora. You aren't under arrest and you aren't accused of anything. Perhaps there's been a misunderstanding. We need to ask you a few questions, purely as a witness."

"A witness to what? I haven't witnessed anything."

"Do you know Signora Grimaldi?"

"Yes, I do, there's no crime in that."

"Do you know her husband?"

"No."

"Do you know her son, Damiano?"

"I'm an acquaintance of Signora Grimaldi's, so it's only natural I should know the boy."

"You know he's missing, don't you?"

"Why would I? They don't tell me things like that."

"Things like what?"

"The kind you're telling me, missing children, that kind of thing. You may know there's a missing child, I don't."

Every time you think you're used to it, Fenoglio told himself, every time you think nothing will ever again shock or surprise you, and every time you encounter someone who's capable of setting your nerves more on edge than ever before. The woman had an irritating face and an attitude that was hard to swallow.

"Your name is Maria Pia, is that right?" Pellecchia asked.

"Signora Maria Pia Scaringella," she said.

"Listen to me, fucking Signora Maria Pia Scaringella. Listen to me carefully: don't play games with us. Don't fuck us around, because whenever anyone tries to fuck us around, we get really pissed off. Now I'm going to ask you a few questions and you'll answer me and tell the truth. If you don't, I swear we'll go to your house and give it a thorough search, we'll smash everything up and then we'll arrest you for aiding and abetting. Then you'll be able to talk to a lawyer before you get put inside. Have you got that?"

She didn't reply. Her facial expression had changed, every trace of certainty gone.

"Have you got that?" Pellecchia repeated, almost shouting, and giving the woman's back a violent slap. She jumped, then slowly nodded.

"Signora, don't force us to treat you badly," Fenoglio said. "We know Grimaldi's son was kidnapped, we know a ransom was paid. The family are refusing to cooperate with us. We know that you know everything. It's pointless denying it, it just wastes our time. You have to help us. The information in your possession could be vital in identifying those responsible and, perhaps, in saving the child."

"I haven't done anything wrong," Scaringella said, looking around as if searching for a way out.

"We know that. You simply helped a friend. That's an admirable thing. The best thing would be if those scoundrels had brought back the child after you took them the money. But they didn't do that, and we need help to find them and the boy."

"I can't —"

"Nobody will ever find out."

The woman sighed. She opened her bag, took out a paper handkerchief and wiped the sweat from her forehead with it.

"Can I get you a glass of water, a coffee, anything else?"

"A glass of water."

"Of course." Fenoglio went to the door and opened it just as someone was about to knock. It was Montemurro.

"What is it?"

"Could you come outside for a minute?"

The young carabiniere looked agitated.

Fenoglio went out and closed the door behind him.

"What's happened?"

"We've had an anonymous call to say the boy's down a well in the countryside near Casamassima. They even explained how to get there."

# 12

Fenoglio already knew the boy was dead. If you kidnap someone, demand a ransom, the ransom is paid and the kidnap victim doesn't come home within a short space of time, it means only one thing: he or she is dead.

There is no plausible reason for kidnappers to hold on to the person they've kidnapped – dangerous material to guard – once they've got what they wanted.

He already knew it, and so he shouldn't have felt that shock in the sternum, as if someone had punched him; he shouldn't have been aware of that intolerable sense of anger, emptiness, futility; he shouldn't have felt that shameful weakness in the legs, as if they were about to give way. None of this should have happened, he thought, pinching his chin and cheeks while the car, with its light flashing – but without its siren on – drove through the bright and strangely pale countryside. With him were Captain Valente and Pellecchia; Montemurro was driving; nobody spoke.

When they reached the scene, a few cars and a fire engine were already there. Getting out of their own vehicle, they were enveloped in a primordial silence. There was no sound of motors – the main highway was a long way away – and nobody was speaking. Every now and again a gust of wind passed through the leaves of the olive trees, and the rustling was like the laboured breathing of time.

To get to the well, they had to walk along a narrow path, a winding white strip between trees and clumps of brown, almost red earth. A lot of people had already walked along that path. Any possible trace of whoever had taken the boy there was irredeemably lost.

The well was about three feet across, in the middle of a square of old concrete; against it stood a metal lid. Fenoglio wished he were somewhere else. He knew what he would be seeing in a few minutes' time, and he had no desire to see it. He knew what the smell would be like, and he had no desire to smell it. He knew it would fall to him to inform the boy's parents, and he had no desire to do that either.

He approached the opening and looked down. It was dark. Black. Black, he repeated mentally, as if it were an important observation.

All black.

Someone said something that Fenoglio didn't hear; someone aimed a powerful torch at the inside of the well. Now it was possible to make out what appeared to be a body, bent in an unnatural position. Of course he was in an unnatural position. He was dead. What's more unnatural than death? Damn it.

The firefighters were ready to go down. They were just waiting for authorization.

"The prosecutor will be here soon," Fenoglio said, and his voice sounded to him like somebody else's.

Just before leaving the station he had called D'Angelo to inform her, and had asked her if she wanted to be present. If she preferred, they could take care of everything. She had replied by asking him to send a car for her immediately.

The duty pathologist arrived. He nodded at those present. There were no handshakes. He didn't seem eager to take part in this process either.

A few minutes later, D'Angelo arrived. She came along the white path between two very tall uniformed carabinieri, and the sequence helped to emphasize the tragically surreal tone of the situation. She exchanged a few words with the captain, whom she was meeting for the first time, and said they could proceed. The pathologist handed round a kind of balm with a strong menthol smell. It was to put under the nose, to overcome the stench of death. Fenoglio didn't take it. He knew it was no use. In fact, it was worse. Afterwards, for hours or even days, the obscene odour you thought you had beaten stayed with you anyway. On your clothes, on your skin, in your head. So you might as well avoid the ointment, which was almost equally nauseating.

A short, thin, dark-complexioned firefighter wedged himself into the well with a handkerchief covering his mouth and nose – like a bandit in a Western, Fenoglio thought incongruously – and with a harness for the corpse. He worked down there for a few minutes, then came back up. His face was grey; his dismayed expression said what he had seen at the bottom of the well. With the help of a pulley, his colleagues pulled out the body.

The boy was curled in on himself, as if he had tried to embrace something or someone.

They put him down, and he looked the way you'd expect a human being to look when he's been dead for a few days and left in the country, in a place where there are rats, and other small predators, and flies.

"My God," D'Angelo whispered. Almost at the same moment, they heard a noise like the sound of a bucket of water being emptied onto the ground. A young uniformed carabiniere who had come too close had thrown up. Two others turned away, to avoid looking.

Fenoglio had seen lots of dead bodies. If you do certain jobs, it's unavoidable. You get used to it, obviously. You *have* to get used to it, it's a matter of survival. That's what any detective would tell you. But any detective, even the most hardened, would tell you that there's one thing you never get used to.

The violent death of a child.

# 13

The worst part isn't seeing the bodies. That's unpleasant, sometimes *very* unpleasant, but it isn't the worst part. The worst part is breaking the news to the victims' relatives. Especially if the victims are children and the relatives you have to break the news to are the mother and father.

There is nothing more unacceptable than a child dying before its parents. When that happens, every semblance of meaning in the world collapses like the proverbial house of cards. The death of a child opens wide an abyss of pain and madness so deep you can't see the bottom. Fenoglio didn't know anyone who had really recovered from that experience.

Breaking the news puts you in contact with the abyss. And yet it's up to you, partly because you've seen how others do it and you think that those parents, whoever they are, deserve something more than phrases like: "Today we unfortunately discovered the lifeless body of your son ..." and so on.

For a few seconds, he stood there with his finger suspended in front of the entryphone. He lowered his hand and looked around. The large apartment block communicated desolation and danger. There were no colours, just shades of grey. The walls were peeling, the pillars in some places showing the iron reinforcement rods. Looking up, he could see bars at the windows and unauthorized aluminium verandas. Some children were playing football beneath the grim colonnade.

"Wait for me here," he said to the young carabiniere who had come with him: a newcomer to the team whose name he couldn't remember. He pressed the button. A woman's voice, raucous, heavily accented, filled with violence, replied after some thirty seconds.

"Who is it?"

"Carabinieri, please open up."

"What do you want?"

"Are you Signora Grimaldi?"

"I'm her mother."

"I'm Marshal Fenoglio. I need to speak to your daughter, we've been told she's with you. Please open."

A few seconds went by, then the door opened with a buzz and a sharp click, like something snapping. The interior of the apartment block was as grim as the exterior, dense with unpleasant, solidly packed smells. From food to bleach to some kind of disinfectant or insecticide to the dampness of the walls, which looked like poor-quality cardboard and wouldn't last long.

Grimaldi's mother-in-law lived on the third floor. The door of the apartment, unlike the others, was white, with garish handles of gilded brass. There was something incongruous, funereal, almost obscene about it. It opened before Fenoglio could ring the bell. Two women appeared: they were mother and daughter, but looked like sisters, and not because the older woman seemed young. Grimaldi's wife might have been about thirty-five but looked at least fifteen years older. The skin of her face was grey, dry and toneless. She had deep, mournful shadows under her eyes.

"Have you found him?"

"Can I come in?"

The two women reluctantly moved aside, opened the door a little more and let him in. The inside of the apartment looked like a mad interior decorator's nightmare. Fake Versailles chairs, armchairs and sofas; fake Murano chandeliers; a mosaic table top. A ceramic leopard; an alabaster copy of Michelangelo's David. A huge black television set; a painting of a hunting scene. There was a smell of cheap deodorant and wax floor polish.

"Where is your husband, signora?"

"I don't know. What's happened?"

Fenoglio took a few seconds to gather his strength. "Unfortunately, I have bad news. Perhaps you'd like to sit down?"

The woman remained standing next to her mother, whose face was as motionless as a funeral mask. "Is he dead?"

Fenoglio thought of the woman holding the newborn baby in her arms. She must have been happy then. Normally happy, and unaware. How can you ever imagine, at a moment like that, that one day someone will come and tell you that your child has been murdered; that he was found in a well, half eaten by rats; stripped of dignity, like all murder victims. How can you imagine that?

"Yes, signora. Sadly, yes. I'm very sorry —"

"Where is he?"

Fenoglio had the impression she couldn't breathe, like someone suffocating at night. "We've taken him to the Forensics Institute."

"I have to see him. I have to go there right now."

"Talk to your husband first, signora. Unfortunately, the child ... I mean, he was out in the country for a few days ..."

He wanted to tell her that the wretched body in the morgue had little to do with her son; he wanted to tell her that it was better for her not to see him, that it was better to remember his face when he was alive, rather than have those terrible, disfigured features fixed in her memory. He wanted to tell her these things, but he soon realized the woman had stopped listening to him or even looking at him. Nothing existed any more but her grief.

"I have to see him. Right now, right now," she repeated, shaking. Then her mouth twisted in a grimace and her voice turned into an animal sob.

# 14

Between Sunday 17 and Monday 18 May, many things happened.

In the afternoon, Nicola Grimaldi, also known as Blondie, also known as Three Cylinders, was summoned to the station, where condolences were expressed and his statement was taken. He denied paying a ransom; he denied receiving any requests; he denied having any suspicion as to who might have kidnapped and killed his son. As he was about to leave, having refused to sign the statement, he merely whispered that he would tear the heart out of him and eat it. Nobody asked him who he was referring to. They all knew he was talking about Vito Lopez.

The following morning, the post-mortem took place. The pathologist gave them a summary of the conclusions he would put in his report. The child had rope marks on his wrists and lesions on his head. Someone had hit him, but the blows weren't the cause of death. The post-mortem had shown the existence of a congenital defect of the interatrial septum: basically, a cardiac defect that is sometimes diagnosed only in adulthood and which can be activated by stressful situations. The consequence of this activation is hypoxia – a shortage of oxygen – and possible cardiocirculatory arrest. The blows, the sudden fright, the physical constriction, were all possible preliminaries to a cardiocirculatory attack and death, the pathologist said.

Asked a specific question, the doctor answered that the post-mortem had revealed no signs of sexual violence.

In the afternoon, someone set fire to the house of Pasquale Losurdo, one of the brothers of Simone Losurdo, the likely victim of an underworld execution. Someone else broke into the houses of Vito Lopez and Antonio Losurdo, another of Simone Losurdo's brothers, destroying the furniture and tearing the doors and window frames off their hinges. All three houses were empty. The working hypothesis, supported by informants, was that the two Losurdos, Antonio and Pasquale, had left Bari to join Lopez in his war on Grimaldi's group and avenge their brother Simone. Sources did indeed point to Nicola Grimaldi as being behind the murder of Simone Losurdo and the hiding of his body.

That same afternoon, a report came in from the Carabinieri's criminal investigation unit in Pescara, where the car used in the shoot-out at Enziteto had been stolen, indicating that Lopez had apparently spent the last two weeks in Pescara, as the guest of known local criminals. Right now, though, he was believed to have left the city. His current whereabouts were unknown.

The general feeling was that even more serious incidents were imminent. Detectives and criminals alike were of the opinion that Lopez and his friends were responsible for the kidnapping and death of young Grimaldi.

The boy's father certainly wouldn't stop at the destruction of a few wardrobes or the burning of a house.

\*

Fenoglio was closing the files and getting ready to go home when Pellecchia came in without knocking, an uncharacteristically excited expression on his face.

"I'm sorry, chief, you can't leave."

"Why not?"

"Lopez."

"Has he been killed?"

"No. He's in a bar near here, the one on the corner of Via Dalmazia and Via Gorizia. He called the switchboard and asked if De Paola was around."

"The corporal?"

"Yes, he asked for him, they know each other." He noticed Fenoglio's puzzled expression. "De Paola arrested him once, many years ago. He says he treated him well, and since then they've kept in touch. I think he's even given him a few tip-offs from time to time. Anyway, luckily, De Paola was in the station and took the call."

"What does he want from De Paola?"

"We don't know. All he said is that he needs to see him urgently. He asked if he could join him in that bar, without telling anyone."

Fenoglio could distinctly hear his own heart beat faster. The turning point he had been waiting for might have arrived.

"He wants to cooperate."

"That's what I think, too. What shall I tell De Paola?"

"To get going in ten minutes' time. That's how long it'll take to inform the captain and take up position around the bar."

# ACT TWO

## *Società Nostra*

# 1

The room, which was on the ground floor, was large and anonymous. It looked out on an enclosed courtyard – like those in which prisoners in solitary spend their exercise hour – and there were bars on the windows. It smelled musty and contained only an old desk, a few chairs and an empty shelving unit.

The captain looked around. "Maybe we should put the heating on, it's cold in here. We don't want to look bad when the prosecutor arrives."

It was something said just for the sake of it. Fenoglio shrugged. They were well into May, so obviously there was no question of putting the heating on.

"Vito Lopez," Valente said. "Known as the Butcher, because of his father's job, if I remember correctly."

"That's right. Actually, they use a Bari dialect word for 'butcher' – but I don't think either of us should try to pronounce it."

The captain smiled. Fenoglio was Piedmontese, from Turin, while he himself was from Marche. Pronouncing the Bari dialect would have been an absurd undertaking for both men.

"While we're waiting for them to get here, tell me something more about him."

Fenoglio didn't beat about the bush. Lopez was a highly dangerous criminal. According to informants, he had been responsible for a number of murders – between six and nine, depending on who you spoke to – but had never been arrested for any of them. His wasn't the classic story of the young man led into a life of crime by social deprivation. His father owned a butcher's shop and wasn't at all short of money. Lopez had studied to be a surveyor, although he had never graduated: he had been failed twice for reasons of conduct – in one case for beating up a teacher – and had dropped out of school. His record was like a compendium of criminal law: it went from theft to driving without a licence, from drug dealing to assault, from smuggling foreign tobacco to extortion. And these were only the crimes for which he had been sentenced. Most of what he had done had never reached court.

"Have you ever arrested him?" the captain asked.

"No. Once, though, I was in the station when he was brought in by some colleagues. I can't remember for what, but nothing serious. Maybe resisting arrest. I had a little chat with him and you know what struck me?"

"What?"

"How normal he was. A normal man. He spoke calmly, as if we were equals, he wasn't either arrogant or submissive. And he was well spoken. I mean, it's immediately obvious that he's a cut above those in his circle. It'll be interesting if he really does cooperate."

Valente was about to add something when the door opened and Assistant Prosecutor D'Angelo came in with Sergeant Calcaterra, who was acting as her secretary and factotum. Calcaterra had never been much of a detective. In fact, he had never been a detective at all. He was a clerk who just happened to be in the Carabinieri. But he did have one quality that marked him out: he was a very fast typist. First with mechanical typewriters, then with electric and electronic ones, now with computers, he was capable of writing at the speed of the spoken word, making hardly any mistakes. You dictated as if talking normally, he would write, and at the end the transcript was there, ready to use.

"Where's Lopez?" D'Angelo asked the captain, after exchanging greetings.

"They're bringing him in, they should be here any minute."

"What made him decide to hand himself in?" she asked, lighting a Chesterfield.

"We haven't even talked to him yet, dottoressa," Fenoglio replied. "About an hour ago he called the station and asked for an officer he knew, Corporal De Paola. The corporal joined him in a bar and Lopez told him he'd decided to cooperate with the law, that he had a lot of things to tell us about, including the events of the last few weeks. He made it clear he would only make a statement to you."

D'Angelo sat down on the edge of the desk. "Who is this Corporal De Paola?"

"I don't think you've ever met him, he's a veteran officer. He used to be on the streets, but for years now he's been behind a desk. He arrested Lopez many years ago and, as sometimes happens, a relationship grew up between them. Luckily he was here when Lopez phoned."

D'Angelo looked at her half-smoked cigarette, the precariously balanced little column of ash. "Is there an ashtray here?"

"I'll have one brought in," Fenoglio said.

Just then, footsteps and indistinct voices were heard in the distance, out in the corridor. Gradually, the voices faded and the steps grew louder. Someone knocked at the open door; then, without waiting for a response, Pellecchia looked in with the usual cigar butt in his mouth.

"Come in, Corporal Pellecchia, just you for now, and please close the door," the captain said. "Is he here?"

"Yes, sir, he's with De Paola."

"What impression did you get, corporal?" D'Angelo asked. "Does he really want to cooperate?"

Pellecchia hesitated for a moment. Without realizing it, he glanced at the captain and Fenoglio, as if asking permission to reply. He wasn't used to the idea of a woman being in charge. He sniffed, as he always did when he was uncomfortable. "I think so, yes. With what he's done, Lopez is a dead man walking. We're his only hope."

"Who's his lawyer?"

"It's always been Romanazzi, in other words, the same one as Grimaldi. Obviously he doesn't want him this time. We've called in a lawyer who's the cousin of one of our officers. She's a civil lawyer, but she's willing to defend him."

"Is she already here?"

"We've sent a car to pick her up. In the meantime, if you like, we can get Lopez in here."

D'Angelo let the ash fall on the floor. "All right, bring him in."

Lopez was just as Fenoglio had described him. Normal. Medium height, medium build, a prematurely receding hairline. Dark jacket and blue shirt, like an office worker who has just removed his tie on leaving work. He moved warily, as if checking there was nothing dangerous in the room. His face was a little red. He said good evening and immediately turned to the assistant prosecutor.

"Are you Dottoressa D'Angelo?"

"Yes."

"You need to be careful, dottoressa. Grimaldi has bad intentions towards you."

"What do you mean?" Fenoglio asked.

"Grimaldi kept saying that the dottoressa was causing him a lot of trouble. She'd arrested several of his men for extortion, and he got very pissed off about it, especially when the lawyers said they'd be out soon and they're still inside. He said we needed to teach her a lesson, so that she'll think twice next time."

"What kind of lesson?" D'Angelo asked. A well-trained ear would have caught a slight crack in her voice.

"It hadn't been decided. But Grimaldi had you followed, so we knew that when you get home you drive your car down into the garage. We talked about it. Grimaldi wanted to have you shot there. I told him it would be a stupid thing to do, because if you shoot a judge or a carabiniere the shit really hits the fan – pardon the expression – and it only makes things worse."

"How long ago did this conversation take place?" Fenoglio asked.

"A few months ago. Nothing was decided, but Grimaldi was obsessed with the idea that Dottoressa D'Angelo here needed to be taught a lesson, that way everyone would think twice before … before causing us trouble."

"Everyone meaning the judges, the police, the Carabinieri?" the captain asked.

"Yes. After we talked, a few months ago, the shit really did hit the fan, all kinds of things happened, things I'll tell you about, and I didn't hear anything more about the plans to take out the dottoressa. But I know Grimaldi: when he gets an idea in his head it stays there, and sooner or later he decides to do something about it. So I thought it was only right to mention it from the start."

"You did the right thing," Fenoglio said. "Where are your wife and son?"

"I've left them with relatives of my wife, near Piacenza."

"Give us the exact address. Then call them and tell them that someone will collect them tomorrow and take them to a safe place. Do you have any other close relatives we need to worry about?"

Lopez shook his head. "My brother left Bari many years ago. He said he didn't want to live in the same city as me. My mother joined him after my father died. They live in Switzerland, in a little village I don't even know the name of."

There was a knock at the door. "Avvocato Formica has arrived," a uniformed carabiniere announced, looking in.

Avvocato Formica was a blonde young woman, thin and slight. She looked around, lost. She was from the chaotic, boring but safe world of the civil courts. A world with few accidents and no dangers. And now here she was, on the verge of entering totally unknown territory. Perhaps, Fenoglio thought, she was wondering right now if it had been a good idea to accept the brief.

# 2

At 21.30 on 18 May 1992 in Bari, at the offices of the Criminal Investigation Unit of the Carabinieri, Vito Lopez, alias the Butcher, born in Bari on 7 July 1964, resident there in Via Mayer, currently under investigation for offences as laid out in Articles 416b, 575 and 629 of the Penal Code and Article 73 of the unified code regarding narcotics and other matters, appears before the Public Prosecutor as represented by Assistant Prosecutor Gemma D'Angelo, assisted in the drafting of the current document by Sergeant Ignazio Calcaterra, and also in the presence, for the purposes of the investigation, of Captain Alberto Valente, Marshal Pietro Fenoglio and Corporal Antonio Pellecchia, all detectives in the Criminal Investigation Unit of the Carabinieri of Bari. Lopez is assisted by Avvocato Marianna Formica of the Bar Association of Bari, whose office he has elected as his domicile for all legal purposes.

The Public Prosecutor informs Lopez that

a) his statements may be used in evidence against him;

b) except where laid down in Article 66.1 of the code of procedure, he has the right to remain silent in response to questions, although proceedings will nevertheless continue.

Vito Lopez declares: I intend to answer and preliminarily renounce my right to have my lawyer prepare a defence within a fixed period of time. I have asked of my own free will to confer with yourself because I have decided to cooperate with the law and therefore to report all that I know about the criminal activities directly committed by me or of which I have knowledge due to my belonging to criminal circles.

I acknowledge that I will be able to enjoy the benefits laid down for those who cooperate with the law only if my statements are complete and exhaustive, without any omissions. I also acknowledge that said benefits will be revoked if it transpires that I have made incomplete, reticent, mendacious or slanderous statements.

QUESTION Before beginning a detailed chronological account of your activities, I would like to ask you if you are in a position to provide us with information with regard to arms caches or with regard to any imminent criminal acts.

ANSWER I can help you recover the arms with which my group was equipped, by taking you personally to the *cupa*. The expression *cupa* in our jargon refers to a hiding place for weapons, ammunition and explosives. When I say "my group" I am actually referring to a small group of three people: myself and the brothers Antonio and Pasquale Losurdo.

I will explain to you how and for what reasons said group was formed: as the result of a split from the criminal organization dominating the area of Santo Spirito and Enziteto, known as Società Nostra, under the leadership of Nicola Grimaldi, known as Blondie or Three Cylinders (a reference to the cardiac defect from which he suffers), and will report on the conflict in which it has engaged against said organization.

Some of the weapons I will help you recover are clean, in other words, they have never been used in any acts of violence, while others have been used for assaults, kneecappings and murders.

Apart from the *cupa* where our arms are, I can take you to other hiding places used by Grimaldi and his associates. I am not in a position to tell you if the arms are still in these places or if they have been moved, which is more likely. In one of these hiding places there is even a bazooka from the former Yugoslavia.

I can in addition indicate to you the places, all related to individuals without criminal records and unaffiliated to Grimaldi's criminal organization, in which considerable quantities of narcotics were (and perhaps still are) kept. I will explain for what reason and by what methods these individuals without criminal records were induced, often against their will, to cooperate with that organization.

Last but not least, I want to point out to you that for some time now Nicola Grimaldi has been considering the possibility of an attack on yourself, Dottoressa D'Angelo. It is known to everyone that you have not been provided with bodyguards, while your investigative activities have for some time been considered very harmful to the interests of said group. In particular, the possibility has been considered of an assault inside the garage of your building, at a time when you go there to get your car and drive to your office. I specify that my information on such a plan dates back several months.

# 3

They moved well after nightfall, to minimize the risk of encountering any of Lopez's old friends.

They had three cars. In one were Dottoressa D'Angelo, the captain and his driver; in the second, Fenoglio and Pellecchia; in the third, Carabiniere Montemurro, Sergeant Grandolfo, Corporal De Paola and Lopez.

They drove along the ring road as far as the Palese exit; then they took a parallel road and, a few miles further on, a dirt road the entrance to which was almost invisible. A smuggler's path, Fenoglio told himself, hoping they didn't run into any. Tonight wasn't the night for any kind of distraction.

It took them a quarter of an hour, driving through the countryside in the ghostly moonlight, to reach a small clearing in which stood a tiny plastered shed, the kind that farm workers use to keep their tools in. Getting out of the car, Fenoglio felt nervous because of all that moonlight, even though the place seemed deserted. He had never liked guns and avoided carrying his pistol whenever he could, but at that moment he reached for the stock of the Beretta 92 stuck in his belt. It was an automatic gesture, a kind of charm. It was unlikely there were any of Grimaldi's men lying in wait for Lopez, but in some situations it's the unlikeliest things that scare us the most.

"Where do we go now, Vito?" Pellecchia asked in a low voice, precisely as if there might be someone around who wasn't supposed to hear.

"The door's at the back," Lopez replied. "I have the key."

They opened the door. Inside, it was pitch-black and smelt of damp, hay, earth and dried dung. Montemurro and Grandolfo lit two large torches and flashed them nervously, creating cones of light. The small shed was almost empty. A few hoes and a few billhooks, two demijohns, and some jute sacks heaped up in a corner.

"There," Lopez said, pointing.

Under the bags there was a wooden trapdoor and under the trapdoor a small square compartment, made of tuff, less than three feet across and perhaps five feet deep.

"Can I go down?"

D'Angelo said he could and with a nimble, athletic movement Lopez jumped in. He worked on the floor for a few minutes, shifted two large tuff bricks and removed some bundles wrapped in material. He handed them up to the carabinieri and pulled himself out without bothering to put things back in place.

"Since nobody's going to use this any more," he commented, with a smile that had something strangely helpless about it. There were no objections.

He placed the bundles on the floor. D'Angelo lit a cigarette. Lopez asked for permission to smoke, too. He was civilized, Fenoglio told himself. A *civilized* murderer. He even seemed quite likeable. An absurd word – likeable – to use about a man who had spent his life robbing, trafficking, extorting and killing without mercy. It wasn't the first time that Fenoglio had made this kind of observation. There were criminals who were stupid, brutal, nasty and hateful. They were the way criminals ought to be in order to correspond to a simple, reassuring vision of the world. You're different from us. You're the bad guys and we're the good guys. Everything clear and easy to figure out.

But there were also – he had met lots of them – intelligent drug dealers, likeable robbers, murderers capable of unexpected and selfless gestures of humanity. They complicated things, made classifications less simple.

They opened the bundles containing Lopez's arsenal. There were guns of every calibre, from a 6.35 to a .44 Magnum by way of a number of semi-automatics; there were pump-action rifles, a sawn-off shotgun, a Skorpion submachine gun, a Kalashnikov, hand grenades that looked like small brown pineapples and so much loose ammunition as to look like an army of sleeping cockroaches.

Dottoressa D'Angelo let out a whistle. Pellecchia sniffed. Fenoglio rubbed his one-day growth of beard. The others probably also reacted in some way in the semi-darkness.

"None of them are loaded, are they, Lopez?" Fenoglio asked.

"None of them are loaded, marshal. The grenades are on safety, don't worry."

D'Angelo knelt and picked up the assault rifle. "This is a Kalashnikov."

"Yes, dottoressa," the captain replied.

"This is the first one I've seen live. In Calabria, I had lots of people arrested for possessing or carrying these things, but this is the first time I've touched one."

"Do you mind if we check the barrel, dottoressa?" the captain said. "Sometimes there's a bullet left in."

"It's completely unloaded, don't worry," Lopez repeated.

"I thought it would be heavier," D'Angelo said, holding the weapon in her arms as if it were a child.

"Unloaded, they weigh seven and a half pounds," Sergeant Grandolfo said. "With the magazine full, nearly nine."

There was something a tad theatrical about the scene. It lasted some thirty or forty seconds, then practicality prevailed.

"Let's take it all and go," D'Angelo said.

The carabinieri wrapped the bundles back up again, took them outside and put them in the boots of the cars. With a gesture that seemed like a metaphor, Lopez himself closed the door and stood there in the moonlit clearing with the key in his hand.

"Give it to me," Fenoglio said. "You don't need it any more."

Five minutes later, the small procession of vehicles, each with the same occupants as before, was winding its way through the countryside, between the olive trees.

"What do you think about this story of an attempt on the dottoressa?" Fenoglio asked Pellecchia, who was relighting his cigar. "Do you think it's credible or did he only say it to make himself look important in her eyes?"

"I think Grimaldi is a lousy son of a bitch. He's genuinely capable of doing something like that. And Lopez, as far as I know, is a serious criminal. Not someone who talks bullshit."

"That's what I thought."

"What do you think of the woman?"

"What woman?"

"D'Angelo."

Fenoglio shook his head. The *woman*. Pellecchia was incurable.

"She's good, she's tough. If I were a lawyer I wouldn't like to come up against her. There's something about her I can't put my finger on, I'm not sure what." He paused for a few seconds. "That was a stupid thing to say. If I can't put my finger on it, then of course I don't know what it is."

Pellecchia gave a hoarse laugh. "And now what do we do?"

"We go back to the station, we put these arms under lock and key, and we go home to bed. Tomorrow we make out a seizure report, then I assume we'll continue taking our new friend's statement."

"If he really spills the beans, it's going to take a while. The bastard has a hell of a lot of things to tell us. How do we proceed?"

"D'Angelo will decide that, but I think Lopez will have to start with the most serious things committed by him, to demonstrate that he isn't playing games. Murders, major drug deals, extortion."

"And he'll have to tell us about the boy."

Fenoglio didn't reply immediately. He looked out through the window, massaging the elbow he had broken years earlier and which still, for no specific reason, gave him sudden unpleasant shooting pains every now and again. He took a deep breath, feeling the tiredness suffuse his whole body like a wave.

"If it was him."

Pellecchia turned to look at him, neglecting the dirt road for a few moments. "What do you mean? Who else could it have been?"

Fenoglio shrugged. "You're right. Who else could it have been?"

# 4

At 10.00 on 19 May 1992 in Bari, at the offices of the Criminal Investigation Unit of the Carabinieri, Vito Lopez, whose particulars have already been stated in other documents, currently under investigation for offences as laid out in Articles 416b, 575 and 629 of the Penal Code and Article 73 of the unified code regarding narcotics and other matters, appears before the Public Prosecutor as represented by Assistant Prosecutor Gemma D'Angelo, assisted in the drafting of the current document by Sergeant Ignazio Calcaterra, and also in the presence, for the purposes of the investigation, of Captain Alberto Valente, Marshal Pietro Fenoglio and Corporal Antonio Pellecchia, all detectives in the Criminal Investigation Unit of the Carabinieri of Bari. Lopez is assisted by Avvocato Marianna Formica of the Bar Association of Bari, whose office he has elected as his domicile for all legal purposes.

The Public Prosecutor informs Lopez that

a) his statements may be used in evidence against him;

b) except where laid down in Article 66.1 of the code of procedure, he has the right to remain silent in response to questions, although proceedings will nevertheless continue.

Vito Lopez declares: I intend to answer. Preliminarily, I declare that I wish to appoint Avvocato Formica here present, previously appointed by the court, as my defence lawyer.

QUESTION Signor Lopez, first of all I would like you to summarize for us, in chronological order, all the acts of violence in which you have been directly involved. I remind you once again that the benefits the law concedes to those who cooperate depend on the completeness of your statements. If any omissions are discovered, or if any of your statements are found to be false or slanderous, that may lead to the immediate revocation of all protective measures and all procedural benefits. Are you aware of all this?

ANSWER I am aware of it and I confirm that I intend to cooperate fully and to report everything I know about the criminal activities of my group – Società Nostra – and of those allied or opposed to it.

I shall talk about the murders and acts of violence in general; the organizational structure, the rules relating to it and the process of affiliation; the activities of extortion and loan sharking; the traffic in narcotics and the network of dealers; the system of controlling the territory as regards both legitimate and illegitimate activities; the relations with local politicians and the support given to certain candidates at election time.

As requested by you, I shall begin with the acts of violence. I am personally responsible for seven murders and one attempted murder. I would like to make it clear that I am able to report useful elements relating to a much larger number of murders, if we include those in which I was not involved but of which I am aware thanks to my role in the organization.

QUESTION Tell us about the murders for which you were responsible. We can deal with the others at a later stage.

ANSWER The first murder committed by me dates from September 1987, in other words, when I was twenty-three. The victim was a young man of whom I recall only the nickname: Curly, because of his hair. I should point out that I was never investigated for this murder, or even suspected of it.

This young man was dealing heroin on behalf of Nicola Grimaldi, but there were nasty rumours about him: it was said that he was a police informer. I believe that Grimaldi did look into the matter. It is possible he set a trap for him, passing him a piece of information to see if it reached the police, which in fact it did, but I cannot now remember this with any accuracy. Anyway, Grimaldi decided that he had to die and that he would deal with it himself, together with myself and another of his men, Michele Capocchiani, known as the Pig.

QUESTION Why did Grimaldi ask you and Capocchiani to participate?

ANSWER Capocchiani was one of his most experienced men and was always given the most dangerous and demanding jobs. He was a good driver, a good marksman, he was ruthless and fearless. Grimaldi wanted me there, too, because he wanted to find out how reliable I was. I had joined the organization at the beginning of that year and Grimaldi had taken a liking to me. Getting me to participate in such a dangerous and demanding operation was the prelude to granting me a more important role.

QUESTION Did Grimaldi offer you money for this job?

ANSWER No. I want to make clear that only hitmen – a category to which, strange as it may seem, I do not feel I belong in any way – receive payment for committing a murder. It would have been a lack of respect towards me on the part of Grimaldi if he had offered me money, but, above all, it would have been a serious lack of respect towards him on my part if I had asked him for any. In the circles to which I belong, participating in a murder is a mark of distinction and respect. The person assigning that role shows trust in the assignee; the person given the role appreciates this trust and wants to show that he is deserving of it in order to strengthen his sense of belonging to the organization.

QUESTION Tell us what happened.

ANSWER We knew that Curly always did his dealing outside a pool hall in Santo Spirito. We drove past it just before lunch and stopped for a beer and a chat. Then, as if the idea had only just occurred to him, Capocchiani suggested we go to Giovinazzo and get some raw mussels from a fishmonger friend of his. Curly, who loved seafood, fell into the trap and asked if he could come, too. Naturally we said yes. Curly soon realized that we were not going in the direction of Giovinazzo and were instead driving into the countryside around Bitonto. He asked for an explanation and it was then that Grimaldi pointed a gun at his head. I should make it clear that Curly was sitting in front on the right, Capocchiani was driving, and Grimaldi and I were in the back. Our destination was a plot of land that could only be reached down a country lane, a long way from the main road. It was a place in which it was very unlikely that anyone would appear by chance. On that plot of land, there was a farmhouse that was sometimes used for hiding stolen goods, weapons and narcotics. It was there that we took Curly, after tying his hands with wrapping tape that we had brought with us for that purpose. Then Grimaldi passed me the pistol – Capocchiani had another – and began hitting Curly, telling him that he had to confess that he was a lousy snitch. He hit him with brass knuckles (he had a set in silver that a jeweller friend of his had made for him); I remember that Curly's face was so covered in blood that you could hardly see it.

QUESTION Did Curly confess?

ANSWER Yes and no. He said that he pretended to pass information to the police, that he would tell them half-truths just to keep them happy.

QUESTION Had he realized that you intended to kill him?

ANSWER No, I think not. He thought we would beat him up and then let him go.

QUESTION What happened after this partial confession?

ANSWER Grimaldi told Curly to get down on his knees. That was when he realized, and he started crying and begging us not to kill him. He said that he had done nothing wrong, he had a child and things like that. Grimaldi told him he should have thought of the fact that he had a child before, when he was being a lousy snitch. Then, because Curly was not kneeling, he hit him again with the brass knuckles and forced him to his knees. He nodded to me as if to say: "Now shoot him." I raised the gun, which was a calibre .38 with six bullets, and realized that my hand was shaking very badly; I had to hold it still with the other hand.

At that moment Curly realized that I was pointing the gun at him – I was at his side – and wet himself. I thought that if I did not shoot immediately, I would not be capable of it afterwards, because of the shaking of my hand and the smell that made me want to vomit and all the rest. So I shot him in the head, in the temple.

QUESTION Did you fire just one shot?

ANSWER Yes, I fired a single shot. Capocchiani shot him another two or three times once he was on the ground. He did not like it if he did not get a chance to shoot, too. Then Grimaldi told me to open the boot of the car and fetch the can of petrol that we had brought with us. I left the farmhouse and vomited, making sure I was not seen. Then I went back in with the can, doused Curly in petrol and, still following Grimaldi's orders, set fire to him.

QUESTION Why did he make you do everything?

ANSWER As I said, dottoressa, it was a kind of test, to see if he could rely on me for the most difficult operations. As I started the fire I thought I noticed Grimaldi and Capocchiani exchanging knowing looks, as if to say: "He is a good boy, he has passed the test." When Curly's body caught fire it moved for a few seconds and I thought he was still alive, even though we had shot him several times. I said: "Is he still alive?" and Capocchiani started laughing and replied that they were just mechanical movements produced by the fire. I could not honestly say if Capocchiani was right or if Curly was still dying.

QUESTION Then what happened?

ANSWER We left the farmhouse while the body was still burning – I had doused him in two gallons of petrol – we got back in the car, and went and hid the guns in a wrecking yard owned by one of Grimaldi's men. There, we cleaned ourselves carefully to remove any possible gunshot residues, in case we were stopped by the police or the Carabinieri. Then they drove me home. On the ride back Grimaldi said that I had done well and that I deserved to "move forward".

QUESTION What did he mean by that?

ANSWER That I had proved worthy of being promoted within the hierarchy of the organization.

QUESTION And did this happen?

ANSWER Yes, a few weeks later.

# 5

Lopez had immediately shown himself to be an ideal witness: he understood the questions and answered in kind, accurately, without wandering off the subject, and without too much coarseness of speech. Of course, his words were then transformed into the somewhat surreal language of a legal transcript, but the man gave the impression that he would handle himself well in court, even under cross-examination.

Dottoressa D'Angelo had left for a few hours: she had wanted to drop by her office where she had a few papers to sign and motions to deal with. The captain and the others had gone to lunch. Fenoglio had stayed with Lopez. They had had sandwiches and beer brought in, and they ate in silence.

As soon as he had finished, Lopez asked if he could smoke.

Fenoglio replied yes and opened a window.

"What happens when I've told you everything?" Lopez asked after a few drags.

"We'll take you to your family. Then we'll check what you've told us, and if any of it turns out to be false you'll lose all your benefits. When I say 'false', I don't mean inaccuracies. I mean falsely accusing people or deliberately omitting something important. Never forget that."

"What do you think of my lawyer, marshal? Do you think she's okay? She seems a bit insecure to me. I was keen to appoint her, but I don't know how she'll be when we get to court."

"She's a civil lawyer. If we'd called in a criminal lawyer, there was a risk that news of your cooperating might get out too soon. When we get to court, you can decide whether to stick with her or get someone else, maybe someone from outside who has no connections with Bari."

Lopez finished his cigarette, extinguished it and walked over to the window. Beyond the bars, the courtyard was deserted.

"What were you thinking when I talked about how we killed Curly?" he said, still looking out.

"Why do you ask me that?"

"It disgusted you, didn't it?"

Actually, the immediate and correct answer would have been: no, it hadn't disgusted him. Not because it wasn't a repulsive act, but because it was more or less what he had expected to hear. It hadn't disgusted him because that was his job, because he had heard or come across many similar stories. It hadn't disgusted him because he was used to it, he had been anaesthetized, he'd developed that mechanism common to all detectives by which the horrors of life are reduced to forms and files. The mechanism by which, when you're told about some poor guy being tortured, beaten to a pulp, killed like a dog and burnt, perhaps still alive, all you're thinking about is the inquiries you'll have to conduct, the cases you'll have to reopen, the corroborating evidence you'll have to find. But if you don't have that functioning system of defences, you'll just go crazy.

So no, it hadn't disgusted him, but telling that to Lopez didn't seem appropriate. It didn't seem *right*. So he kept silent. His expression said only: go on, if you want. Lopez lit another cigarette.

"The day we went to kill him, I felt strong. My life was about to change, I was going to become someone, not the loser I'd always been. You know when I stopped feeling that way?"

"When?"

"When I made him get down on his knees. I told you his face was all bloody from being hit with the brass knuckles, but I didn't give a fuck about that. I'd beaten up lots of people. It was normal. But the moment I made him get down on his knees and he realized we were going to kill him and I realized that Grimaldi was making me do it, I started to feel … what can I call it?"

"Panic?"

"Panic, I felt panic. I felt like running away, and almost did. And then it occurred to me that if I ran away, they'd kill me, too. Capocchiani would kill me, because the son of a bitch liked killing people. Have you ever been afraid of death, marshal? Not death in general. Have you ever thought you might be about to die?"

"Yes, I have."

"Then you know what I mean. I felt I was going to shit my pants, I really had to hold it in, and in fact I later threw up. When Grimaldi told me to shoot him, I was shaking all over and didn't want to show it, so, as I said, I took the gun in both hands and killed him, to have done with it. Then I dreamt about it for a week. I dreamt that he was begging me, telling me not to kill him, I dreamt that he was burning alive. Once I even dreamt that my father – who was already dead by then – was standing there after we'd burnt Curly, asking me what I'd done."

Fenoglio wondered why Lopez was telling him all this. Assuming there was a reason.

"Don't you ever smoke, marshal?" Lopez asked, holding out the packet of cigarettes.

"Almost never," Fenoglio replied, shaking his head.

"Then, gradually, I stopped dreaming about him," Lopez resumed, as if he had left an important part hanging.

"What about the other murders?"

"You want me to tell you about them now?"

"No, I just want to know what you felt."

Lopez was silent for a while. He didn't seem surprised by the question, and appeared to be searching for the right words – which are almost always the simplest.

"You know something, marshal? I didn't feel anything. A few months later, I committed another murder. It was meant to be just a kneecapping, but it went wrong. By the next day I'd already forgotten it. And the third even less. He was a junkie, Capocchiani and I killed him, and then I went and had a meal."

Fenoglio felt the need to drink a sip of beer, but his bottle was empty.

"The problem, marshal, is that you can get used to anything. Even murder."

Yes, that was the problem: you could get used to anything.

# 6

At 15.30 on 19 May, in the presence of the same persons as previously indicated, the interview is resumed.

QUESTION When we suspended the interview, you were telling us about your promotion within the hierarchy of Grimaldi's group. Before continuing with this account, can you explain to us the various ranks in the criminal organization to which you belonged, and what the qualifications for affiliation or promotion are?

ANSWER The ranks – or to be more exact: the gifts – of the organization, according to rules which, with a few differences, are valid throughout Apulia, are as follows: *Picciotteria, Camorra, Sgarro, Santa, Vangelo, Trequartino* and *Diritto di medaglione.* Actually, the rank of *Picciotteria* is never used, in the sense that new members join the organization as a *camorrista* or even a *sgarrista.* For example, I was affiliated directly as a *sgarrista,* which is referred to as the 'third', meaning the third gift.

QUESTION For what reason is the first rank never used, and for what reason were you affiliated directly into the third rank, the rank of *sgarrista?*

ANSWER It is necessary to say something first. The organization of which I was part, which is headed by Nicola

Grimaldi, comes out of the Apulian prison Camorra established at the beginning of the 1980s, the leaders of which were – and as far as I know, still are – Giosuè Rizzi from Foggia, known as the Pope, for the northern part of Apulia, and Pino Rogoli from Mesagne, known as the Bricklayer, for the southern part. Giosuè Rizzi is the head of the Società Foggiana, while Rogoli is the head of the Sacra Corona Unita. When I speak of prison Camorra, I am referring to the fact that this organization, to which many Apulian prisoners from various places eventually belonged, was born within the prison system. Up until the end of the 1970s – I speak here of things I was told and of which I have no direct knowledge – there were no Mafia-style organizations in Apulia, only criminal cliques devoted to specific activities such as smuggling, gambling, prostitution and, obviously, narcotics. With the exception of the town of Andria, in which a dangerous and highly respected group devoted to kidnapping had been active for some time, Apulia was a region of little significance from a criminal point of view. That was the reason for the particularly harsh prison conditions imposed on Apulian prisoners, who were considered second-class criminals: apart from having to bear the normal rigours of the prison regime, they were forced to endure harassment by prisoners from other regions in the south, especially from members of the Neapolitan Camorra. The situation became intolerable, and some Apulian prisoners decided to react. First of all, as I said, Rogoli and Rizzi, having been affiliated and promoted by major Calabrian Mafia bosses (Di Stefano in the case of Rizzi and Bellocco in the case of Rogoli, I believe), and therefore having acquired some personal prestige in criminal circles, started in their turn to affiliate others in large numbers in order to form self-defence groups within the prisons, with the aim of countering the bullying and violence of the Neapolitans. The idea was that in Apulian prisons, the Apulians should be in charge, and not, to use Grimaldi's expression, those "scumbags from the Neapolitan Camorra". It is no coincidence that the Apulian prison Mafia was born out of a narrow relationship with the Calabrians, absorbing the rituals and hierarchy of the 'Ndrangheta almost wholesale. The very need to establish large groups within a short space of time led them to speed up the procedures, affiliating people directly into the second or third rank, as in my case. I've never met anyone who had the first rank, the *Picciotteria*. It exists in the theoretical framework of the organization, but it has never been used, at least not by us.

QUESTION I repeat the previous question. For what reason were you affiliated directly into the third rank? Where and how did your affiliation take place?

ANSWER Grimaldi had taken a great liking to me during a brief period of imprisonment together. I was in prison for a robbery for which I had been arrested as a consequence of being identified by the victim from photographs. Immediately after the arrest, I was beaten for a long time, very harshly, to make me inform on my accomplices, but I did not do so. When I entered prison – Grimaldi was already there – I still had visible marks of the beating on me, and word soon spread that I was a young man who respected *omertà*. One day, during the exercise hour, Grimaldi came up to me and said that he knew how I had conducted myself during my arrest and afterwards, and he said he appreciated that. Then he said that he knew something else about me, something that had made a good impression on him.

QUESTION To what was he referring?

ANSWER Sometime earlier, I had gone to dinner with two friends of mine with whom I had done a number of jobs – Vito Colella and Franco De Carne – in a pizzeria in the San Girolamo district. I do not remember the name. After eating and drinking a lot, we got up to go without paying, which is what we did in a lot of places. Usually, nobody said anything because the owners of the restaurants and the pizzerias knew us and preferred to avoid trouble. In that case, though, I think the management of the pizzeria had changed, because a young man – the son of the owner – followed us, caught up with us at the door and said with great determination that we had to pay the bill. Colella, who was the most drunk of all of us, tried to punch him, but the fellow dodged the blow and reacted by hitting him repeatedly in the face. We would later find out that the man was a black belt in karate, even a national champion, I think. De Carne also tried to hit him, but suffered the same fate. While this fellow was beating De Carne, I grabbed a bottle of beer from a table and struck him violently on the head several times with it. He fell to the ground. He may have been knocked unconscious. What is certain is that I had hit him until he bled, in front of the other customers and the waiters. The next day, I discovered – even the newspapers talked about it – that the man I had hit was a martial arts champion. The news spread, and this increased my criminal reputation. As I said, even Grimaldi had heard about it (although he did not know that I had used a bottle and assumed I had got the better of a martial arts expert with my bare hands) and had been impressed.

When he left prison a few days later – he was acquitted of a charge of loan sharking and extortion – he told me to go and see him once I, too, had got out. I replied that this would not be for some time, given the seriousness of the charge against me. He gave me a strange smile, patted me on the back and said: "Who knows?" At the time, I did not understand what he meant, but it soon became clear to me because the witness to the robbery, when asked to identify me by the examining magistrate, did not do so and I was released. I later found out that some of Grimaldi's men had been in touch with him and told him not to identify anyone.

QUESTION They threatened him, obviously?

ANSWER I do not know the details, but I would say there was no need for overt threats. If the witness knew who these people were and on whose behalf they were speaking – and of course I believe that he did know – a request devoid of any overtly threatening content would have sufficed.

QUESTION Were you responsible for that robbery?

ANSWER Of course, and the witness had seen me very clearly.

QUESTION What did you do when you got out?

ANSWER What Grimaldi had told me to do. I went to see him, he asked me if I wanted to become one of his men and I said yes. He told me that he had gathered a great deal of information about me and that it was all positive. That was why he had decided to do something out of the ordinary, which was to affiliate me directly into the rank of *sgarrista*. He told me it was an honour, and I was perfectly well aware of that.

QUESTION What information had Grimaldi gathered about you?

ANSWER Grimaldi knew practically everything about me and my criminal career, which had started with petty thefts when I was still a little boy and continued with smuggling and robbery. I do not know who he had talked to, but he had become convinced – as he told me quite openly – that I was a young man who could act, talk and keep quiet when each of these things was necessary. Such a judgement from a figure as important and prestigious in criminal circles as Grimaldi filled me with pride. At that moment I would have done without question anything he had ordered me to do.

QUESTION Tell us about your affiliation.

ANSWER I should point out that for the proper conduct of an affiliation or a promotion, a baptized place is necessary. When I say "baptized" I mean it must be a place expressly and stably equipped for affiliations in a ceremony of baptism, or else a different place but one that has first to be subjected to a kind of purification.

QUESTION Can you describe this?

ANSWER For this ritual, as for the others (affiliations, promotions), specific formulas are laid down. I have to say that I have long been fascinated by these rituals and have learned them all by heart. Someone like me, who is able to speak every formula without the help of a written text, is said in our jargon to "shine". The purification of the place is carried out following a ritual dialogue between the head of the group and the other participants in the ceremony. The boss begins thus: "Good evening, wise companions." The others reply: "Good evening." The boss: "Are you ready to baptize these premises?" The others: "We are ready." The boss: "In the name of our ancestors, the three Spanish knights Osso, Mastrosso and Carcagnosso, I baptize these premises. If previously I recognized it as a place haunted by policemen and informers, from now on I recognize it as a sacrosanct and inviolable place where this honoured society may form and dissolve."

QUESTION Was the place where your affiliation was celebrated a place permanently devoted to these rituals, or was it baptized specially for the occasion?

ANSWER It was a house between Palese and Santo Spirito. I do not know who the owner was, but it was clearly at the disposal of Grimaldi and his men. It was a place permanently equipped for affiliations, and in fact it was also there that I was raised to the rank of *santista*.

QUESTION Who took part in your affiliation ceremony?

ANSWER Grimaldi, who was the Godfather or Leader in Chief; Capocchiani, who was the Tirade; a man named Lattanzio who later died of natural causes, who was the Bookkeeper; a young fellow from Foggia whose name I cannot remember, who was the Favourable, and someone named Oronzo, from Lecce, who was the Unfavourable.

QUESTION What do these terms mean?

ANSWER They are the roles that have to be filled for the ceremony of affiliation or promotion to be valid. The Godfather is the one who grants the gift; the Bookkeeper represents the organization's responsibilities towards its members, who will always be helped in times of need; the Tirade (an expression that refers both to the formula of affiliation and the person who recites it) is the one who represents the training and traditions of the organization; the Favourable is the one who delivers his opinion on the affiliation or promotion of the initiate; the Unfavourable is the one who has the task of checking that the procedure is being performed correctly.

QUESTION Describe to us briefly how it went.

ANSWER After the formulas of affiliation had been recited, a small cut was made on the index finger of my right hand (the trigger finger) and the blood allowed to drip onto a small image that I burnt while holding it in my hand. Then I recited the oath which I had learned by heart and can still remember. If you like, I can even recite it now.

QUESTION Go on.

ANSWER I swear on the point of this dagger bathed in blood that I will be loyal to this constituted society and disown mother, father, brothers and sisters to the seventh generation; I swear to share, hundredth part by hundredth part, thousandth part by thousandth part, to the last drop of my blood, with one foot in the grave and one on the chain, embracing imprisonment wholeheartedly.

At the end of the ceremony I was congratulated and then we had dinner to celebrate. My affiliation was passed as news to all the other members, both inside and outside prison.

QUESTION "Passed as news"?

ANSWER In our jargon, passed as news means communicated. When there is a new affiliation all the members of the organization, both those at large and those inside, must be informed immediately. Another thing that is done after a new affiliation is what is known as "giving the portions". That means offering cakes or cigarettes to celebrate the admission of the new member. I should point out that those members at large are offered cakes and those inside are offered cigarettes, red Marlboros to be specific.

QUESTION So this is the ceremony in which you were affiliated. You said that after the murder of Curly you were granted the rank of *santista*. Can you explain what it means to receive and hold the rank of *santista*?

ANSWER As I said earlier, the *Santa* is the fourth of the ranks in the hierarchy. It is an important rank, which involves some duties of command, and can be granted only to someone who has committed a murder or at least, but only in exceptional cases, an act of violence in which the victim did not die. I have been told that in the Calabrian families it took, and still takes, many years to reach that rank. With us, for the reasons I have explained (the need to establish a structured organization with the requisite hierarchy within a short period of time), things happen more quickly. In concrete terms, I was affiliated with the rank of *sgarrista* in February 1987 and received the *Santa* in November of that same year after the murder of Curly.

QUESTION Who was present at the ceremony in which you were given the rank of *santista*?

ANSWER I should point out that the ceremony for the promotion to the rank of *santista* involves three celebrants, not five. All three are godfathers and are conventionally known as Giuseppe Garibaldi, Giuseppe Mazzini and Alfonso La Marmora.

QUESTION What have Garibaldi, Mazzini and La Marmora got to do with a criminal organization?

ANSWER In the tradition of the 'Ndrangheta, which was later taken up by our Apulian organizations, Garibaldi, Mazzini and La Marmora are considered the founders of the *Santa*. I am unable to tell you the reason, although an elderly Calabrian did once tell me that the 'Ndrangheta began during the Risorgimento as the Carboneria. It was not an argument that interested me, and I did not look any further into it.

QUESTION Let us go back to who was present.

ANSWER Grimaldi, a Calabrian named Barreca, who was the highest in rank, and a man from Foggia named Agnello or Agnelli, who was killed a few years later. The ceremony is much more complicated than a simple affiliation and requires among other things the use of various objects. The three members of the *capriata* – the name we use to refer to the group of persons who carry out the affiliation or the promotion – and the initiate sit around a table on which there have to be a cyanide pill (in ceremonies conducted in prison, a normal pill is used) which symbolizes the suicide the *santista* must be ready to commit rather than betray the organization; a sawn-off shotgun (in prison, this is represented by a plastic fork with only two prongs), to be used to shoot the initiate in the mouth if he betrays; a ball of cotton wool, which symbolizes Mont Blanc, that is, a sacred thing; a lemon, which is used to treat the members' wounds; a needle that represents weapons and is used to prick the initiate; a sacred image; three white silk handkerchiefs, which symbolize purity of heart; and the "portions", that is, pastries or cigarettes.

QUESTION Was the formula the same?

ANSWER No, for every transition from one rank to another there are different formulas and rituals. As I said, I know them all by heart and over the years I have taken part in numerous affiliations, reciting said formulas. The ceremony for conferring the *Santa* is complicated: the blood and the lemon are mixed, the image is burnt, a lot of things are done and it all lasts quite a long time. If you like, I can describe it in detail.

QUESTION Let us move on for now. We can proceed with a detailed description of these rituals at a later stage. Let us go back: what are the conditions of eligibility for the organization?

ANSWER There are positive requirements – having shown that you are a man of action, reliable, able to respect *omertà* and of good conduct in general – and negative requirements. Basically, you must not be a member of any law enforcement agency, or a relative of a member of any law enforcement agency, and you must not be a drug addict or a homosexual. I should make it clear that when I say drug addict I mean heroin addict; they are particularly unreliable because when they are without their fix they are capable of anything, even talking to the police or the Carabinieri.

QUESTION So there is no bar against those who take other forms of narcotics, or those who are heavy drinkers?

ANSWER With cocaine and marijuana, there has never been a problem. We all consumed a lot of cocaine, and I would even say it was our principal pastime – along with going with prostitutes – when we were together. As for drinking, the question is evaluated on a case-by-case basis. There is no problem with the consumption of alcohol, even heavy consumption, but an alcoholic, a real drunk, cannot be affiliated.

QUESTION What if someone becomes an alcoholic or a drug addict after being affiliated?

ANSWER That can be a major problem. In the rare cases where that happened, the individuals were disposed of.

Once I was forced to kill a young man who had started consuming heroin daily and had become a risk. As I have already said, heroin addicts can easily become police informers.

# 7

D'Angelo left with the loyal Calcaterra and two other carabinieri who had been assigned to her by the colonel while
waiting for the prefecture to decide about giving her bodyguards. Nobody thought of underestimating Grimaldi's
"bad intentions" towards her.

Pellecchia and Montemurro accompanied Lopez to
the Carabinieri station on the edge of town where he was
being housed and kept under surveillance, even though
not officially in custody.

The captain invited Fenoglio to get something from
the canteen.

"Sometimes I think our work is a mixture of the tragic
and the ridiculous," he said, knocking back a glass of
Prosecco.

"In what sense, sir?"

"I was thinking about what we write in transcripts and
reports. Today, for example, in a phrase attributed to Lopez,
there was mention of criminal cliques. Obviously he would
never have used the word 'clique' himself, although I must
say, he's one of the most intelligent criminals I've ever met."

Valente really was a strange officer: he seemed to be
playing – with some difficulty – a role that wasn't his, a role
he couldn't get used to.

"You're right, it's a surreal language. Have you ever read Calvino?"

"I read *The Baron in the Trees* in high school, but didn't like it very much. Actually, my favourite is *The Nonexistent Knight*."

"Mine, too. We all identified with Agilulf."

"Why did you ask me about Calvino?"

"Many years ago he wrote an article in a newspaper, I can't remember which one. He imagined the transcript of a witness statement about the theft of some bottles of wine. The witness says: early this morning, and the sergeant takes it down as: in the early ante meridiem hours; the witness talks about lighting the stove, and the sergeant takes it down as: activation of the thermal equipment; the witness says: I found bottles of wine, and the sergeant takes it down as: I made a chance discovery of a number of oenological products. And so on."

The captain smiled. "Very true to life."

"Yes, completely true to life and very amusing. If I can find it, I'll show it to you. The most interesting thing, though, is what Calvino says about why transcripts are written in that way."

"Why?"

"Calvino talks about what he calls semantic terror. The idea is that the language of transcripts should avoid words with common, concrete meanings because the person writing wants unconsciously to emphasize that he's on a higher level than the material things he happens to be dealing with. It's an attempt to keep a distance from the concreteness of the real world. Anti-language, Calvino calls it. A language far from meaning and far from life."

The captain had his glass refilled. He took another sip. Fenoglio played with an olive and ate it. Twice, the captain seemed on the verge of saying something and twice he thought better of it.

"It seems correct, yes. But maybe he simplifies too much. Maybe he's imposing an ideological interpretation."

It was certainly impressive to hear a captain in the Carabinieri, a career officer, talking about ideological interpretations.

"Why does it strike you as ideological?"

"I think reducing everything to the transcriber's supposed sense of superiority over the material being transcribed is, as I said, simplifying it a little. There are also practical reasons. If I have to make a summary transcript, which by definition doesn't contain every word that's been said, I'm forced to use words that summarize, even though they may not fully correspond to the vocabulary of the person speaking."

"I agree. But we need to be very aware of what's being done. D'Angelo's good, Lopez is intelligent, and these interviews are going well. Apart from anything else, I think he's so bright that he's learning as she takes the statement. I won't be surprised if we hear him using expressions like 'criminal cliques' in court."

What a bizarre dialogue, Fenoglio thought. A captain and a marshal in the Carabinieri discussing linguistic niceties in the context of an interview with a homicidal Mafioso. Like news from a parallel world.

"But leaving D'Angelo and Lopez aside," Fenoglio resumed after this quick private digression, "it doesn't generally take much for an overly formal transcript, caused by the reasons Calvino spoke about, to twist the meaning of what the witness or the suspect said."

They were both silent for a while.

"We don't often get the opportunity to have this kind of conversation in a place like this," the captain said.

"No, you're right," Fenoglio replied.

"There was a game I used to play when I was a child. I'd choose a word and repeat it out loud lots of times until it lost its meaning and became just a sequence of letters."

"I did that, too," Fenoglio said.

"Yes, I think it's quite common. I sometimes still do it even now. It's interesting – even quite scary – to see how fragile the link is between things and words. The world is based on the connection between words and things, but it's a connection that can be broken in two minutes with a child's game. I've always said to myself: it must mean something, something important. But I've never quite figured out what."

Language is a convention, an implicit pact between people. There is no law of nature that says that a certain sequence of signs – consonants and vowels – corresponds to a particular object. That's the fascinating and slightly frightening aspect of the matter. Fenoglio thought these things, but didn't say them. After a long pause – and after finishing his drink – it was the captain who spoke again.

"I don't think I'll be an officer in the Carabinieri all my life. I ended up in this job, but I never thought I was right for it, not even at the start."

"This may be armchair philosophy, but I think certain jobs should be done by *those who don't feel right for it*, to use your expression. Feeling a little out of place helps to make us more vigilant. Someone who feels *absolutely right for it*, for example, doesn't notice the absurdity of the way we write transcripts. He doesn't notice important details."

"I'd never thought of it that way."

"Nor had I. It's an idea that came to me as I spoke."

"How old are you, marshal?"

"Forty-one."

"I'm thirty-five. As a boy I thought I'd be a famous stage actor by now. What about you?"

"I think I'd have liked to write. Journalist or novelist, it was all the same in my imagination. The idea was that I would earn my living writing, one way or another."

Valente nodded, as if that was exactly the answer he'd been expecting. "In some ways, it's what you do. Your reports are the best I've ever read."

Fenoglio had always been uncomfortable with compliments. He didn't know what to say and felt compelled to change the subject. "Can I ask you a question, sir?"

"Of course."

"You call all your subordinates, even the twenty-year-olds, by their rank and surname. Why?"

The captain smiled, like a little boy caught in the act. "It makes me seem unfriendly, doesn't it? The men think I'm arrogant and like to keep my distance, I know. But let me tell you an anecdote. Once, when I was a child, I went with my parents to visit some friends of theirs. They were landowners, they had a farm and children who were older than me: the oldest might have been sixteen. At a certain point, I heard that boy call an old farm labourer by his first name, and give him orders, and the old man reply by calling him sir. I've never forgotten the sense of unease that scene gave me. Maybe it's because of that episode that I can't bring myself to call someone by his first name if I can't tell him to do the same to me. And I think you'll agree that it wouldn't be a good idea if I told all the men they can call their captain by his first name."

"No, you're right, it wouldn't be a good idea," Fenoglio replied with a smile.

# 8

Over the following two days, Lopez told them the story of his criminal career. Above all, to explain his gradual rise in importance and prestige within the organization, he told them, in chronological order, about the murders for which he was directly responsible. In this kind of investigation, there's a basic rule: you want to cooperate with the law and obtain the corresponding benefits? Then talk first about what you've done, maybe things you weren't even suspected of. It's a basic prerequisite if you want to be believed about everything else.

The second murder, after Curly, was that of a night-watchman who had refused to let the members of the Grimaldi clan into a household appliance warehouse to commit a robbery. Such an act of rebellion was intolerable and could not remain unpunished. Grimaldi ordered him to be kneecapped. Lopez and two other members were assigned to the job. They waited for the guard outside his building and shot him in the legs, but one bullet severed the femoral artery. The man bled to death before he could reach the emergency ward.

When Grimaldi found out what had happened he said that, when it came down to it, it was better that way. The lesson would be clearer to everybody.

The third murder was that of the member who had become a heroin addict. They had told him to stop; they had even told him to go to a detox clinic. He had replied that he didn't need to, that he did a little heroin every now and again, but that he wasn't an addict and could stop whenever he liked. He even became aggressive and disrespectful. He ate and drank in the bars and restaurants of Santo Spirito without paying. He took heroin on credit from a dealer in the Libertà neighbourhood, providing as guarantee his status as a member of Grimaldi's organization. He didn't pay the debt. They saw him on several occasions talking to narcotics officers – a very bad sign. The last straw was a robbery of a supermarket whose owner regularly paid monthly protection and who, quite rightly, went to Grimaldi and complained: You swore to me that if I paid, nothing would happen, and now this? Grimaldi told him he was right, which meant he wouldn't have to pay the monthly instalment until he had recovered the amount stolen. The incident wouldn't happen again, he concluded.

Two days went by and the junkie was shot down by Lopez and Capocchiani as he was coming out of a café after breakfast. For the last time without paying.

The fourth murder had been committed as a favour to the bosses of the clan in charge in Cerignola, with whom Grimaldi was negotiating to acquire large quantities of narcotics from Milan. There was a war in progress between the Cerignola people and a rival group. The Big Boys (this was the name the four bosses of the Cerignola clan went by) wanted to settle the matter. The idea was to eliminate the boss of the rival group in the most spectacular and terrifying way, and there is no more spectacular and terrifying way than a killing bang in the centre of town, with people around and in broad daylight. For an operation of that kind, you need someone from outside who, even in broad daylight, won't run the risk of being accidentally recognized, perhaps by a local police officer or carabiniere. So the Big Boys asked Grimaldi to do them the honour, as a mark of consideration and respect, and as a way to seal a friendship and an alliance between equals. Grimaldi gave the job to Lopez, who would have a free hand in organizing the operation.

Lopez chose one of the brightest, most determined, most ruthless of the recent recruits, someone who was eager to prove his worth. The Cerignola people provided logistical support. The act was carried out just as the shops were opening. From the criminals' point of view, it was a success.

The fifth murder was the most spectacular and alarming of all. An episode that had become notorious in the criminal history of the region.

A small team of Grimaldi's men had been assigned to kill a man named De Fano, a member of the Montanari clan, which controlled the San Paolo neighbourhood that bordered on Società Nostra's area of influence. The Montanaris were long-time opponents of Grimaldi in a low-intensity war that had lasted for about ten years, with many wounded and a few killed. De Fano, with some accomplices who had not yet been identified, had raped a girl from Enziteto, the niece of one of Grimaldi's associates. If relations between the two groups had been good, Grimaldi could have asked old Nicola Montanari, long-standing boss of the clan that bore his name, to punish his associate himself. As this wasn't a feasible solution, they had to act directly.

De Fano had been riddled with bullets but had survived and, in addition, had got a good look at his assailants, all of whom he knew well. A rumour circulated that, purely out of revenge, he was deciding to cooperate with the law and accuse his attackers. Whether or not the rumour was true, Grimaldi said they needed to complete the job they had left half done, by striking De Fano in the clinic where he was being treated. Once again the task, far from an easy one, was entrusted to Lopez, who took along two other members, both young but already experienced in operations of this kind. Capocchiani, who would normally have taken part in such a strategic action, was in custody at the time.

In the days following the wounding, the police commissioner had arranged for guards to be stationed outside De Fano's room. Then the service had been suspended because of the usual shortage of manpower.

To get into the clinic, they were helped by a male nurse who informed them when there were no more visitors, opened the door to the department, pointed them in the direction of De Fano's room and left, having finished his shift, before the three men got down to work.

They had long-barrelled revolvers with silencers. Lopez put a pillow over De Fano's face, and the other two shot him in the head through the pillow. The only sounds were dull thuds. If anybody heard them, they didn't realize they were shots, and the three men left first the department, then the clinic, undisturbed.

The staff became aware of the murder at least an hour later. The episode caused a huge stir and would greatly increase the prestige of the Grimaldi clan as well as the personal prestige of Vito Lopez, who soon became Grimaldi's right-hand man – basically, the deputy boss of Società Nostra.

It gained him further respect in criminal circles, but also attracted envy and hostility. In addition, with the passing of time, Grimaldi became increasingly paranoid and worried about possible internal betrayals and competition with other organized criminal groups in the city and the province.

These were the conditions that led to things coming dramatically to a head.

# 9

At 9.30 on 22 May 1992, in Bari, at the offices of the Criminal Investigation Unit of the Carabinieri, Vito Lopez, whose particulars have already been stated in other documents, appears before the Public Prosecutor as represented by Assistant Prosecutor Gemma D'Angelo, assisted in the drafting of the current document by Sergeant Ignazio Calcaterra, and also in the presence, for the purposes of the investigation, of Captain Alberto Valente, Marshal Pietro Fenoglio and Corporal Antonio Pellecchia, all detectives in the Criminal Investigation Unit of the Carabinieri of Bari. Also present is Lopez's defence lawyer, Avvocato Marianna Formica.

QUESTION At the end of your previous statement, you hinted at the deterioration in your relationship with Grimaldi. Could you tell us the details?

ANSWER As I said, I had become Grimaldi's right-hand man. I was the only person he trusted, partly because over time there had been various problems within the group: some had been killed, some had been arrested; Grimaldi was afraid that certain others might be police informers and, generally, that his commanding position might be threatened. The more time passed, the more paranoid he became.

QUESTION Who were the members of the group whom Grimaldi feared might be police informers?

ANSWER Let us say that he was worried about a number of individuals, but without any real foundation. In reality, I believe he was losing faith in certain people and for that very reason hypothesized (often, I repeat, with no foundation) betrayals and informers. For example, he was obsessed with the people in Japigia. He had a competitive attitude towards their boss, Savino Parisi. He considered himself superior to him and suffered greatly from the fact that, in the newspapers and in the opinion of the law enforcement agencies, Parisi was considered more important. If he ever found out, or even only suspected, that any of his people had contacts with members of Parisi's group, he immediately thought that it was a plot to oust him.

QUESTION Was there any foundation to this idea?

ANSWER As far as I know, Parisi had no interest in extending his influence over an area so far from the neighbourhood in which he is still the undisputed boss and where, as I believe you know, people come from all over the region and even from outside to stock up with drugs, because of the reasonable prices. Moreover, in many cases, he only imagined these contacts, which were for the most part non-existent. It did happen that some of our people were acquainted or friendly with some of Parisi's people, but, as far as I know, there was no sharing of criminal activities.

QUESTION What about the idea that there were informers?

ANSWER This had more foundation, although Grimaldi exaggerated it. He was obsessed with the idea of *omertà*, not just as a practical instrument to keep us safe from the activities of the law enforcement agencies, but also as a symbolic fact. It is not easy to explain but – this is something I understood as time passed – Grimaldi had and has delusions of grandeur. He likes to think that his organization is as important and respected as the great Mafia organizations in Sicily, Calabria or Naples. I have to say that not even at the height of my criminal career did I ever believe that things were like that. Ours was little more than a local organization, even though we liked to talk a lot about *omertà*, honour and affiliations. Anyway, Grimaldi, because of the obsession of which I have spoken, expected to exercise very strict control over his associates. A few days ago, I told you about the Curly episode, which was one of the first manifestations of this delusion.

QUESTION Who else provided information to the law enforcement agencies, in Grimaldi's opinion?

ANSWER He had become obsessed with two men: Gaetano D'Agostino, known as Shorty, and Simone Losurdo, known as the Mosquito. One afternoon in March, he sent for me and told me that he needed to kill those two. He said, to be more specific, that he needed to kill them and make sure they disappeared, so that not even their own mothers could mourn these two snitches in a cemetery.

QUESTION What did you reply?

ANSWER I asked him why, even though I already knew of the rumours circulating about D'Agostino. He repeated that they were both lousy snitches, that they were talking to the police and that it was necessary to eliminate them in order to send a signal. Among other things, he added, he believed they were engaging in extortion without asking for authorization.

QUESTION Whom should they have asked for authorization?

ANSWER Grimaldi. Or at least they should have told me or another of Grimaldi's lieutenants, Capocchiani or Vito Pastore, and then waited for us to talk to Grimaldi and give them the go-ahead. I have to say, however, that the matter of the extortion was conjecture on Grimaldi's part, and when I asked him to clarify for me how he had reached this hypothesis he replied that he knew and that was it. He had got himself into a real temper, something which had been happening with increasing frequency. I told him that we could kill D'Agostino, even though the increase in the number of murders would lead to an increased presence of the law enforcement agencies on our territory and make things more difficult for us. But there was nothing on Losurdo, and it seemed to me absurd to kill him simply on the basis of conjecture. I should make it clear that I had a personal relationship with Losurdo that led me to defend him.

QUESTION What are you referring to?

ANSWER Losurdo and I shared a passion for dogs. He had a pair of Alsatians. When they had puppies, he gave me one and we had got into the habit of taking our dogs together out into the country to let them run about and to train them. Often, when I had to be away for a few days, Losurdo would go to my place, collect my dog and take it out with his. Partly for this reason, it could be said that Losurdo and I were friends. In fact, I was much fonder of him than of almost anybody else in the group.

QUESTION How did Grimaldi react when you told him that it was not right to kill Losurdo?

ANSWER He said: all right, for now we will kill that piece of shit D'Agostino. Then we shall see if anything comes out about the Mosquito.

QUESTION How long after this dialogue was D'Agostino killed?

ANSWER A few weeks later.

QUESTION Who took care of it?

ANSWER The men involved were Mario Abbinante, known as Little Mario, and Cosimo Lacoppola, known as Snowy because of his dandruff. They shot D'Agostino as he was on his way to police headquarters, where he had to report regularly because he was under special surveillance. They went there on an Enduro motorcycle and used a revolver. Little Mario was the one who fired the shot. Snowy was driving the bike and had another gun with him, a 7.65, I think, although it was not used. I believe no cartridges were found at the scene of the crime. These things were all reported to me by Grimaldi soon after the killing took place and after the two men involved had told him everything.

QUESTION We will talk in greater detail about this episode later. For now, tell us about the disappearance of Simone Losurdo.

ANSWER It happened when I had left for Milan, where I was supposed to be collecting a consignment of cocaine, the purchase of which we had negotiated with the people from Cerignola – of whom I have already spoken – who had direct contact with Colombia.

QUESTION Was it normal for you to be involved with transporting drugs?

ANSWER Grimaldi usually sent me when there were important consignments. In this case, we needed to collect five kilos of cocaine, which was why I did not suspect a thing. I was in the car, near Ancona perhaps, when my wife called me and said that Losurdo's wife had called her. She was worried because her husband had not come home the previous evening. This sometimes happened but, like almost all of us, Losurdo usually warned her if he had to be away. His wife was very worried because he had not even come back the following morning and could not be reached on his mobile phone.

QUESTION What did you do then?

ANSWER I asked if they had checked the little colonial house that Losurdo had in the country between Molfetta and Bisceglie, where he kept the dogs and which we used as a storehouse for stolen goods. For example, we once hid there a batch of forms for identity cards, stolen from the printworks in Foggia; another time, the contents of numerous safe-deposit boxes from a major robbery from the vault of the BNL bank in Reggio Calabria.

QUESTION What did your wife do?

ANSWER She called me back an hour later and told me that they had gone together to check the house. Losurdo was not there, but the most worrying thing was that the dogs were not there either.

QUESTION What did this mean?

ANSWER Losurdo might have gone away without warning because he had some important business to attend to, or it might have been something to do with a woman. In itself, his disappearance was unusual, but not inexplicable and not necessarily alarming. It had happened before, although rarely. If, however, not even the dogs were there, it became much more difficult to hypothesize that Losurdo had gone away because of some unexpected engagement. If he had done that, he would not have taken the dogs with him.

QUESTION What did you think at that point?

ANSWER I was very worried. So I called Grimaldi. He did not reply immediately, and when he did I asked him in an angry tone what was going on. He was strangely agitated, to the extent that I thought he was under the influence of cocaine. He told me not to worry, to do what I had set out to do, and that when I returned he would explain everything.

QUESTION What did you reply to that?

ANSWER I got very angry and told him again that I wanted to know what had happened and that if he did not answer me I would turn back. Grimaldi said that everything was all right, but it was not a good idea to talk on the telephone – it was not yet clear if and how mobile phones could be tapped – and repeated that when I got back he would explain everything.

QUESTION What did you do?

ANSWER I was tempted to turn back, but I had already passed Bologna. So I decided to collect the cocaine as quickly as possible and then come straight back, travelling by night if I had to.

QUESTION Was anyone with you on this mission?

ANSWER Yes, a young man named Marino Demattia was with me. I was his godfather, having affiliated him as a *camorrista* and then promoted him to the rank of *sgarrista*.

QUESTION So this Demattia answered to you and not to Grimaldi?

ANSWER Not exactly. I was his godfather and his superior, so he answered to me, but Grimaldi being the boss, it was obvious that he also answered to him. If Grimaldi ordered him to do something, he would have to do it.

QUESTION And if you did not agree, could you have forbidden Demattia – or any of your godsons – to obey Grimaldi?

ANSWER No, Grimaldi was everybody's boss, even mine. Naturally, over time, I had gained a position of importance in the group and it could be said that I was the de facto deputy, even though there were others of the same rank as me, that is, the *Santa*. I was therefore entitled to challenge his choices and could raise objections to what he was planning to do. If, however, the argument continued, the last word was always his.

QUESTION One thing I forgot to ask you: what rank is Grimaldi?

ANSWER Grimaldi has the fifth rank, that is, the *Vangelo*. As far as I know, in the whole of Apulia only Giosuè Rizzi and Pino Rogoli, whom I have already mentioned, are definitely higher in rank, that is, the sixth or even the seventh. It is likely there are a few others, and I have no idea what the situation is in Salento. I have to add that there exists a kind of regime of secrecy when it comes to the higher ranks, who are known only to those of the same rank. What we knew was that Grimaldi was lower in rank only to the supreme bosses and to the Calabrians from whom they had drawn their legitimacy.

QUESTION How many *santistas* are there in Società Nostra?

ANSWER There were four of us at that time: Vito Pastore, Michele Capocchiani, Nicola Maselli, who had moved somewhere near Turin some time previously, and myself.

QUESTION Let us return to your journey to Milan to acquire the cocaine from the Cerignola people.

ANSWER I got to Rozzano. A dispatch rider was waiting for me at a petrol station just outside the town and led me to an area on the outskirts that I do not think I would be able to find again. The exchange took place in the garage of a very large apartment block with a portico. The same dispatch rider took me out of town and we got straight back into our own car to drive back to Bari.

QUESTION What time was it?

ANSWER It was late afternoon. We drove all night, taking turns, and got to Bari in the morning.

QUESTION On the way back, were you in contact with anyone? Your wife, Grimaldi, Losurdo's wife, or any members of the organization?

ANSWER I spoke to my wife. She confirmed that there was no trace of Losurdo. She even asked me if his wife should report him missing. I told her to wait until I got back. When I arrived, the first thing I did was go and hide the cocaine I had collected in Rozzano. I should point out that I did this after dropping Demattia at his home.

QUESTION Why?

ANSWER Because I had decided to hide the cocaine in a secret place known only to me. I was afraid – and my fears would turn out to be well founded – that the situation might come to a head. I did not want to hand the cocaine over to Grimaldi, thinking that it might finance a possible conflict.

QUESTION So at that moment you had already decided to start a war with Grimaldi?

ANSWER Not exactly. I wanted to confront him, talk to him, demand an explanation. Before anything else, I wanted to ask him if he was responsible for Losurdo's disappearance. I was almost certain he was, but I wanted him to confirm it. Once I had clarified that, if he convinced me that the elimination had been unavoidable – providing me with evidence of incorrect conduct by Losurdo – I would accept it as a natural consequence of the application of the organization's rules. If, on the other hand, I was convinced that the elimination of Losurdo had been an abuse of power, I was aware of the fact that the situation might deteriorate. For a war, arms and money would be necessary, so the cocaine I had hidden might be useful to me.

QUESTION Where did you hide it?

ANSWER In the same place as the arms I led you to.

QUESTION What did you do then?

ANSWER I went to see Losurdo's wife, in the hope of obtaining some useful information. But she was very agitated, almost hysterical. She kept repeating that her husband had been murdered, that she had known it would end like this. Then I went to the farmhouse where Losurdo kept his dogs to see if there were any traces of violence.

QUESTION Were there any?

ANSWER No. I made a rapid search of the surroundings and found nothing. So I decided to go and see Grimaldi.

QUESTION Did you call him before you went to see him?

ANSWER No. I had stopped trusting him, and it seemed to me more prudent to go to him without warning him in advance.

QUESTION What were you afraid of?

ANSWER Nothing specific, but I had become very mistrustful and acted accordingly. So I went to Grimaldi's house, knocked at the door and told him that we should go and have a coffee. Out in the street, I asked him what had happened to Losurdo.

QUESTION What did he say?

ANSWER All he said in reply was to ask me the whereabouts of the cocaine I had collected in Rozzano. I told him it was safe, and asked him again what had happened to Losurdo. At that point we had an argument, because he wanted me to go and get the cocaine and move it to the place previously arranged: the garage of a man without a criminal record, where we kept narcotics and weapons under secure conditions. He asked me in an angry tone why I had not already taken it there. I replied that I had had the impression I was being followed by the police, that I had shaken off the car that had appeared to be following me and that I had hidden my car with the cocaine in a warehouse in the industrial area.

QUESTION But that was not true.

ANSWER No, it was not. As I explained, I had put the cocaine in that particular hiding place, but naturally I had no intention of telling Grimaldi. Such a decision would have seemed a declaration of mistrust and war. The atmosphere of our conversation was very tense from the start, but I was anxious for it not to deteriorate, at least not before I had found out what had happened to Losurdo. I assured him that once I knew that, I would go and get the car and the cocaine and take them to the place agreed upon. Grimaldi calmed down, or perhaps pretended to, and gave me something of an explanation.

QUESTION What did he tell you?

ANSWER He said Losurdo had been killed. When I asked him why, he told me that Losurdo had on several occasions bought drugs from Albanian traffickers without informing him and above all without paying the share owing to the group for activities carried out independently.

QUESTION How much was this share?

ANSWER There was no fixed percentage. Let us say it depended on the kind of activity and how much it was worth. For drug-related activities it was ten per cent.

QUESTION How had Grimaldi found out about the things he attributed to Losurdo?

ANSWER He did not tell me. He said only that he was sure the information was correct, that there was no doubt, and that the only thing to do was kill him. Someone who behaves in that way, breaking the rules of allegiance, was capable of anything.

QUESTION And what did you reply?

ANSWER That in my opinion the person who had told him these things was simply someone who was putting on the tragedy.

QUESTION What does "putting on the tragedy" mean?

ANSWER Saying things that are not true, or only partly true, with the aim of manipulating the other person and stirring up trouble.

QUESTION Who did you think had "put on the tragedy" and accused Losurdo unjustly?

ANSWER Actually, I did not have a clear idea. Mine was an angry reaction to the confident tone with which Grimaldi asserted that Losurdo had done incorrect things. I was well aware – and still am – of how rumours circulate and how easy it is to believe them. Anyway, I dropped the question of the validity of the accusations against Losurdo and asked Grimaldi why he had acted when I had been away. He replied very honestly that he knew I was against the elimination of Losurdo and that was why he had decided to act when I was away. His honesty on this point left me speechless for a few moments. It was then that he told me about the dogs.

QUESTION What did he say?

ANSWER That the bastard had deserved it, but that he was sorry about the dogs. And above all, he was sorry about mine.

QUESTION Why?

ANSWER He said that it had been a fine dog, and a brave one. That when Losurdo had set the dogs on them my dog had been the first to attack and had kept going even after they had shot it. Now I know I am about to say something wrong, I realize that, but the moment I really thought I wanted Grimaldi dead was not when he told me he had killed Losurdo, but when he told me he had killed my dog.

QUESTION What did you do then?

ANSWER By this point, I had made up my mind. So I acted cautiously. Against Grimaldi's obvious expectations, I did not fly into a rage and only repeated that they should have eliminated Losurdo when my dog was not there. Grimaldi appeared relieved and said that I was right, that about this he had been mistaken. He said that he wanted to buy me another dog, a pedigree dog, that we should go together and choose it from the breeders, things like that.

QUESTION What did you reply?

ANSWER That right now I did not want another dog, what I wanted was to know where they had put Losurdo's body. I wanted to recover it so that there could be a funeral and his wife and relatives would have somewhere to mourn him. He told me – and these are his exact words – that not even the Virgin Mary would be able to find the body.

QUESTION Why?

ANSWER Because they had burnt it – and had also burnt the dogs – in a dump, using old tyres as fuel. It was a method he had learnt from people in Trani, who often employed it to get rid of bodies.

QUESTION Why had they burnt him?

ANSWER Grimaldi always said that if there was no body, there was no murder. He meant that if the law enforcement agencies did not find the body, they could not bring charges for murder, because there would always be a doubt about the death. Having said this, I think Grimaldi liked playing with fire. Literally. I do not know quite how to put this, but it seemed almost that he took a kind of pleasure in looking at fire. When we killed Curly and set fire to him he watched the flames with satisfaction and said smugly: "Look how he burns." He was obsessed with fire. What is the word?

QUESTION Do you mean pyromaniac?

ANSWER Yes. He always liked to talk about the times when, as a young man, he set fire to shops whose owners had refused to pay protection. He would throw the Molotov cocktail and then stand watching the flames. Sometimes he had even run serious risks – he had told me – in lingering longer than necessary to look at the fire.

QUESTION What did you reply when Grimaldi told you he had burnt the body?

ANSWER As I have said, I had already made up my mind. So I had no desire for Grimaldi to know my true feelings. But nor could I show indifference about something that clearly involved me quite a lot. I had to find a point of balance. So I merely showed displeasure at the fact that Losurdo's body had been destroyed by fire. In this way, his family had been denied the possibility of a funeral or the chance to visit their loved one's grave.

QUESTION Did you ask him who had actually carried out the murder?

ANSWER Yes, immediately afterwards. I asked him who had gone with him – it was clear from what he had said so far that he himself was there – and what method had been used.

QUESTION What did he reply?

ANSWER At first he was evasive. He said something like: He is dead and gone now, why are we still talking about him?

We need to think of the future. But I insisted: if he did not tell me, he would be showing me a lack of respect, which seemed to persuade him. And so he told me.

QUESTION What did he tell you?

ANSWER There were four of them, Grimaldi in person, Capocchiani, a fellow from Trani whom I do not know, and Abbinante, the man who had killed D'Agostino. They knew that in the afternoon Losurdo went to feed the dogs and they knew that the place where he kept them was isolated and a long way from prying eyes. So they followed him when he left home. First he dropped by my place to collect my dog because, as I have said, he used to take it with him to let it run and enjoy itself when I was away. They stayed behind him as he drove through the countryside, keeping at a distance.

When Losurdo saw them coming, he called to the dogs. The men got out of the cars and Grimaldi told him to put the dogs on leads. He did not do so, and asked Grimaldi why they were there.

QUESTION Did Grimaldi tell you all this?

ANSWER Partly Grimaldi, partly Capocchiani.

QUESTION When you went to see Grimaldi, was Capocchiani also there?

ANSWER No, I spoke to Capocchiani the following day. He told me more or less what Grimaldi had told me, although in a little more detail. The four men arrived and told Losurdo they had to talk and so it was only right that he should tie up the dogs. But Losurdo did not do so. Grimaldi told me that the dogs went and stood in front of him, as if to protect him. He had realized that something was wrong, and he told the four men not to come any closer because if they did he would set the dogs on them. Capocchiani took out his gun and again ordered him to tie up the dogs or else he would kill them. It was at this point – I believe – that Losurdo fully realized why they had come to see him and, in a desperate attempt to escape the ambush, ordered the dogs to attack. As they ran forward, he started to run in the opposite direction. There was a first burst of gunfire, in which the dogs were killed. Abbinante and the man from Trani were wounded, because the dogs had managed to bite them before dying. Then Grimaldi and Capocchiani ran after Losurdo. They fired at him several times and managed to hit him. He staggered and fell. They reached him and killed him, shooting him several times in the head.

QUESTION All this happened in open country. Were they not afraid that a passing person, a farm worker perhaps, might see them?

ANSWER As I said before, it is a very isolated area, where it is unlikely that anyone would pass by chance. In that very area, to show you how far out of the way it was, in previous years some guys from Bitonto had kept an enormous plantation of cannabis. They cultivated it for more than two years without anybody noticing a thing.

QUESTION Is the plantation still there?

ANSWER No, they decided to stop cultivating it for reasons that I do not know. But it is true that nobody ever noticed that plantation, and we are talking about several hectares of land. So as I was saying, that was the reason the area had been chosen for the attack. Having said this, there is no doubt that the situation had got out of the hands of Grimaldi and his men. They had not planned on the reaction of the dogs and they were certain that they would do everything just outside the farmhouse, not go on a prolonged chase through the countryside.

QUESTION What did they do after killing Losurdo?

ANSWER I should point out that this part of the story was told to me by Capocchiani the following day.

QUESTION Before continuing, would you tell us how your conversation with Grimaldi ended?

ANSWER Yes. Basically, he told me that they had disposed of the bodies of Losurdo and the dogs by burning them. I did not ask him any further questions because I was disgusted by the whole thing. So I concluded by repeating to Grimaldi that I was not happy about what had happened, but that life and business had to continue. He repeated to me in his turn that he was sorry about the dog and would make it up to me. Then he asked me what we should do to recover the cocaine that I had collected in Rozzano. I replied that I could recover it the next day, and he told me that Capocchiani would go with me. It was what I had been expecting, and at that moment I decided that I would begin my revenge by killing Capocchiani, whom I had always hated anyway.

QUESTION What happened the next day?

ANSWER Capocchiani picked me up in a car belonging to a nephew of his. I had taken care to arrange for him to pick me up far from my home, specifically in the vicinity of the Quintino Sella underpass, in order to reduce the risk of our being seen together. I had two guns with me: a Beretta 6.35 and a .38 Tanfoglio. They are two of the weapons I led you to. Capocchiani seemed in a very good mood. I gave him directions to the place where I had said I had hidden the cocaine, although in fact it was not there. During the ride I asked him to tell me about the killing of Losurdo and especially about how they had disposed of the body.

QUESTION Did this not make Capocchiani suspicious?

ANSWER No. It should be said that Capocchiani was not especially intelligent. He owed his reputation to the fact that he was a madman, capable of the most daring acts and the most ruthless behaviour. Apart from that, out of pure luck, until that day he had escaped a number of ambushes, and this had contributed to his fame. Besides, it was quite natural for me to ask about what had happened.

QUESTION So Capocchiani was quite willing to talk?

ANSWER Very much so. Grimaldi had already informed him that I knew. And he liked to boast.

QUESTION Tell us what he told you and if it differed in any way from Grimaldi's account.

ANSWER His account of the killing of Losurdo and the dogs was practically identical to Grimaldi's. But Capocchiani also told me in detail how and where they had disposed of the bodies of Losurdo and the dogs.

QUESTION Where did they take the bodies?

ANSWER To an unauthorized dump between Trani and Bisceglie where drums of toxic waste from Northern Italy were dumped, along with wrecked cars and objects of all kinds. They laid down tyres as a base, put Losurdo and the dogs on it, covered them with more tyres and set fire to them. It is unusual for the tyres to go out, even if it rains; with this method, nothing remains of the bodies.

QUESTION Did they remove anything from Losurdo's body? Papers, his watch, anything like that?

ANSWER They did not tell me. But I doubt it: there was no reason to do so.

QUESTION To transport the bodies, had they been placed in the car boots?

ANSWER Correct. After the bodies were completely burnt, Grimaldi and the others – who had watched the burning until the end – went and cleaned the cars.

QUESTION Why not burn the cars?

ANSWER That is the usual procedure when the car used for an operation is stolen. In this case, though, the two cars were not stolen, but belonged to Abbinante and the man from Trani. The discovery and identification of the burnt-out wrecks (through the chassis numbers, which often withstand burning) would have drawn attention to the two men. You also need to take into account the fact that Losurdo's body had been completely burnt and his disappearance would be classified as a gangland execution.

QUESTION So they had used their own cars for this murder?

ANSWER It does happen. When murders have been planned for some time stolen cars are used, which are then burnt. In this case the act was decided on following my departure to collect the cocaine in Rozzano. As I have already said repeatedly, Grimaldi knew that I was not happy about it.

QUESTION Is it not the case that your departure for Rozzano had been planned for some time?

ANSWER No, that is not the way it works. When the merchandise arrives, they call you and you go to pick it up. Consignments, partly for obvious reasons of caution, are never planned in advance. Grimaldi had already decided to eliminate Losurdo, but the fact that he was often in my company and that our wives were friends constituted a problem. He could not risk acting in my presence, and he certainly could not ask me to take care of it myself. So he seized the opportunity of my departure and obviously had no way of getting hold of cars. In addition, since they had decided to do it in the country, in the total absence of potential witnesses, the need to use stolen cars was much less strong than for an operation to be carried out in a residential area. I should, however, emphasize that all this is speculation, because I did not ask either Grimaldi or Capocchiani for what reason they had gone to kill Losurdo in the cars belonging to Abbinante and the man from Trani.

QUESTION You said that they went to clean the cars. Where?

ANSWER In a car wash.

QUESTION Were they not afraid that the staff of the car wash would notice the bloodstains there must have been in the cars?

ANSWER One of Grimaldi's men was working on day release in the car wash. I remember only his nickname, Kojak, which he owes to the fact that he is completely bald. He was given the job of working carefully on the two cars, on his own. Capocchiani told me that even before taking the cars to be washed, they had disposed of the rugs that had been in the boots where the bodies of Losurdo and the dogs had been placed.

QUESTION Now tell us about the killing of Capocchiani.

ANSWER I should say first of all that I did not know whether or not he was armed. Strictly speaking, he should not have been carrying a weapon without a specific reason: to do so meant running the pointless risk of being arrested if stopped by the police or the Carabinieri. But I could not be sure. Moreover, Capocchiani was highly dangerous and capable of the craziest, most absurd gestures. I had once seen him leap on someone who was threatening him with a gun. The other man had pressed the trigger, but the gun had jammed, and Capocchiani had then beaten him to death. I should point out that, in my opinion, such behaviour was not only crazy, it was stupid. The fact, though, that he had survived so many dangerous situations had created around Capocchiani the aura of a legend. Capocchiani had, among other things, an incredible capacity for bearing physical pain. In regard to this, I can tell you another episode. Once the car in which he was travelling together with other men was stopped by the Carabinieri. Capocchiani replied badly to a request from one of the officers, who gave him a slap. Capocchiani said that nothing had been done to him and that they were the slaps of a pansy. He meant: not very manly slaps, which did not hurt. Anyway, to cut a long story short, the carabinieri laid into him, it was a real beating. But with every blow, Capocchiani said that they had not done anything to him, so in the end they had to stop, without his having given in. In short, what I am trying to say is that it had to be taken into consideration that he could act in an unpredictable and uncontrollable way. So I had to be very careful. Moreover, I want to add that Capocchiani, in addition to being a madman devoid of any sense of danger, had a bad temperament. He was the worst. To explain the kind of person he was, I have to tell you about one of his hobbies. He had a couple of his men capture all the stray cats they could find and put them in a room into which he could look through a window, after which he invited some of his friends with pit bulls, freed two of the dogs into the room, and they bet on which one would kill the most cats.

QUESTION Did you ever witness this?

ANSWER No. I love animals, and the idea of making them suffer just for the pleasure of it has always disgusted me. I would never have tolerated a spectacle like that without intervening. But what I have told you is widely known.

QUESTION Did you make your move inside the car?

ANSWER No. It was impossible to predict what he would do if I pointed a gun at him while he was driving. He would have been quite capable of throwing the car off the road in an attempt to disarm me. Besides, Losurdo's two brothers, Pasquale and Antonio, were waiting for me at the hiding place. I had got them involved because they wanted to avenge their brother's death.

QUESTION Were the Losurdos members of the organization?

ANSWER Only Pasquale Losurdo, who had the rank of *sgarrista*. The youngest, Antonio, was a robber, but he had never wanted to join.

QUESTION Why did the Losurdos agree to go up against a criminal organization as powerful and dangerous as Grimaldi's? How did you manage to persuade them?

ANSWER I repeat: they wanted to avenge their brother's death. I told them what Grimaldi had told me. That would have been enough. Then I added that I had five kilos of cocaine and that we could use it to finance a war against Grimaldi. We would make our base in Abruzzo, in Pescara, where I had friends – Roma who trafficked narcotics and committed robberies – who would help us to sell the cocaine for a good price and would provide us with a safe base. I said that we would carry out the various operations travelling from there and going back there immediately afterwards. They would not know where to look for us.

QUESTION But what were you thinking of doing?

ANSWER I cannot say for sure. Thinking back on it now, in the cold light of day, the idea of exterminating all of them was absurd and impracticable. But at the time, we imagined that if we managed to kill Grimaldi we would be able to take his place and control Enziteto and Santo Spirito. I did not think I would have any difficulty in getting myself accepted as the new boss by the other criminal groups that ruled over the various areas of Bari: the Parisis, the Capriatis, the Mercantes, the Laraspatas. I had an important rank – the *Santa* – that was recognized even by the members of other important criminal organizations from outside the region, and I thought that I would be able to explain what had happened and become the new boss of Società Nostra.

QUESTION Let us get back to the killing of Capocchiani.

ANSWER We got to the place. I had said that the cocaine was under a trapdoor in an inner courtyard. We got out of the car and set off towards the abandoned warehouse. When we got to within a few yards of the entrance Losurdo's younger brother came out, armed with a pump-action rifle. It was actually one of the two pump-action rifles in the cache I led you to. Capocchiani turned towards me, as if to ask me what was happening. I had taken out the Tanfoglio in the meantime, and I shot him twice without saying a word. He fell to the ground. I kept my gun aimed at him in case – as I told you – he was armed and was able to retaliate. But he made no attempt to take out a gun and in fact was unarmed, as we ascertained after killing him. Losurdo's younger brother went up to him, pointed the rifle at his chest and said: "This is for my brother, you piece of shit." After which, he shot him in the chest two or three times. At that distance the high-calibre bullets actually tore the flesh. Death was instantaneous.

QUESTION What did you do with the body?

ANSWER We put it in the car and threw it down a well, after destroying his phone. As far as I know, the body has not yet been found. Naturally, I can take you to the place. After throwing him down the well, we drove his car about twelve miles and set fire to it. Subsequently, we went and hid the weapons in the cache I led you to.

QUESTION What did you do after that?

ANSWER The Losurdos drove me home in their car. All three of us were aware that we had to get out of Bari as quickly as we could, because within a short time there would be a violent reaction from Grimaldi and his men. We could not rule out the possibility that they might even attempt to hurt members of our families. So we decided that we would leave the following morning, taking with us the cocaine I had collected in Rozzano. When the Losurdos left, I switched back on the mobile phone I had deliberately switched off earlier to prevent Grimaldi from contacting me. I was certain that, not hearing from Capocchiani about the recovery of the cocaine, he would start to look for me. And in fact a few minutes after I had switched the phone back on, his call came in.

QUESTION What did he say to you?

ANSWER He asked me what had happened and why my phone had been off. I said that I had not switched it off, but that there had probably been a problem with the network. He asked me if I had gone to collect the cocaine and why I had not brought it to him. I told him that Capocchiani had not picked me up and was not replying on his mobile. That was why I had not gone to get the cocaine.

QUESTION Did you speak openly about the cocaine?

ANSWER I did not, and nor did he at the beginning of the call. Then, as I am about to tell you, he lost his composure, especially when, playing my part, I asked him if he knew what had happened to Capocchiani.

QUESTION And what did he say?

ANSWER He flew into a rage. Naturally, he did not believe me. He screamed that I should be telling him what had happened to Capocchiani, that I was a lousy snitch, that I had to recover the cocaine immediately and take it straight to him. Perhaps if I did that, he would not kill me like my friend Losurdo. Otherwise, he said, he would have me quartered like a pig and leave me to bleed to death. He was beside himself, so furious that he abandoned all caution on the telephone, speaking freely about drugs and killings.

QUESTION What did you reply?

ANSWER I tried to keep calm. I reminded him that he was talking on the phone, I said that if he stopped acting crazy I was always ready to reason with him and to find a solution. That pissed him off even more. He screamed a few more insults at me, said he was coming to get me and hung up.

QUESTION What did you do then?

ANSWER I told my wife to pack the essentials and get our child ready. I went and recovered some weapons – not those used to kill Capocchiani – specifically, two 9 x 21 calibre semi-automatic pistols, a sawn-off shotgun and a Kalashnikov. All with the corresponding ammunition.

QUESTION Where did you go to get these weapons?

ANSWER I am sorry, dottoressa, but I prefer not to say. The person holding them for me was a clean young man, who has never done anybody any harm and who was keeping the weapons partly out of friendship, partly out of fear.

QUESTION Let me remind you that you do not have the luxury of choosing what to say and what not to say. Cooperating with the law – and enjoying the corresponding benefits – requires statements completely devoid of any kind of reticence. So I repeat the question: who was keeping these weapons?

After a long hesitation, the suspect asks for the interview to be suspended in order to consult his defence lawyer.

# 10

Lopez and Avvocato Formica went into another room, to talk alone. Fenoglio took advantage of the break to go to his office. In reality, he had nothing to do, but it was an opportunity to stretch his legs and try to clear his head.

He only managed the first of these things.

He knew what would happen soon. Formica, even though inexperienced in criminal law, would confirm to her client what D'Angelo had already put on record: the decision to cooperate with the law and the benefits that may derive from it are incompatible with any kind of reticence. Lopez would go along with it, revealing the identity of the "clean young man … who was keeping the weapons partly out of friendship, partly out of fear", and getting him in serious trouble, given that the possession of assault weapons is a serious offence liable to severe punishment.

Of course, the legal rules were clear, as was the solution; there was no room for reflection or speculation. But were the ethical rules governing a case like this equally clear? From the point of view of individual morality, was it right to get someone who has helped you out of friendship – or fear – into trouble? It was the kind of question that Fenoglio asked himself with tiresome frequency, whenever similar cases arose. By law, close relatives of a defendant or suspect can refuse to testify; in other words, legal reticence is allowed for ethical reasons, because the idea of forcing someone to testify against his or her own mother, father or child is unacceptable.

But what about in other cases that are ethically similar, however different from a legal point of view?

Once, they had arrested a girl who was buying blocks of hashish and selling them on in small portions at friends' parties. Dubious behaviour, and certainly illegal. But forcing her closest friend to testify against her about these episodes, under threat of arrest, had struck Fenoglio as an unpleasant thing to do, although legally irreproachable.

More generally, even being obliged to tell the truth is never as clear-cut as it may seem at first sight.

Walk with an honest, upright person for half a mile and he will tell you at least seven lies. Who had told him that? Fenoglio couldn't remember, but that sentence contained a basic truth. Our daily lives, the things we say, are riddled with lies of which we are seldom aware. The same thing happens in the world of investigations and legal proceedings, where everybody lies, often in good faith and with the best of intentions, often without even realizing it.

He had once brought up these arguments with Serena, who had found them hard to follow. In order to explain, he had given her an example, something that had actually happened.

Imagine an anti-drug operation, he had told her. Imagine that the presumed dealers have been observed at a distance exchanging something – sachets of some kind, apparently – with some youths. After a while, the carabinieri decide to intervene, and the dealers run away. There begins a chase during which, at times, the carabinieri lose sight of the dealers, although in the end the latter are caught up with and stopped. The problem is that a rapid search reveals that they don't have the drugs on them. So the carabinieri retrace their steps and find a small packet filled with doses of cocaine lying on the ground. Nobody has seen anyone throw this small packet away, but you can bet that both the arrest sheet and the seizure report will state that the suspects were *seen* getting rid of the package as they made their escape. The person who writes this – in other words, any carabiniere or police officer who has found himself in a situation like this – doesn't think of it as a lie, let alone that there's anything wrong in writing that he's seen something he hasn't in fact seen.

Fenoglio's mind was shifting dangerously from ethical speculations to the memory of Serena when Pellecchia arrived to tell him that the interview was resuming.

# 11

After a suspension of about twenty minutes, the interview is resumed in the presence of the same persons as previously indicated.

QUESTION Having conferred with your defence lawyer, have you decided to reveal the name of the person who kept weapons on your behalf?

ANSWER Yes, but I want to emphasize again that he is a decent person, a young man with a job, who has never taken part in any criminal activity. His name is Gaetano Cellammare, he owns a metal workshop near the cemetery – they make mostly door frames – and on a few occasions he has indeed held weapons for me. He kept them in the scrap iron section. On the three occasions when I went to collect the weapons, it was he who went to the back of the workshop and returned with the weapons wrapped in cloths. This is what he did the last time. I have not seen him since then. As I have already said, I do not believe that Cellammare has ever been involved in any criminal activity.

QUESTION What happened then?

ANSWER After collecting the weapons, I phoned Rocco Bevilacqua, a Roma living in Pescara who is quite highly placed in organized crime in Abruzzo. I had done business with him in the past and it was a kind of personal friendship. I told him that I needed his help, that I required a house that was quiet and possibly spacious in his area and that when I was there I would talk to him about a thing for which there were great prospects of gain. As Bevilacqua knew me well, he did not ask any questions, apart from asking me when I needed the house. When I told him that I needed it the next day, he did not make any comment, but simply replied "Okay."

QUESTION To what were you referring when you spoke about great prospects of gain?

ANSWER I intended to let him have the cocaine I had picked up in Rozzano.

QUESTION What was the value of this cocaine?

ANSWER I should point out first of all that it was good-quality merchandise and that we had paid the Cerignola people in Rozzano 580 million lire, which was a discount price, the initial request having been for 600. Sold in doses, after being cut with mannite or lidocaine, it might bring in more than a billion and a half, perhaps even two. Naturally, in the urgent situation in which I found myself, I could not envisage being involved in the packaging and selling, which requires, among other things, the availability of a network of dealers. My intention was to sell it to Bevilacqua, hoping to make as much as possible, although the conditions of the sale would obviously not be advantageous to me. In fact, in the end, we agreed on 450 million, with the understanding that we would keep a hundred grams for our personal use.

QUESTION Was Bevilacqua in a position to get hold of such a large sum?

ANSWER Actually, he needed a few days to get the money together. But he is an important figure who runs a lot of illegitimate and profitable businesses in that area.

QUESTION Continue with your story.

ANSWER After talking to Bevilacqua, I called one of the Losurdo brothers and told him that I was bringing forward my departure for Abruzzo. I would be leaving that very evening. I explained that it was urgent, given that by now Grimaldi had realized that I had taken possession of that consignment of cocaine. But they could take their time, perhaps even wait until the next day, because at the moment there was nothing to connect them with the killing of Capocchiani. They called me back soon afterwards, telling me that they would come that night as well. I had the impression that this decision was influenced by their worry that I might disappear with the cocaine. Whatever the case, just before dawn, we left in two cars. There was myself, my wife, my three-year-old son, Antonio Losurdo with his wife (or perhaps his partner, I am not sure) and Pasquale Losurdo, who was alone.

QUESTION Doesn't Pasquale Losurdo have family?

ANSWER He is separated and on very bad terms with his wife, who has moved up north. After the separation he moved back in with his elderly mother.

QUESTION What happened when you got to Pescara?

ANSWER We met with Bevilacqua, and the first thing he did was take us to the house he had found for us. It was a spacious, partly furnished house on the outskirts, in a very decent condition. He did not tell me whose it was, and I did not ask him. That same morning, we discussed the matter of the cocaine. The day before, I had made sure to take a sample so that he could test it. I did not tell him that I already had the cocaine with me.

QUESTION Why?

ANSWER Because it is good to trust people, dottoressa, but better not to. Bevilacqua was a friend, but it is hard to predict how someone will react when so much money is involved. Anyway, he tested the cocaine and admitted it was very good. So we sealed the deal – but only after he had asked me what had happened and why I had had to leave Bari.

QUESTION Did you tell him the whole story?

ANSWER The essentials, which were that there had been a rift with Grimaldi, that the situation had become untenable and that I feared for my safety. I told him that I wanted to stay there for a while before deciding if I should go back to Bari or move north for good.

QUESTION Did Bevilacqua ask you where the cocaine came from?

ANSWER No. I think he had guessed some of it, but he did not ask me anything.

QUESTION How did you arrange for payment?

ANSWER We came to an understanding that when he had the money he would inform me, and I would go down, pick up the cocaine and hand it over to him. As I have said, though, I already had the cocaine with me. When he left, I found a closet in the cellar of the house and hid it there.

QUESTION Was the deal completed?

ANSWER Yes. Three days later, Bevilacqua called to say that he had the money and we agreed to meet the following day. As far as he knew, I had to travel to recover the consignment. In actual fact, I did decide to come back to Bari, because I wanted to talk to some people and get an idea of the situation.

QUESTION Had you heard from anyone since you had left?

ANSWER Only Cosimo Pontrelli, an associate whose job was to fix up stolen cars or prepare them for robberies, as well as producing keys for opening them. I had called him, firstly because he was my godson – I had been the head of the *capriata* at his affiliation – and secondly because I knew he was well connected in criminal circles but not too close to Grimaldi.

QUESTION Did you tell Pontrelli what had happened?

ANSWER No. I used an excuse to justify the call – I asked him how long it would take him to get hold of a couple of Lancia Themas for me – and I told him I was away on business.

QUESTION What did he say? Did he know about what had happened between you and Grimaldi?

ANSWER If he did know, he gave no indication. He spoke to me quite naturally – he said that it would take two or three days to get the cars if I confirmed it, and I replied that I would let him know – and above all, he did not even mention Capocchiani. So, unless he was pretending, which I do not think he was, the news had not yet got out.

QUESTION Was Grimaldi not looking for you?

ANSWER I have no idea. I had got rid of my old telephone and the corresponding number and had acquired a new one before leaving.

QUESTION Did you drive down by yourself?

ANSWER Yes. Even though the absence of the Losurdos would soon be noticed and Grimaldi and his men would be bound to assume that they had gone with me, I did not want the matter to be clear immediately.

QUESTION I can tell you that in subsequent interviews you will be shown photographs and asked to make identifications, but for now I would ask you to indicate to me briefly the number of people affiliated with Grimaldi.

ANSWER To answer that question with any accuracy it is necessary to clarify that some affiliates do not live in the area and are not organically part of the group. These are people who have received the flower from Grimaldi or his godsons but who belong to different clans, from other parts of the region.

QUESTION Can you explain what "receiving the flower" means?

ANSWER It is one of the expressions we use to refer to affiliation or promotion from one rank to another. The flower or the gift are, basically, the privilege of affiliation or promotion.

QUESTION Let us go back to the number of affiliates.

ANSWER Yes, as I was saying, there are many affiliates who derive their status in the organization directly or indirectly from Grimaldi. I could not give an exact figure, but I would say at least 200, perhaps more. The operatives are naturally fewer in number, approximately some fifty people. To this number should be added the network of street-level dealers, who are not affiliates (although the best of them are affiliated after a period of observation) but who still have to account to the clan and respect all the rules laid down for these activities. I refer in particular to the division of the territory into areas and to the type of drug that each person is authorized to deal.

QUESTION How were you thinking of waging war on such a large organization with the help only of the Losurdo brothers?

ANSWER I had a plan. The idea was to practise a kind of guerrilla war, getting help with logistical matters from others in the territory, but keeping their identities hidden to avoid reprisals. Not being on the spot was an advantage to us because they would not know where to look for us. I thought that, once I had killed two or three important members of the clan, I would be able to bring other people over to my side and then launch a final assault. An alternative to this plan was to strike two or three times then offer to make peace with Grimaldi. In actual fact, though, this second hypothesis never struck me as too feasible.

QUESTION Let us go back to your trip from Pescara to Bari to look around. What emerged from that?

ANSWER Not very much. I met with a few people, but nobody important. A couple of people told me that Grimaldi was looking for me, but they did not give me the impression they knew why. Then I went back to Pescara. I met with Bevilacqua, he gave me the money and I gave him the cocaine. At that point I asked him if he could get hold of weapons for me. He asked me what my intentions were. He was worried that I wanted to do something in his area, which would cause trouble for him. I made it clear that I needed the guns for a robbery in my own area and assured him that I would not keep them in that house. Having received these reassurances, he agreed and told me that he would be able to get me a few pistols, a semi-automatic rifle and, if I wanted it – although it would cost me a lot – a Skorpion machine pistol. I replied that the Skorpion and a .44 Magnum revolver with the serial number erased would be fine. I chose the Skorpion, which I had already used in the past, because it is a very versatile weapon: it can be carried like a normal pistol but fires as rapidly as a machine gun and, with the stock folded, becomes a genuine sub-machine gun, but one which it is possible to aim accurately. The .44 Magnum is a very powerful gun, suitable for operations in which it is necessary to penetrate car doors and bodywork with some certainty of achieving results. A few hours later, Bevilacqua brought them over, together with the corresponding ammunition. He asked me for two million, to which I agreed without arguing. These weapons, too, are among those to which I led you.

QUESTION Why did you ask him for these weapons? Did you not have enough already?

ANSWER Not enough to safeguard us against possible emergencies. My idea was that in order to act with relative safety, it was necessary to have at least a couple of weapons per head.

QUESTION What did you do then?

ANSWER At that point we had to organize the expeditions to Bari. As we would have to come from outside and then get away quickly, we needed an easily identifiable objective which would not require lengthy preparation. That was why we chose Gennaro Carbone, known as the Cue, who was easy to find outside the amusement arcade in Palese that he ran for Grimaldi.

QUESTION Before going into details, could you give us an overview of the actions undertaken in your war with Grimaldi?

ANSWER We launched five excursions from Pescara to Bari and the immediate vicinity. On the first, we killed Gennaro Carbone; on the second, we drove for a few hours between Palese, Santo Spirito and Enziteto, but could not find anyone to hit; on the third, we found

Francesco Andriani, although he noticed us and managed to get away inside a building; on the fourth, we went to a jewellers' shop in San Girolamo that belonged to Grimaldi, although officially it was in someone else's name, and robbed it; on the fifth, there was a shoot-out in Enziteto between us and some of Grimaldi's men.

QUESTION I notice that you do not include the kidnapping of Nicola Grimaldi's son in the list.

ANSWER Because I had nothing to do with that.

QUESTION Let me point out to you that the temporal coincidence between your attacks on the Grimaldi clan and the abduction of the son of that clan's boss makes it hard to believe that you had no involvement in such a serious incident. I invite you to reflect on your answer.

ANSWER As you have been able to observe in these first interviews, I have already accused myself of crimes of which I was not even suspected and for which – without the benefits of cooperation – I would be liable to life imprisonment. It would be absurd to deny that incident if my friends and I were genuinely responsible for it. I would not gain any advantage, on the contrary I would run the risk – if evidence against me emerged from other sources – of losing all the benefits of cooperation.

QUESTION Why did you not tell us immediately that you had no involvement in that incident?

ANSWER I could say that nobody has asked me about it specifically over the past four days. Of course, I knew perfectly well that this was one of the matters in which you were and are most interested. I chose not to deny responsibility for kidnapping the Grimaldi boy immediately, as soon as I appeared before you, because I was afraid that beginning in this way would arouse an instinctive mistrust on your part. I wanted to tell you immediately about the most serious acts I have committed in order to make it clear that my decision to cooperate with the law is definite and irrevocable, thinking that after such statements it would be easier to convince you that I was not involved in the kidnapping.

QUESTION If you and your friends did not kidnap young Grimaldi, who could have done it?

ANSWER I have asked myself that question, too, but have not come up with an answer. If the kidnappers belong to the underworld, I feel duty-bound to say that they are mad. If their identities are discovered, Grimaldi will inevitably take his revenge. Apart from anything else, for something like that he could ask for help from anybody, inside or outside the region. Everybody would help him. In short, once identified, the people responsible for that act would be hunted down without mercy.

QUESTION So what do you think?

ANSWER I think it could have been a pervert, someone who did not know whose child the boy was.

QUESTION Did you know a ransom was paid?

ANSWER No. This is the first I have heard of it.

QUESTION Are you really sure you have nothing to do with the incident? In the criminal circles of which you have been talking, everyone is convinced that you and your friends were responsible.

ANSWER I realize that, and I would think the same thing, but I can only repeat that I was not involved.

QUESTION Have you ever been involved in a kidnapping?

ANSWER Yes, a lightning kidnapping.

QUESTION What is a lightning kidnapping?

ANSWER A criminal activity developed in the area of Andria and Cerignola, which has spread here in the last few years. It is very simple. To explain it, I will describe the one that I myself carried out with Simone Losurdo.

QUESTION The same Simone Losurdo who was later killed by Grimaldi and his men?

ANSWER Yes. We knew a meat wholesaler who did most of his business off the books and so had a lot of cash at his disposal. We grabbed his son on the outskirts of Triggiano, where he lived, just as he was about to get into his car. Immediately afterwards, we telephoned the father and told him that we wanted fifty million within an hour. If we did not get it, we would cut the boy's throat. We got the boy to talk to him on the telephone to demonstrate that it was not a joke. If he handed over the money, his son would be released immediately, completely unharmed. Needless to say, we told him not to get in touch with the police or the Carabinieri. I should point out that the technique of lightning kidnapping involves asking for a relatively low sum that can easily be found. In this particular case, we were sure that the man had that sum in cash, because of what I have just told you.

QUESTION How did it go?

ANSWER Like clockwork. We told the wholesaler to wrap the money in newspaper and put it under a dustbin. One of my men went to pick it up, we checked that the amount was what we had asked for and that the notes were good, then we released the young man in the country, informing the father that he could go and collect him. After getting the money, I paid the share owing to Grimaldi, according to the rules. The crime had been committed in the territory of which he was the boss. Given my position, I could engage in operations of this kind without informing him in advance and without asking for his permission, but I still had to pay him the regulation ten per cent.

QUESTION How old was the young man you kidnapped?

ANSWER He was an adult, about twenty. As I said, he was just getting into his car when we went up to him and threatened him at gunpoint.

QUESTION Do you know if the kidnapping was reported?

ANSWER No. In fact, I do not think any of these kidnappings were ever reported. I suspect it is a crime that does not even figure in the police statistics. Apart from anything else, you generally choose someone who has something to hide and would find it hard to justify the availability of all that cash, like that wholesaler, who is a big tax evader. As I said, he did almost everything off the books and would certainly not have wanted anybody to ask questions about how he had managed to get his hands on fifty million in less than an hour. In short, I cannot think of a single case where things did not work out.

QUESTION Apart from that of young Grimaldi.

ANSWER Apart from that of young Grimaldi, of course. Among us it was said that lightning kidnapping was the perfect crime, because it paid well, it paid quickly and it was almost impossible to verify. We knew that some people in the police and the Carabinieri were aware of the phenomenon, but we were not worried because, I repeat, it is a crime that leaves no trace, and we were sure that neither the kidnap victims nor their family members who had paid the ransom would ever say anything. Apart from the general and widespread fear of organized crime in the territories in which we were active – I very much doubt that a similar criminal procedure would work in areas where organized crime and a general climate of intimidation are less dominant;

I certainly would not have risked an operation of that kind in Florence, for example, or Bologna – there was the sense of vulnerability that came from having suffered a kidnapping so close to home, and also the impression of having had a narrow escape, in fact of having got away relatively unscathed. My understanding is that anyone who had been subjected to something like that would want to forget it as soon as possible.

QUESTION You said that there were members of the police and the Carabinieri who were aware of the phenomenon. How had they found out about it?

ANSWER I have a feeling that a number of carabinieri – I do not know from which department – asked a few questions and received confirmation of the existence of the phenomenon.

QUESTION I put it to you that the modus operandi you describe in such detail corresponds to the initial phase of the kidnapping of young Grimaldi.

ANSWER I know: it was the usual method, although sometimes, instead of the relatives being phoned directly, it was a go-between who was called. Having said that, I can only confirm what I have repeatedly stated today: I cannot tell you about something I did not do. I would like to point out that I came to you to cooperate after learning of the discovery of the child's body. I had hoped that whoever had taken him would have returned him. First of all because I hoped that the boy would return home, then because in this way my responsibility, which everyone seemed to be taking for granted, would be ruled out. The child himself would have said – perhaps not to you, but certainly to his father – that I was not the person who had taken him. Among other things he knew me well, since I had been to his house

167

many times and had even eaten there. When I heard that the boy was dead, I realized that my only option was to cooperate with the law, to save myself in general and to be able to say, with some likelihood of being believed, that I had no involvement in that incident. If I had not handed myself in, I would have been hunted down forever, and not just by Grimaldi's men.

At this point, at the request of the defence lawyer who wishes to confer privately with her client, the interview is briefly suspended at 19.15 and resumed at 19.30 in the presence of the same persons.

QUESTION Do you have anything to add concerning the kidnapping of young Grimaldi?
ANSWER No. My lawyer has also asked me to think it over and to tell the truth, in case I was keeping silent about anything. I confirm all the statements I have made until now, with no modification.

At 19.40 the transcript is read, approved by those present, and signed.

# 12

D'Angelo and Fenoglio met up in the captain's office. Valente had had to leave for an unspecified engagement but had made his office – obviously the most comfortable in the station – available to them.

"What do you think?" D'Angelo asked, collapsing into an armchair. "Do you believe him?"

Fenoglio suppressed the impulse to tell her that right from the start he'd had his doubts that Lopez and his men had been responsible for the kidnapping.

Don't take an investigation as an opportunity to show that you're better than anybody else, he often told himself. It's one of the reasons – perhaps the main reason – why the worst mistakes are made, why innocents end up behind bars and criminals are left at large.

It was true, though: he'd had his doubts from the start, although he had then dismissed the thought as an example of his tendency to doubt everything, and in particular to distrust overly obvious solutions. The fact is that the most obvious solutions are usually the right ones. In most cases, human actions and conduct follow consistent lines and things are just as they seem. Consequently, most cases are solved that way, taking note of the statistical data and applying it to concrete situations. The vast majority of murders are committed by male individuals known to their victims. This is the obvious premise of any investigation into a violent death, one that any detective has to take into account in formulating and verifying his hypotheses. Almost always, the facts match the statistics, and this shouldn't be forgotten.

*Almost* always. This, too, shouldn't be forgotten.

"He strikes me as credible. Of course, it isn't easy to admit you're responsible for the death of a child, irrespective of the practical consequences. So his argument – what would I gain by denying it, given that I've already accused myself of crimes that would get me a life sentence? – makes sense but isn't conclusive. There are things that are hard to admit because they might damage the image you have of yourself. For example: I'm a criminal, but I don't harm women or children. Having said that, I believe him. Apart from anything else, what he says is convincing: if it does turn out to be them – maybe one of the Losurdos decides to cooperate – Lopez will lose everything. He's intelligent, and I don't think he'd run that kind of risk."

D'Angelo lit another cigarette. She said mechanically, yes, thank you, to the corporal who had looked in to ask if they wanted a coffee, and arranged a strand of hair with the ring finger of the hand holding the cigarette.

"What if he's denying it because he's afraid of Grimaldi's revenge?"

"He must be afraid of that anyway. He's killed several of his men, stolen cocaine from him, ruined his reputation in the underworld and will soon be sending him to prison. That strikes me as more than sufficient reason for Grimaldi to want him dead."

"You're right. It's just that I was sure I could close the case of the Grimaldi boy and I'm finding it hard to resign myself to the fact that now I can't."

"I understand that. But we don't have to resign ourselves to not catching the kidnappers."

D'Angelo breathed in the smoke and, with the same gesture as before, again arranged the strand of hair, pushing it behind her ear.

"Actually, there's absolutely nothing to link Lopez and his partners to the kidnapping. Not the hint of a clue. It can't be said that we've neglected anything in order to give credibility to Lopez at all costs. We've asked him, we've insisted, and he's said it wasn't him, while accusing himself of very serious crimes in which he wasn't even a suspect. I think that proves Lopez's reliability, and we can proceed against Grimaldi and the others. The lawyers may create a bit of a fuss, but there's nothing they can actually use against him."

"That's right."

It was right. Why, then, did he feel ill at ease? Actually, it wasn't a difficult question. They would keep listening to Lopez's stories; they would investigate and find the necessary corroborative evidence; they would arrest a whole lot of people, dealing a fatal blow to a criminal organization as despicable as it was dangerous. But the darkest of all the things that had happened lately would remain outside the reassuring circle of those investigations that give meaning to events and assuage anxieties.

Fenoglio knew perfectly well that the kidnapping would obsess him until they managed to solve it. The problem was: there was no certainty that they would. There never is.

The corporal came in with their coffees and two small Neapolitan tarts on a tray.

"You shouldn't show me these things," D'Angelo said, smiling nervously and picking up her tart. "I have a sweet tooth and I'm fat."

Then she drank the coffee and lit yet another cigarette. She really did smoke too much, Fenoglio thought. Just like Serena.

Serena. A stab of pain in his stomach. God alone knew where she was right now.

"There's something I've been meaning to ask you for some time," D'Angelo said, interrupting this painful thought at birth. "You're Piedmontese, aren't you?"

"Yes, from Turin."

"It's a silly question, but I'll ask it anyway, because Beppe Fenoglio is one of my favourite writers. Any relation?"

"In my family, some used to say that we were distant relatives. Frankly, I've never believed it. When you have the same name as a famous person and come from the same area there's always someone in the family who says you're related. It's a way of making yourself feel important."

D'Angelo played with her half-smoked cigarette, looking at the embers as if they hid a crucial mystery. "You do look alike, though."

# 13

At 15.30 on 23 May 1992, in Bari, at the offices of the Criminal Investigation Unit of the Carabinieri, Vito Lopez, whose particulars have already been stated in other documents, appears before the Public Prosecutor as represented by Assistant Prosecutor Gemma D'Angelo, assisted in the drafting of the current document by Sergeant Ignazio Calcaterra, and also in the presence, for the purposes of the investigation, of Captain Alberto Valente, Marshal Pietro Fenoglio and Corporal Antonio Pellecchia, all detectives in the Criminal Investigation Unit of the Carabinieri of Bari. Also present is Lopez's defence lawyer, Avvocato Marianna Formica.

QUESTION Let us resume from where we left off yesterday.
ANSWER I repeat, as I already mentioned in the previous interview, that we made five excursions to Bari and the surrounding area to strike members of the Grimaldi clan. The strategy, if it can be called that, was very simple. Every now and again we would steal a car, always in the Pescara area. We would choose models with powerful engines but small in size, to reduce the risk of being stopped by the law enforcement agencies.
QUESTION What do you mean?

ANSWER What the police and Carabinieri pay greatest attention to at roadblocks are eye-catching cars with powerful engines, with several male individuals on board. So we would procure turbo versions of small cars such as the Peugeot 205 or the Fiat Uno, the same models that are often used for robberies. I should make it clear that after carrying out the operation we would return to the Pescara area in which we had stolen the cars and leave them on the street in such a way that the owners could recover them and police would think that the theft had been an act of bravado. We counted on the fact that in such cases no detailed investigation is conducted and the vehicle is immediately restored to the owner. With the same aim of not being noticed and not being stopped, whenever we left on these excursions we dressed smartly, in jackets and ties. This, too, reduced the risk of being stopped.

QUESTION What would you have done if you had been stopped?

ANSWER We would have slowed down, as if about to pull up, then accelerated abruptly and driven away. I cannot tell you what we would have done if we had been shot at. We were in such a state of excitement that we might even have returned fire.

QUESTION When you left on these expeditions, were you using cocaine?

ANSWER No. Actually, one of the Losurdos wanted to, but I dissuaded him. Cocaine gives an illusion of lucidity, but when the effect wears off it can be very dangerous if you have to undertake a military-style operation. We would consume it on the way back, as a pick-me-up: as I have told you, we had kept a hundred grams from the consignment sold to Bevilacqua.

QUESTION Were the operations themselves carried out in jacket and tie?

ANSWER No. We had disposable builders' overalls which we took off after the operation and threw in rubbish bins. We also wore balaclavas and rubber gloves. We disposed of these in the same way.

QUESTION Could you clarify why you wore overalls, balaclavas and rubber gloves?

ANSWER To reduce to a minimum the risk of contamination from gunshot residue. Having been the object of various murder investigations in the past, and also having discussed this several times with others in the clan, I was aware that the first check the police do on a suspect after an act of violence is a test to ascertain the possible presence – on the hands, the hair or the clothes – of gunshot residue. Covering ourselves in that way, we greatly reduced the risk that if we were stopped it might be possible to ascertain that we had fired guns.

QUESTION Tell us about the first operation you carried out.

ANSWER We decided to hit Gennaro Carbone, known as the Cue because of his love of pool. He was one of Grimaldi's most trusted men (he had reached the third rank, but had been promised promotion to the fourth) and his job consisted, first of all, in collecting and distributing the money intended for the families of prisoners. He also ran an amusement arcade in Palese, at the back of which was a very lucrative clandestine gambling den. For that reason, he was always there and often stood outside the arcade. He would be an easy target, and the operation would not require any planning. Moreover, it should be said that he was the cousin of Mario Abbinante – one of the men who had executed Losurdo – and so an operation against him was also a specific act of revenge. We had considered the possibility of directly hitting Grimaldi, but it would have been very difficult, given that he is always very cautious and always has bodyguards with him when he goes out. He is also under special surveillance and has to report every day to police headquarters. We had thought of hitting him on the way back from there, but we dismissed the idea as being too dangerous. Anyway, our plan of action against Carbone was flexible. If we had met any of Losurdo's killers or any high-ranking member of Grimaldi's clan on the street, perhaps even in the vicinity of the amusement arcade, we would have attacked them. As did in fact happen, although not on our first expedition.

QUESTION Let us keep to chronological order. Tell us about the operation against Carbone.

ANSWER As I have already mentioned, we stole a small but powerful car, in this case a Renault 5 GT Turbo. We left in the afternoon, dressed in jackets and ties. We had the Kalashnikov and the Skorpion with us in the boot, already loaded and ready to fire. We also had the overalls and the rest of the gear. I was carrying the .44 Magnum. We drove past Carbone's arcade and saw him next to the entrance, as was his habit and as we expected. Together with him was another of Grimaldi's men, named Dangella, a recent affiliate, with the second rank, but promised promotion to the *Sgarro*. We decided to kill both of them.

QUESTION How did you proceed?

ANSWER We went and changed in a garage in the immediate vicinity to which we had the keys. We took off our jackets, put on the overalls – which are very easy to put on and take off – and all the rest. Then we quickly drove back to the arcade. When we got there, we saw that Dangella had left – or perhaps had simply gone inside – but Carbone was still there. Pasquale Losurdo remained behind the wheel, while Antonio Losurdo and I got out of the car. When he saw us coming, Carbone did not immediately realize that we were there for him, or at least gave no indication that he had realized. I almost had the impression that he was about to say something to us, perhaps to ask us who we were or what we wanted. Losurdo let off a burst of machine-gun fire, and Carbone fell to the ground. I went closer and shot him twice with the .44. Then we got straight back in the car and quickly drove away. As we escaped, we took off the overalls and put them with all the rest in a large rubbish bag, which we threw in a dustbin after a few miles. Then we went and dropped the weapons in the usual *cupa* and drove back to Pescara. We got there at night, abandoned the car – after cleaning it – not far from where we had taken it and went back to the house on foot.

QUESTION Were you aware that a passer-by was wounded in the course of that operation?

ANSWER Yes, we heard about it on the radio, on the way back.

QUESTION Tell us about the second expedition.

ANSWER It was a week later. We had decided to seek out one of Grimaldi's trusted men who controlled Enziteto, in charge among other things of the unauthorized occupation of municipal apartments. It is a very lucrative business – there are a great many illegally occupied municipal apartments – but above all a basic way of controlling the territory.

QUESTION What do you mean?

ANSWER Managing the municipal apartments, deciding who is allowed one and who has to be evicted, is an important manifestation of criminal power. If you are in a position to do something like that, you are effectively the law in a particular area. As if you were the State or the mayor, or a judge. You are the person who is really in charge of the place, you are the one people need to go to, not only to buy drugs or engage in other criminal activities, but also to resolve disputes, to obtain the things due to you that the State is not able to guarantee. Hitting someone who was in charge of this important area of criminal activity would be an act of war with strong symbolic value. It would mean attacking the control of the territory at its core.

QUESTION So you planned this operation. How did it go?

ANSWER We left Pescara in the morning and set off for Enziteto. On the way, we dropped by the *cupa* where we had hidden the weapons. We drove around Enziteto for an hour, but did not encounter anyone. A lot of people noticed us, which we did not mind, because it meant that everyone knew we were there and were launching our challenge. We could not do it for too long, though, because there was a risk that Grimaldi's men would arrive in force or that someone would inform the Carabinieri. To cut a long story short, after an hour of fruitless driving around, we left with nothing accomplished.

QUESTION Let us move on to the third expedition.

ANSWER It took place three days later, I think, and it was very similar to the second one, except that we went to Enziteto in the evening. In this case we succeeded in locating one of Grimaldi's trusted men, Francesco Andriani, but he noticed us in time. We got out of the car and fired, but from a distance, and he managed to get away by taking shelter in an apartment building.

On the fourth expedition, we went to a jeweller's shop in San Girolamo, which belonged to Grimaldi even though it was in someone else's name, and robbed it. I should point out that among us there was a debate about what to do, in the sense that one of the Losurdos also wanted to kneecap the jeweller, who in fact was only an assistant. To be more specific: the jeweller was the original owner of the shop, but had had to resort to loan sharks, was unable to pay the enormous interest demanded and in the end had been forced to give up his activity, while remaining the official owner and continuing to work there, but only as an employee.

QUESTION You said there was a debate between you about whether or not to kneecap the jeweller.

ANSWER Antonio Losurdo wanted to shoot him in the legs, but I said it was not right. The jeweller was not affiliated with Grimaldi. In fact, in his way, he was one of Grimaldi's victims, therefore it was not right to hurt him. The other Losurdo agreed with me, so the idea was rejected.

QUESTION When did you find out about the kidnapping of young Damiano Grimaldi?

ANSWER Two days after the last expedition, the one in which there was a shoot-out in Enziteto. At the point at which that happened, the kidnapping had already taken place, but we did not know that.

QUESTION Tell us about that episode.

ANSWER We had gone back to Enziteto, once again in search of Grimaldi's associates or, possibly, lieutenants. We had been driving around without any result for nearly half an hour when we noticed a BMW with four men on board. Among them, I recognized two, of whom at the moment I can remember only the nicknames: Pelé and Crazy Gino. The other two I could not see well, so I did not recognize them. Pelé and Crazy Gino are both very dangerous characters, who specialize in robbing security vans. They are not affiliates, but they are very friendly with Grimaldi. When they saw us they stopped their car and all got out, armed with pistols and a rifle. I was behind the wheel of our car; I spun it around and managed to get our car into a partly sheltered position behind a lorry.

QUESTION How were you able to do a manoeuvre like that in a city street?

ANSWER We were not in a normal city street. We were in Enziteto, where the streets are wider and clearer. Many blocks do not even have cars parked on them.

QUESTION What happened after that?

ANSWER All three of us got out and started shooting wildly. They did the same. I cannot tell you how long the encounter lasted, probably ten seconds at the most. A number of bullets hit our car, but none of us was hurt. I cannot say if any of them were hit. I did not see anybody fall to the ground.

QUESTION How did that episode end?

ANSWER During a pause in the shooting – both sides had emptied their weapons – we got back in the car and drove away. They tried to follow us, but I soon managed to lose them. I think in reality they gave up following us because it was too dangerous, partly because the police or the Carabinieri might have intervened.

QUESTION What did you do with the car?

ANSWER We burnt it near San Ferdinando di Puglia. Obviously, we could not do as we had done with the others, that is, leave it where we had stolen it to ensure that it was recovered. Before disposing of it, we dropped the weapons in the *cupa*, the one I led you to.

QUESTION How did you get back to Abruzzo?

ANSWER In San Ferdinando, I had a friend and comrade, Giuseppe Curci. I called him and told him that I had an emergency and needed a clean car. He did not ask any questions – apart from anything else, he owed me a number of favours – and within half an hour he had one of his men bring me a Fiat Ritmo, in which we returned to Pescara.

QUESTION Was Curci aware of the war that you had launched against Grimaldi?

ANSWER I have no idea. I certainly did not mention it to him, and he did not ask any questions.

QUESTION We were talking about when and how you came to hear about the kidnapping of the boy.

ANSWER Yes. After the shoot-out of which I have just spoken, some of Grimaldi's men went to the house of my wife's sister, beat up her husband Raffaele De Bellis, shot him in the legs and told him that, if the boy was not handed back immediately, they would return, rape and kill his wife in front of him, then burn him alive. Obviously, he had no idea what they were talking about, but they told him to pass on the message.

QUESTION Is your brother-in-law involved in criminal activities?

ANSWER No, he is a quiet lad, completely clean, who works as a bricklayer. My wife's sister called her on her mobile and told her everything. My wife became very angry with me and asked me what was going on and if we really had kidnapped a child. I was flabbergasted and swore to her that we had nothing to do with it, that I knew nothing about it.

QUESTION What did you do then?

ANSWER I made a few telephone calls to people I trusted. They told me that Grimaldi's son had been kidnapped by someone who had demanded a ransom. Everyone thought it had been us, and both Grimaldi's men and the various law enforcement agencies were looking for us.

QUESTION What did you think?

ANSWER I got very worried. When I told the Losurdos, they both went into a panic and, after long discussions, they said that they wanted to get out of there. There was no way to dissuade them. Besides, they were not wrong. With what was happening, the situation was becoming very difficult to sustain. It was one thing waging war on Grimaldi, although that was dangerous enough in itself; it was quite another being suspected of an exceptionally serious operation like the kidnapping of a child and being the targets in a manhunt that united the Grimaldi clan and the law enforcement agencies.

QUESTION Did the Losurdos leave?

ANSWER Yes. They asked me for their share of the kitty, that is, the money from the cocaine and the proceeds from the robbery of the jeweller's shop. Realizing that it was impossible to make them change their minds, I handed over the money and they left, with the intention of crossing the Adriatic and settling in Montenegro, where they have a cousin involved in cigarette smuggling and where there is no danger of their being arrested and extradited.

QUESTION Where is the share of the money that you kept for yourself?

ANSWER I left it with my wife.

QUESTION Are you aware that you will have to surrender the money to us, as well as the proceeds from all the other illegitimate activities in which you were involved, and that this is a condition of your receiving the benefits of your cooperation?

ANSWER Yes, I am aware of that. I confirm that I intend to cooperate fully, including in the matter of assets.

QUESTION Do you know if the Losurdos managed to reach Montenegro?

ANSWER I have no idea. I have not heard from them.

QUESTION At this point, what did you decide to do?

ANSWER The situation quickly came to a head. The police had found the burnt-out and bullet-riddled car we had used for the last expedition and had traced it back to the area where it had been stolen.

QUESTION How did you find out about this?

ANSWER Bevilacqua told me. He came to see me. He was very worried. The police and the Carabinieri were causing a lot of trouble in the area with searches and roadblocks, and he had realized that it was all to do with us. He asked us to leave the house as soon as possible. He did not care about what I had done, but he did not want to be involved.

QUESTION And you?

ANSWER We did not have much choice. Even if we had not agreed, it was impossible to stay if Bevilacqua did not want us there. Apart from being our host, he was, in a way, the boss of the territory. He could have come with his men and got us out by force, or else he could have informed the police or the Carabinieri of our presence. But apart from that, I myself was convinced of the need to leave: it was just a matter of time before the police and the Carabinieri found us. So I reassured Bevilacqua that we would leave the house within a few hours.

QUESTION How did you arrange things?

ANSWER I took my wife and son to some relatives of ours who lived near Piacenza, where you later went to get them to take them to the safe location. When we got there, I heard on the radio the news that the boy's body had been found. At that point I realized I had no choice. After a few hours' rest I got back in my car, drove back down here, contacted a carabiniere I had known for a while and informed him of my intentions. That same evening, I met with you for the first interview.

QUESTION We are now going to show you an album of photographs. For each photograph, tell us if you recognize the person shown, if you know his name and/ or his nickname, and if he is someone who belongs to the organization of which Grimaldi is the boss or to any other criminal group. Where you are not sure that you recognize him, please say so.

Lopez begins to examine said album.

At 18.50, before proceeding with the identifications, but after the interviewee has already viewed the first pages of the photograph album, the interview is suspended for serious reasons unrelated to the object of the present procedure.

Read, confirmed and signed.

# 14

Lopez had just started looking through the photograph album when someone knocked at the door.

"Come in," D'Angelo said, suppressing a gesture of annoyance at the interruption.

The door opened slowly and Colonel Morelli looked in. It was the first time he'd put in an appearance since the interviews with Lopez had begun. The other carabinieri got to their feet. So did Lopez after a few moments. Morelli didn't come in.

"I'm sorry, dottoressa, may I speak with you for a moment?"

There was something strange about the colonel's hesitant tone. Morelli was normally very military in the way he moved and spoke. Lacking in half-tones, perfectly commensurate with the traditional idea of how a commanding officer should behave.

Now, though, his voice and movements were uncertain; and he was alone. This, too, was unusual, Fenoglio thought. Commanding officers rarely go about on their own; there is always someone with them, as if to symbolically underline their role in the hierarchy they represent.

That afternoon, though, Morelli was alone. No hierarchy, no symbols, no rituals. Something was wrong.

D'Angelo looked around for a few seconds. "Of course," she said, getting to her feet and picking up her packet of cigarettes.

"You too, Valente," the colonel said to the captain, disappearing into the corridor.

"The colonel looked odd," Pellecchia commented after a few minutes' silence.

"What can have happened?" Avvocato Formica asked.

Something very serious, Fenoglio thought. Someone had been murdered, maybe a relative of Lopez's. Something had happened that was bringing the situation to a head.

D'Angelo came back some ten minutes later, without the captain. Her eyes were moist and there was a lost expression on her face. She seemed to recognize neither the room nor the people in it.

"We have to suspend the interview. I mean, we have to … We can't continue."

"What happened, dottoressa?"

She didn't reply. She probably didn't even hear Fenoglio's voice. "Write this, sergeant," she said, staring straight ahead. "At" – she looked at her watch, staring for several seconds at the dial – "18.50, before proceeding with the identifications, but after the interviewee has already viewed the first pages of the photograph album, the interview is suspended for serious reasons unrelated to the object of the present procedure."

She pronounced the words emphatically, but it was as if her voice was coming from somewhere else.

"Please print the transcript. We'll resume on Monday. I'm sorry, Avvocato, I'll let you know the time of the next interview. I'm sorry," she repeated, "but something's happened."

Her words hung there for a few moments, perhaps longer.

"There's been an explosion on the highway."

"Where?" Fenoglio asked.

"In Palermo. Apparently there are survivors, apparently Falcone and his wife are being taken to hospital."

In the most tragic situations, we tend to remember apparently insignificant details. What remained in Fenoglio's mind was Sergeant Calcaterra's face. It was usually unmoving, expressionless, as if the only thing that interested him was getting statements down on paper, transforming terrible, bloodthirsty events into bureaucratic, aseptic language, sterilizing them, draining them of the incomprehensible violence of life, domesticating them, making them the material of files and records.

But now Calcaterra looked shocked. His lips quivered two or three times, then he rubbed his eyes and blew his nose several times. "I'm from Palermo," he whispered, in dismay, almost as if to justify his reaction.

They went into the captain's office and heard the TV newsreader, Angela Buttiglione, announce that Giovanni Falcone had died at 19.07.

"I'd like to get a bit of air," D'Angelo said, after a few interminable moments of silence. "I'm walking home. And please, I don't want any bodyguards."

The captain was about to say something – It isn't possible, don't make things harder for us at a time like this, we can't let you go home without bodyguards. Something like that.

"I'll go with you, dottoressa," Fenoglio said.

She looked at him as if he had spoken in a foreign language and his words needed to be translated. "All right," she finally said.

Within a short time they were outside, walking along the seafront. The air was cool and dry. D'Angelo kicked a beer can. Fenoglio was aware of a multitude of incongruous thoughts passing through his head. But was that any different from usual? We usually only pay attention to the stream of our thoughts – which are always incongruous – when one of them becomes particularly nagging.

"Did you ever meet Judge Falcone?"

"Yes," she replied immediately, as if she had been waiting for that very question. "A few years ago, at a study day held by the Superior Council of Magistrates. A session on organized crime for those young magistrates among us who would be working in Sicily and Calabria."

"Was he giving a lecture?"

"Yes. Although I remember almost nothing of the lecture itself, I mean its actual contents. At the time I thought it was interesting, that he spoke well and was easy to follow, but I wouldn't be able to tell you today what he talked about. Obviously about investigating the Mafia, but I can't remember anything specific. Lunch, though, when the morning session was over: now that, I remember well. In the restaurant there were these big round tables, each seating ten people, with no assigned seats. I was with colleagues from my year and with others I didn't know. At the last moment, when there was only a single seat left, just next to mine, he came in and asked if he could sit down. We said yes, of course he could, and that was how I met Giovanni Falcone. It was a very … peculiar sensation. I can't find a more appropriate word."

"Why peculiar?"

"You have to imagine … I don't know, a historical figure, or a character from a novel, in other words, someone who's too remote to be real, coming and sitting down at your table, starting to chat to you, calling you by your first name, and he's ... Well, he's normal. Likeable, even. Quite likeable. Not too much, though. That's not a euphemism for saying he was unlikeable. You have to be careful with words. No, I mean exactly what I said: he was quite likeable. Very relaxed, very much at his ease. Normal, I can't think of another word. But you know perfectly well that he isn't normal. You're familiar with what he's done and is doing, and it crosses your mind that at that very moment, there are highly dangerous people thinking about how to kill him, this normal man you're having a normal conversation with. And being young – I was twenty-seven – you ask yourself: Who'll win? Us or them? I was thinking this while I was trying to say things he might remember me for, but I don't think I succeeded. So it can't even be said that we knew each other. If anyone had asked him: 'Do you know Gemma D'Angelo?' he would have replied that he was sorry, but he didn't think he remembered her. At least that's what I think."

She stopped in one of the little public gardens facing the sea. It was getting dark now. She sat down on a bench and Fenoglio did the same. He was a little embarrassed, and at the same time the situation struck him as natural. She took out her packet of cigarettes and with a mechanical gesture offered him one. This time he took it.

They sat side by side, smoking and looking out to sea. His thoughts began shifting about again, uncontrollably. When are you ever able to control your thoughts? Fenoglio didn't really feel like going home. It occurred to him that he ought to be angry with Serena but, absurdly, he wasn't. It occurred to him that all he wanted was for her to come back. A man passed with a big mongrel pulling on its lead. The dog came up to D'Angelo, and she stroked its muzzle with the gestures of someone who is very familiar with animals and has never been scared of them.

"Do you have a dog, dottoressa?" Fenoglio asked as soon as they were alone again.

"I had one as a child. When I was with my parents. I'd like to have one now, but how can I, living alone? What about you?"

"No. I think about it sometimes."

"He had an ironic smile, Giovanni Falcone. But it was an irony that was barely hinted at. As I looked at him, sitting there at the table, I told myself it was like an antidote, that almost invisible irony. Normality and irony. Maybe that's how you confront the monster. There you are: the lesson of that study day wasn't the content of the lecture, the lecture I can't remember. The lesson was about sitting normally at the table, that vaguely ironic smile, that being on first-name terms with the students. It was as if he was saying: we all know I am – but actually: *we are* – in the middle of a deadly game. But that's not going to stop us from smiling. If it did, the others would already have won."

She extinguished her cigarette and immediately lit another.

"Why did you decide to become a prosecutor?"

D'Angelo smiled and shook her head. "For me, it was a kind of mission. Falcone and the others were my idols. I wanted to be a prosecutor because I wanted to be like them."

Fenoglio nodded.

D'Angelo put her feet up on the bench and hugged her knees. She let several minutes go by without saying a word. "You know something absurd, marshal? I'm hungry."

"It isn't absurd. It's one of the many forms the survival instinct takes."

"Maybe you could walk me to a pizzeria and leave me there. I can get home on my own, don't worry."

"Dottoressa, don't make things difficult for me. We shouldn't even be here, sitting on a bench like this. You shouldn't have come out alone with me, without your bodyguards. I'll walk with you, but I won't leave you on your own. Let's call —"

"Please, I don't want them. They're good men, but I don't want to be with them right now."

"Then I'll wait. You eat your pizza and then I'll take you home."

"Don't even think about waiting for me. But you can be my guest, and then you can walk me home, if that makes you feel any easier."

"Yes, it does make me feel easier."

"Only I wouldn't want to cause you any problems with your family. They must be waiting for you at home."

"No problem, I was thinking of having a bite to eat myself."

She seemed about to ask him something, but thought better of it.

They went to a small pizzeria in Madonnella and found a table at the back, with Fenoglio sitting in such a way that he had a clear view of the entrance.

"My girlfriends and I used to come here in my university days," D'Angelo said, lighting yet another cigarette.

"Are you actually from Bari, dottoressa?"

"My father's from Bari, my mother's Sicilian. He's a civil lawyer, she teaches literature at high school."

My wife also teaches literature. But she's not at home any more. She may have someone else. I don't know.

"What was your first posting?"

"I did three years in Palmi."

"Always in the Prosecutor's Department?"

"I was an examining magistrate, and for a few months, when the new code came into force, I was also a judge at preliminary hearings. Then I was transferred here."

"Palmi can't have been a holiday."

She smiled again. "No, it wasn't."

The waiter came with *taralli*, olives, chunks of provolone and two beers. He took the order for the pizzas – they both ordered the one with turnip tops, anchovies and breadcrumbs – and slipped away as only some waiters can.

"When we were sitting on the bench, you started telling me about your mission."

She again took out her packet of cigarettes, looked at it as if she had never seen it before, and put it back. "I really am smoking too much. The next one after dinner."

"Good idea."

"My mission, yes. We were young and we wanted to change the world. Some thought they could do it through politics. I thought the best way was to become a magistrate. Without any compromises. On one side there were the bad guys – tax evaders, corrupt officials, polluters, Mafiosi, crooks of all kinds. I'd be on the other side, fighting them. Rather a naive idea, let's say. It took me quite a while to realize that things are more complicated."

She drank a little beer, ate a *tarallo* and a piece of cheese. Fenoglio did the same, in the same order.

"You know what the happiest moment of my life was?" she said.

"What?"

"We were waiting for the results of the written exams. One morning we heard they'd come out. To find out what they were, you just had to call a number at the Ministry of Justice. You gave your name, and the person there would tell you if you'd been accepted for the orals. A friend of mine – we'd studied together for the written exams – had already called and been told she'd passed. I don't know why, but I got it into my head that she'd asked about my result, too, and that they'd told her I hadn't got through but she hadn't had the courage to tell me. So I called, feeling a real sense of desperation – and that's no exaggeration. I gave my name to the person at the other end, stammering, I think. He leafed through the register – I could hear the rustling of the pages – and asked me: Did you say Gemma D'Angelo? Yes, I replied, barely able to breathe. Congratulations, dottoressa, you've been accepted, and he read me my marks. And I realized what it means to be crazy with happiness. Even now, when I think about it, I get the same blissful expression on my face that I went around with for at least two days."

Fenoglio smiled.

"I'm making you laugh."

"You're making me smile. That's different."

"Is it true that you're a literature graduate?"

"I studied literature. Then I joined the Carabinieri, for reasons it would take quite a while to explain, and dropped my studies. Sometimes I think I'd like to go back to university and get my degree, but I imagine it's just a whim. I still had five exams to take."

"Why literature?"

"I liked books and I didn't think I had any particular qualities. And the situation hasn't changed even now. I still like books and I still don't think I have any particular qualities. Apart, perhaps, from a certain stubbornness."

"And do you like being a carabiniere?"

"There are lots of things I *don't* like. But there are some I like."

"What don't you like?"

"I don't like the brutality. I don't like the abuse of power, especially when it's done in the name of supposed justice. I don't like some of your colleagues, I don't like many lawyers – but on the other hand there are some I like a lot – I don't like the hierarchy, I don't like some officers. Obviously I don't like criminals. Some are truly repulsive."

"There has to be something you like a lot to make up for all that."

"I like finding out what happened. In so far as it's possible. I like it that people trust me and decide to tell me what they know, even in the most unexpected situations. I like it when what I do – and it does happen – gives a little dignity back to those who've lost it. It gives meaning to chaos. And I like some of the people I come across in my work. A few of your colleagues, a few of my colleagues, even a few criminals. Some are pleasant people." He paused, surprised by what he had just said. "That was a pathetic little outburst."

"No. It really wasn't. I like the idea of giving meaning to chaos."

The pizzas arrived, and for a few minutes the conversation was put on hold. It was Saturday evening, the place was full, the voices from the various tables mingled in the discordant symphony typical of a crowded downmarket restaurant.

"You know what my first moment of disillusion was?" D'Angelo said after eating the last triangle of pizza with her hands.

"When people you'd sent down were acquitted in the appeal court?"

194

She gave a little laugh. "No, no. It was long before that."

Fenoglio pushed his plate to one side.

"Immediately after I graduated, I enrolled on a course to prepare for the magistrates' exam. It was given by a famous Neapolitan judge, who was said to be very good. And having attended the course I can vouch for that: he really was very good. To cut a long story short, I enrolled, did the trial month, then went to him and asked him how to make the payment, if a cheque from my father would be all right. He smiled, looking at me the way you'd look at an innocent little girl – which is exactly what I was – and said no, unfortunately he couldn't take cheques, I had to pay cash."

"It was all off the books."

"Precisely. I stammered something, said I didn't have the cash and if he didn't mind I'd bring it the following week. He said that'd be fine. It made me feel really bad. He was there to help us become magistrates, he was such a good teacher, and he was a tax evader. Without any embarrassment, without any shame, as if earning money – a lot of money, there were a great many people on the course – and not paying tax on it was completely normal. I didn't think it was right, I thought it was inadmissible, intolerable. I thought of not continuing. I was already kicking up a fuss in shops and restaurants if they didn't give me a till receipt, just to give you an idea."

"But you did continue."

"Yes, I did. And I paid on time every month, in cash like everyone else. I can still see it: us giving him the money, just like that, all rolled up, and him taking it without looking at it and putting it in his pocket."

Fenoglio smiled and shrugged. Life is made up of compromises.

"But it was thanks to him that I passed the exam. If I hadn't followed his course, in all probability I wouldn't have got through."

The waiter came over. Gerardo, his name was, and he had dyed black hair with an incredible comb-over and white roots.

"Would you like a dessert, marshal? Panna cotta, tiramisu, *sporcamussi?*"

Fenoglio looked at D'Angelo. She shook her head. "Nothing for me, thanks."

"Thank you, Gerardo, just bring us the bill, please."

"You know what they say about you?" D'Angelo said when the waiter had again disappeared.

"Who?"

"People. Even a few of my colleagues."

"What do they say?"

"Basically, that you're good but not likeable. Do you know why?"

"I can imagine."

"What do you imagine?"

"I imagine I won't make myself likeable by saying it."

She laughed. She looked much younger when she laughed, Fenoglio thought.

"Go on, be brave, or you'll make yourself not very likeable, even to me."

"Many of your colleagues, and almost all my superiors, love the rituals which ensure that other people acknowledge their authority."

"Is that a way of saying that they want to be respected?"

"More or less."

"And you don't bother with the rituals. Which makes you unlikeable."

"It's a reasonable simplification."

"And what do they say about me?" she asked, playing with a cigarette but without lighting it.

"That you're good but not likeable. But I have to add that so far, in the circles I move in, I've never heard of a female magistrate being considered likeable."

"So I can take some consolation from the fact that it's a stereotype?"

Fenoglio smiled. "Yes, I think you can."

"Dropping the question of likeableness, a few of your colleagues, and a few police officers, too, have told me that you're good at making people talk, that they tend to confide in you. Is that true?"

"I think so."

"Why?"

"I assume they realize I'm not trying to trick them."

"Is that enough?"

"No, not really."

"What, then?"

"I think it's also important to see things from their point of view. Which of course isn't the same as justifying their acts."

D'Angelo nodded pensively, then finally lit her cigarette. "God alone knows what it must be like to see things from the point of view of whoever pressed the button to set off that bomb," she said grimly.

D'Angelo lived in a 1970s apartment building behind the main railway station. Fenoglio walked her to the front entrance, looking around to make sure there were no unusual presences. He didn't think there was likely to be any attempt on her life just yet – Grimaldi was too busy with other things – but being careful wouldn't come amiss.

"Thank you," she said.

"You're welcome, as they say."

"I'm not referring to your walking me home."

"I know."

"Is there any point in going on with our work, with what's happened?"

"Yes."

For a long time she stood there thinking, her head slightly bowed, as if Fenoglio had given her a long, complicated, well-thought-out answer that required careful consideration. But probably it did. At last she raised her head and looked Fenoglio straight in the eyes.

"All right. Let's meet on Monday at the station, at nine, and resume with Lopez. I want to speed things up."

# 15

And speed things up they did.

The initial phase of interviews with Lopez lasted until 28 May.

Then, for ten days, Fenoglio and his team worked without a break. They made a large number of on-the-spot inspections, accompanied by Lopez. They reopened files, looked through duty reports, recovered phone-tap transcripts, statements, old arrest and seizure reports.

From the photographs, Lopez had identified sixty-eight individuals as members of Società Nostra. The Carabinieri found significant corroborating evidence for forty-one of them and submitted a report of more than five hundred pages to the Prosecutor's Department, requesting their detention.

D'Angelo shut herself up in her office, and after four days the detention orders were ready. The charges went from criminal association to homicide; from robbery to extortion; from drug trafficking to the possession and carrying of arms and explosives. Plus many other minor offences.

The first phase of the operation excluded the whole network of street-level drug dealers. Lopez had explained that they were not affiliates of the organization; they were much less dangerous than the others, and establishing their individual positions would require rather more time. Another thing that was postponed until a later stage was the corroboration of Lopez's statements concerning politicians, municipal employees, police officers and carabinieri who – for a payment – would pass on confidential information to the men of the clan. All of this would take a lot more investigation – delicate investigation, at that – and was incompatible with the urgent need to make arrests.

And so on the evening of 12 June 1992, Captain Valente and Marshal Fenoglio went to the Prosecutor's Department to collect the warrants to be served that night. They were accompanied by four carabinieri: given the number of suspects on whom the warrants were to be served, they were needed to carry all the large boxes containing the copies of these warrants. It was raining, and the thermometer indicated the unbelievable temperature of eleven degrees.

Weather metaphors are among the most effective and powerful. Fenoglio had read that somewhere, he couldn't remember where.

"Our superiors want to give a name to the operation," the captain said, with a hint of embarrassment. "It's something we always do, as you know. The people in Rome need it for the press release, for the newspapers and the TV channels."

D'Angelo looked at him without saying anything. Fenoglio felt sure she was going to light a cigarette, but she didn't.

"Maybe you have a name we can give the operation, dottoressa?"

It was dark outside, and the rain was falling with an autumnal rhythm.

"Cold summer."

"Yes, it is, it's incredibly cold," the captain replied. "Although to be exact, it's still a few days to 21 June."

"I meant: *Cold Summer.* The name you were asking me for. It'll be really difficult to forget."

It was true. That summer would be very difficult to forget.

Nobody went to bed. The assembly of forces in the battalion barracks, where the patrol groups would be formed – one for each individual to be placed under arrest – and instructions given as to how to proceed, was scheduled for two in the morning. One hundred and fifty men were involved. The colonel gave his contribution, stipulating that, once the warrants had been delivered, a helicopter should be sent up; he was told that a helicopter wasn't necessary, because there was no risk of anyone going to ground in countryside inaccessible to normal wheeled vehicles. He replied that a helicopter was indispensable for the TV channels. As he was the colonel, the argument appeared unassailable, nobody felt up to objecting and the matter was settled.

At three on the dot dozens of cars left the courtyard, each with an address and a name. Fenoglio, the captain and Montemurro, accompanied by a second car in support, went straight to the house of Nicola Grimaldi, also known as Blondie, also known as Three Cylinders.

It had stopped raining. The streets were deserted, black and shiny. Nobody spoke. You may have done this kind of work for many years, but when you're about to enter the house of a multiple murderer at night, in order to arrest him and take him to prison, nothing is certain. Career criminals don't usually cause any trouble when you go to arrest them. They know it isn't a good idea, for many reasons, and so they let themselves be handcuffed, in the hope that their expensive lawyers will find a way to unlock those handcuffs. But you never know: it's impossible to predict every reaction.

They got to Santo Spirito after leaving the ring road. As they entered the built-up area, they found Marshal Fornaro's car waiting for them, greeting them with a flash of headlights: yet more support. The three vehicles glided silently past anonymous apartment blocks, houses and shabby gardens, with the occasional brief glimpse of the sea, sensed rather than seen.

They passed a bakery with its shutter half open and its door ajar. Fenoglio could imagine the smell of the loaves, the focaccias, the sweet buns.

The neon sign of a closed pub flashed in the darkness in sporadic bursts, as if sobbing.

Five minutes later, they were outside Grimaldi's house. For at least ten yards on either side of the gate, there were no cars at the kerb, as if this were a no-parking zone. But there was no traffic sign. Clearly the local people knew better than to leave their vehicles here. There was no need for signs.

Fenoglio pressed the entryphone button. After a minute spent waiting for an answer, he pressed it again for a longer time. A woman's voice replied.

"Who's there?"

"Carabinieri. Open up."

"What do you want at this hour?" There was hatred in that voice, and anger, and a touch of hysteria. It was Grimaldi's wife, and she knew perfectly well what the Carabinieri want when they come to your house at 3.30 in the morning.

"Open up. We have to speak to your husband."

The woman didn't open, didn't say anything more. All that could be heard was the discordant crackle of the old entryphone.

"Signora, if you don't open up we'll have to knock down the gate, and then the front door."

Another ten minutes or so went by and then the gate emitted a rapid, muted buzz, followed by a click. Fenoglio, the captain, Montemurro and Fornaro walked up the two flights of steps. The other carabinieri stayed at the bottom, keeping an eye on the cars and the situation in general. Soon, when they started to serve the arrest warrants, the neighbourhood would become a lot more agitated.

They found Grimaldi waiting for them at the door in his vest and pyjama trousers. His light brown hair, too long for a man pushing fifty, was dishevelled.

He looked with a calculated expression of scorn at the guns that Valente, Montemurro and Fornaro were holding in their hands, their arms down by their sides, the barrels pointed at the ground.

Fenoglio's hands were free. "Get dressed, Grimaldi," he said. "You're coming with us."

"What have I done?" Grimaldi said, without moving away from the door.

"Quite a lot of things, apparently," Fenoglio replied, handing him the warrant. "Move aside, we have to search the house."

The search was a formality – nobody imagined that Nicola Grimaldi would keep arms, drugs or other illegal material in his own home – but still took half an hour. In that time, Grimaldi got his lawyer out of bed, dressed, had his wife prepare a large bag of clothes for prison and started looking through the warrant. Fenoglio noticed that he handled it with the expert gestures of someone who, although never having studied law, was nevertheless extremely familiar with legal documents.

"That lousy snitch, that piece of shit," he growled at a certain point in thick dialect, loudly enough for everybody to hear him. You didn't need an interpreter to know he was talking about Lopez. "I'm going to tear his heart out and eat it. Even if I die five minutes later, I'm going to eat his heart."

The captain seemed on the verge of saying something in reply, but Fenoglio gave him a nod, as if advising him that it was better to leave the man alone to let off steam.

They put the handcuffs on Grimaldi.

"Did that lousy piece of shit at least tell you how he killed my son? What are you going to do now, give him a medal for being a fucking snitch?"

There was a brief silence.

"He says it wasn't him," Fenoglio replied. Slowly, in a low voice.

Grimaldi looked at all of them, one by one, his eyes full of incredulous rage. "Bastards, you and that bitch of a female judge."

And he spat on the warrant, just where the heading was: Prosecutor's Department of the Court of Bari, Regional Anti-Mafia Section.

# ACT THREE

## The Wild Bunch

# 1

Leaving his solitary apartment to go to work, Fenoglio found himself thinking again about Grimaldi's son and wondering what he had been like before he became a victim of circumstance.

Because everyone is a victim of circumstance, even in premeditated murders.

The previous evening he had reread an extract from Carlo Emilio Gadda's *That Awful Mess on the Via Merulana*: "Unforeseen catastrophes are never the consequence … of a single motive, of *a* cause singular; but they are rather like a whirlpool, a cyclonic point of depression in the consciousness of the world, towards which a whole multitude of converging causes have contributed."

That digression into philosophical speculation was the most obvious sign of his frustration as a detective. You never start speculating – in excellent company, for heaven's sake – about chance, fate and the concept of converging causes if your brain has something concrete to work on. What was the child like? What had he *been* like? That was the one thing missing from the mountain of paperwork in the file – statements, reports, post-mortems. Had he been a normal child born into the wrong family? Had he been a little fool who would have become a criminal like his father? Or did he have some skill, some talent, some special, hidden gift?

The boy had been on his way to school. Cheerful, calm, bored, angry, whatever, but unaware of everything. Unaware, too, of the defect in his heart – that fatal inheritance from his father. All at once, everything had changed. And then everything had ended.

God alone knew what he had thought when they grabbed him. God alone knew what he had thought – but do you think at moments like that? – when he had felt his heart give out. What was it, a spasm? An excruciating pain? Something exploding inside you? Fenoglio had once heard in a documentary that people attacked by wild animals lose consciousness even before they are aware of the physical pain. It appears that the body releases an analgesic substance, a kind of anaesthetic that ensures a peaceful death, without pain and without fear. Was that true? Was there even such a thing as a peaceful death? He had always thought of death as bitter and nasty: he had seen lots of dead bodies and almost none of them had looked serene or dignified. What had always disturbed him, like a symbol of obscenity, were the rigid, half-open mouths of people who had been murdered, their teeth fully exposed, almost as if the killing had restored them to a feral condition and deprived them of all decency.

He made an effort to dismiss from his mind the image of the Grimaldi boy when they had found him. The state he was in, the smell he gave off, after more than four days in that well.

What had Pietro Fenoglio thought when he was a little boy? When he went to school or came back home, or on certain endless winter afternoons, without a television?

He didn't know. He had no idea. The absence of memories of his own thoughts was so total as to instil in him a sense of panic. As if his inner life as a little boy had never existed. He remembered a certain number of events from the outside world, but nothing of what he had thought, nothing of what he had dreamt.

But then, he told himself, does anyone really remember his thoughts as a child? Or his past thoughts in general? Maybe it wouldn't be a bad thing to ask a few people. Maybe it would help him to put things in their true perspective, to feel less abnormal, less uprooted from his inner life.

He went into the Caffè Bohème to have breakfast. Nicola had put on the aria "Lascia ch'io pianga" from Handel's *Rinaldo*. One of his favourites. Fenoglio thought of the trip he and Serena had taken a few years earlier to Salzburg. A woman had sung "Lascia ch'io pianga" in the street. He suddenly remembered the atmosphere of that holiday, the cool and gently dazed air of the city, with elderly couples in evening dress, even though it was afternoon, coming in and out of the theatres. He felt a pang of nostalgia and of other painful emotions. I love you, Serena, he caught himself saying under his breath.

He found himself back in his office without realizing it. Without remembering the route he had taken to get there, although he had walked for half an hour. It struck him that in a few years' time he wouldn't remember the thoughts of that morning, of any of those days. He wouldn't remember them. Nobody would remember them. All gone, lost forever.

He switched on the little stereo he kept in his office, and stood there by the unit for a few seconds, undecided as to what to listen to. He told himself he wanted something lively, something filled with light, and chose Mozart's Concerto for Flute and Harp. He had heard it an infinite number of times, which is the good thing about music, if you're looking for a little peace and quiet.

From a drawer he took the pad with his notes on the case of the Grimaldi boy. A neurotic gesture, to gain time. What was written there he knew by heart, yet he started leafing through it all the same, rereading the brief sentences in their clear, square handwriting.

At that moment, someone knocked rather energetically at the door.

"Come in!"

Pellecchia entered. He was back after a few days' leave and seemed to be in great shape, tanned and slimmer, with his hair cut short. He wore a well-ironed white shirt, instead of his usual slightly torn-looking T-shirts. He looked as if the sun had cleansed and wiped him.

"Tonino."

"Marshal." Pellecchia looked him up and down for a moment. "You're not looking too good, you know that? Haven't you taken a few days off?"

"No."

"Have you been shut in here all day, as usual?"

Fenoglio got up and lowered the volume of the music to a minimum. "Actually, yes, more or less."

"What about your wife?"

"She's chairing the board for the school examinations in Pesaro."

Pellecchia appeared to ponder this, as if to interpret the situation and develop a strategy. "Listen, Pietro, my partner has a lot of single girlfriends. Some aren't bad at all. Attractive forty-somethings, divorced, in good shape. A couple of them are really hot. I'll tell Agnese to organize something one of these evenings. We can make up a four-some, go out to dinner —"

"Thanks, but I'm not quite ready to go out with any attractive forty-somethings who are divorced, in good shape ..."

"... and really hot."

"... and really hot, yes. As soon as I'm ready, you'll be the first to know."

Pellecchia sniffed. There was something more genuine in his expression now, as if he were renouncing the role he had played for so long.

"Have you been away?"

"Five days on the Tremiti Islands. Do you know them?"

"It's beautiful there. But I seem to remember there were jellyfish."

"No jellyfish this year. I went diving, sunbathed, ate, drank and all the rest. If you know what I mean."

Another pause.

"You're still obsessed with the boy, aren't you?" Pellecchia said, his tone of voice changing.

Fenoglio nodded.

"Wasn't it you who said we need detachment in this job, otherwise we'd go mad?"

"Yes, that was me. Consistency isn't one of my qualities."

Pellecchia took a cigar butt from the breast pocket of his shirt and put it in his mouth. "Have you found anything?"

Fenoglio gave an involuntary grimace and shook his head.

"It's like a brainteaser. Whichever way you look at it, it doesn't make sense."

"Lopez and his men would certainly have been the perfect guilty parties."

"If it was them and we couldn't figure it out, maybe we should just give up this job and retire to a farm. But if it wasn't them, who could it have been? Who'd have crazy enough to run that kind of risk?"

Pellecchia shifted on his chair. It struck Fenoglio that he seemed a little uncomfortable. "Mind if I light up?"

"Go ahead."

Pellecchia lit his cigar with a Swedish match and blew out a dense cloud of grey smoke. If this had been a scene from a novel, Fenoglio thought, the hypothetical author would have written "pale blue smoke". In the real world, though, he had never seen pale blue smoke, like many things that are talked about in novels.

"And the idea that it was a pervert?"

"I thought about it, even looked into it. Though remember, the pathologist did rule out sexual violence, despite the marks where the boy had been beaten. The kid had a heart defect, like his father. Nobody knew it. He had a heart attack, probably at the very moment he was kidnapped, or soon afterwards."

"Anyway, the idea of a pervert doesn't fit in with the ransom demand. I can't see some raging sex maniac planning to extort money from someone like Grimaldi, can you?"

"A psychopath might do something like that."

"A psychopath meaning a crazy guy?"

"A psychopath meaning someone with a personality disorder. Psychopaths aren't crazy, they're completely affectless – they don't have any kind of feeling – and they're manipulative. They think quite logically and they can rape, torture and kill without feeling even a smidgen of remorse. Serial killers, for example, are usually psychopaths." Fenoglio broke off and smiled. "I'm playing teacher's pet, aren't I?"

"You're certainly playing the teacher. But I get the picture. Someone who's really bad, maybe even a pervert, but may be intelligent. Someone who smiles at you while he's cutting your balls off."

"Precisely. Books on criminology are full of stories about people like that. In theory it could fit."

"So?"

"So, working on that hypothesis, it struck me that whoever it was can't have been a beginner. It couldn't have been the first time. To do something like that, apart from having the disposition, you'd need practice. You'd need to have done a kind of apprenticeship. In addition, to know who Grimaldi is – and to know that he can get together a lot of money in a short time – you'd need to be from the area. So I did a bit of research on local individuals with the appropriate records."

"And what did you find?"

"I checked those with records for rape, indecent assault or indecent behaviour, and who were living in the north of Bari. A fairly arbitrary yardstick, not much more than random, I know. But I thought it was worth a try, like putting a chip on a number in roulette."

"How many did you find?"

"Quite a few, at first sight. But on closer inspection, many were just flashers who hang around parks in the evening. Some had been sentenced for indecent assault, but they were isolated incidents a long time ago. Among those with more serious and repeated charges against them, some were in prison and others had moved to another area. In the end, I was left with two who might theoretically correspond to the profile."

"And did you check them out?"

"Yes."

"All by yourself?"

"Yes."

"Why didn't you get anyone to help you?"

"I don't know. Maybe because I didn't even believe in it myself."

"So what about these two?"

"I went to see them. I wanted to look them in the face. One of them is half crazy, a complete maniac. Mentally retarded, and from a dysfunctional family. Sentenced twice for abusing children. You should have seen his apartment in the middle of a housing estate. He doesn't have a licence, can't drive, and with the best will it's impossible to imagine that he was our man."

"And the other one?"

"The other one I saw yesterday. He's in a wheelchair, has been for years. He was accused of raping a little girl, but at the end of his trial he was acquitted and released. A few days later a group of people wearing hoods broke his back. Nobody knows who they were. He hasn't walked since."

"I know the case. It's not true that nobody knows who they were: it was the girl's father and uncles, and they did the right thing. That was the last girl that piece of shit raped."

"I appreciate your concern for civil rights."

"Fucking justice. Anything else?"

"I thought of looking at the lightning kidnappings."

"That thing the snitch told us about?"

"The snitch?"

"Lopez."

"Now I remember why you and I never talked much."

"I need a double espresso."

"So do I. Then we have to go and see someone."

# 2

They both had double espressos in cappuccino cups at the Bar Riviera. Pellecchia put in three spoonfuls of sugar and two of cream.

"Where are we going?" he asked as they left the bar.

"The Libertà district, to talk to a friend."

A few minutes later they were in the bottle-green Arna which nobody apart from Fenoglio wanted to use any more.

"This car is really crap," Pellecchia said, fiddling with the faulty window handle. "The worst ever."

"You're forgetting the Fiat Duna."

"You're right. The Duna was the shittiest model ever. This comes second on the list of shittiness. What's the address?"

"Via Pizzoli. There's a leisure centre —"

"The Albino's place?"

"You know the Albino?"

"Who doesn't? If he's the one you're talking to, it's best if I don't go in with you. We've had … a bit of a misunderstanding. Maybe if I'm there he'll feel uncomfortable and won't be so ready to talk."

Fenoglio was about to reply, then realized that Pellecchia – whatever his misunderstanding with the Albino – was right.

"Okay. Wait for me in the car. I won't be long. I'm just testing the waters."

Vito Marasciulo, alias the Albino, had started out as a burglar, but having once been arrested thanks to his very white hair being recognized "beyond a shadow of a doubt" by a witness, he had decided that for someone like him it was more sensible to stay with the back-room jobs. So he had devoted himself, profitably, to high-class fencing and the running of gambling dens. Every now and again, he was arrested and spent short spells in prison: a kind of business expense he accepted without complaint. He was highly respected, even though he had never been a Mafioso. He had refused – taking care not to offend anyone – all proposals for affiliation that had been made to him over the years.

Few things happened in certain circles, in Bari and the surrounding area, that the Albino didn't know about, or couldn't find out about.

His acquaintance with Fenoglio went back several years.

A patrol car had stopped a young man on a moped who had been weaving in and out among the people in Via Sparano, a pedestrian street. They had confiscated his vehicle, and he had flown into a rage and insulted the carabinieri. They hadn't taken it well. The young man, who was the Albino's son, had been bundled into the car and taken to the station. They were giving him a lesson when Fenoglio had arrived and made them stop. The next day the Albino had come by to thank the marshal, telling him that in future, whatever he needed, he would be at his disposal.

They parked on Piazza Garibaldi. Fenoglio got out, noticing one of the Albino's men keeping an eye on the situation from the corner of Via Pizzoli. Obviously, the man noticed Fenoglio, too: it was his job. The marshal walked over unhurriedly. At the entrance to the centre stood a man with broad shoulders, a prominent belly and disproportionately large, calloused knuckles. Fenoglio couldn't recall seeing him before.

"Is Vito around?"

It wasn't this man who replied, but a hoarse voice from inside.

"Good morning, marshal. I was just going to get a coffee. Want to come with me?"

One coffee at home when he woke up; another on his way to work; the double espresso with Pellecchia just earlier. This would be the fifth, and it was only 10.30.

"Sure."

The Albino came outside into the sunlight. An unfamiliar situation: they always met indoors, in badly lit rooms that stank of smoke. The back rooms of gambling dens, storage closets, dubious offices. The Albino was a creature of the dark.

They set off in the direction of Via Napoli. The man with the knuckles made to follow them, but the Albino stopped him with a gesture of the hand.

Outside the bar there was a small group of young men having a heated argument in dialect. When Fenoglio and the Albino arrived, they fell silent and stood aside to let them pass.

"We'll sit in the back," the Albino said to the barman.

"What can I get you?"

"Coffee and brandy for me. You, marshal?"

"Coffee without brandy."

The back of the bar was clearly not intended for the public. There was a single table with two chairs; around it, crates of beer and boxes of snacks. Beyond the back door could be glimpsed a yard with dirty walls and peeling plaster. There was a vague smell of cats.

The barman brought the coffee and the brandy. The Albino poured half a glassful of brandy into his cup and downed it all in one go.

"How are you, marshal? I haven't seen you in a while."

"We've been busy."

The Albino nodded. "I know. You've been making a lot of people angry."

Fenoglio thought he detected a hint of anxiety in the Albino's voice. He decided to ignore it.

"You know what the problem is?"

"No, what is it?"

"That you've arrested Grimaldi and all those bastards of his. People who aren't worth a damn. They call themselves men of honour, men of *omertà*, and their mouths are full of words like respect, but they're just lousy drug dealers, although instead of pushing the odd sachet on street corners they deal in large quantities. Plus, they're butchers, they like killing people. You did the right thing arresting them, but you know what everyone's saying?"

"What?"

"They're saying that now Palese, Santo Spirito and Enziteto are wide open. That's all anyone is thinking about: what do we have to do to take these places over now that Grimaldi's inside?"

"And who *is* going to take them over?"

The Albino shrugged. "Some guys who were affiliated in prison, who say they're *sgarristas*, *santistas*, all that bullshit. I don't know, but every time someone gets taken out, those who come after him are always worse. With coke you'll never win, it's impossible. It's like sex: there'll always be people who want to sell it because there'll always

218

be other people who want to buy it. The only solution is to make it legal. But nobody will ever dare do that. Coke suits everyone, the underworld and the cops. With coke, cops are never afraid they'll end up unemployed. I don't know if I'm making sense. Maybe I'm just too old. One day, one of those people will even come to me and ask me to pay protection. What should I do then?"

"What should you do?"

"I'm not going to pay those bastards. Either I get them shot, but then that'll start a war that'll end with me or one of my family being killed, or else I pack up and leave. Once you start to pay, you're dead. I'm staying here as long as people respect me and don't ask me for anything. The day I see one of those fucking killers come to my house and ask for money, I'll know it'll be time to shut up shop."

From the breast pocket of his shirt he took a packet of filtered Nazionali and lit one.

"How old are you, Vito?"

"Fifty-two." After a few moments spent pondering that answer, as if he himself were surprised by how old he was, he yelled at the barman to bring him another brandy.

The barman materialized with a small rounded glass full of liquor. After placing it on the table, he whispered something in the Albino's ear. The Albino gave a slight smile.

"So, what do you need?" he said, looking Fenoglio in the eyes.

"You know about Grimaldi's son, don't you?"

The Albino was unable to hold back an expression of disgust.

"You know Lopez says it wasn't them."

"I know. I've read the newspapers."

"Do you believe him?"

"No. True, he admitted to those murders, but it may just be that he's ashamed about the boy. It's a nasty business. Do you believe him?"

"Maybe, yes. And anyway, there's nothing that points to them. I have to look elsewhere."

"How can I help you?"

"You can help me find someone who was kidnapped, paid the ransom and didn't report it."

The Albino stubbed his cigarette out on the floor – there were no ashtrays on the table – and knocked back his drink. "Even if I find him, what are you going to do with him? People who've been kidnapped will never say anything. They're shit-scared, quite rightly."

"I'm not interested in getting a statement from them. I just need to hear what happened, to get some kind of lead. Find me someone, and I'll deal with it."

The Albino sighed, his expression filled with scepticism. "You won't get anything. You're deluding yourself. As far as I'm concerned, it was Lopez and those other two sons of bitches."

Fenoglio didn't reply.

"Okay, I'll try and find them. But I'm not guaranteeing anything."

"Thanks, Vito."

"Do you have a mobile phone?"

"They're too expensive."

"A lot of your colleagues have them. Do they earn more than you?"

"I don't think so."

"Will you be at the station this evening?"

"If you tell me you're coming, I'll be there."

"Around eight. I repeat: I'm not guaranteeing anything."

"That's fine."

"Marshal?"

"Yes?"

"You can tell Corporal Pellecchia I don't bear a grudge. If another time he wants to come in with you, he can come. He doesn't need to wait in the car."

# 3

"Hot, isn't it?"

"It's summer."

"What about the Albino?"

"He told me to tell you that he doesn't bear you any grudge."

"How did he know I was here? I parked two blocks away."

Fenoglio shrugged.

The Arna moved laboriously through the traffic. A moped with a noisy exhaust, ridden by two youths who were trying to look tough, overtook them on the right and slipped between the queueing cars. Pellecchia stared at them with the absent, dangerous look of an old cat watching two stupid mice come too close.

"You never told me what your problem was with the Albino."

"Once, many years ago, during a search, I slapped him in front of his kids. I shouldn't have, but sometimes I can't help myself. You know how it is."

"Yes, I do. And how did he react?"

"He didn't. But he didn't look happy about it. I was careful for months after that. I was almost certain he'd make me pay for it one way or another."

"But nothing happened."

"No, nothing happened."

"It's not the Albino's style, doing something to an officer. He's old-school, he knows there's no point and it causes nothing but trouble."

Pellecchia didn't reply. He started whistling a tune, perhaps without realizing it. He turned into Corso Cavour from Via Putignani and put the cigar in his mouth. "What now? Back to the station?" From outside, someone launched an oath directed at someone else's dead relative.

"I think so. What do you want to do?"

Pellecchia looked at his watch. "It's nearly one. Let's go to Torre a Mare and have something to eat. A friend of mine has a trattoria there where they make incredible spaghetti with sea urchins."

"A friend of yours?"

Pellecchia let a few seconds go by, to see if Fenoglio added anything. "You think I don't pay in restaurants," he said at last.

Fenoglio breathed noisily. That was precisely what he'd been thinking.

"All right, sometimes I don't pay. They're friends, there's nothing wrong if every now and again they offer me lunch or dinner. Sometimes it's on the house, sometimes I pay. With a bit of a discount, but I pay."

Fenoglio wondered whether to deliver his eloquent speech about the fact that a public servant, particularly a law enforcement officer, shouldn't eat for free in restaurants.

He decided not to. It was a period of great confusion, better to drop the moralizing. Not to mention the fact that he could do with a good dish of spaghetti with sea urchins accompanied by a bottle of chilled white wine.

"All right, let's go. Does your friend's restaurant have a car park?"

"Yes, why?"

"Because I wouldn't like us to park a service car on the street, have our spaghetti with sea urchins, and then discover that someone has taken it for a spin."

The trattoria faced the little harbour of Torre a Mare with its fishermen's boats. It had nets hanging on the walls, a counter of fresh fish and an unauthorized veranda.

Predictably, they didn't limit themselves to the spaghetti with sea urchins. Pellecchia's friend – his name was Franco and his head was bound in a knotted handkerchief that made him look like a pirate – said they really had to try the fried fish and the mussels au gratin. Then they really had to try the ice cream affogato. Then, of course, they really had to try the almond pastries and the home-made *rosolio*.


"I've never asked you, do you live alone?" Fenoglio said, pouring himself a little more wild fennel liqueur.

"Every now and again I sleep over at my girlfriend's place, but I have my own apartment. It was my parents', I have all my work things there."

"Your work things?"

"I like doing woodwork." Then, as if to overcome a hint of embarrassment: "I have a big room that I use as my workshop. Agnese isn't even allowed inside."

"Are you happy, Tonino?"

Pellecchia didn't seem surprised by the question. "I don't know what that means exactly. But I don't think I've ever been unhappy. I should remember, shouldn't I?"

Fenoglio laughed. "Yes, I suppose you should."

"Maybe I'm not sophisticated enough to feel sad. I don't think much. In my opinion, it's thinking too much that makes people unhappy."

It was a throwaway sentence, but Fenoglio took it seriously, thought it over as if looking for a hidden meaning.

A car pulled up close to the entrance of the restaurant. Its windows were down and the stereo was blaring out a Neapolitan song by Carmelo Zappulla at full volume. Pellecchia turned in the direction of the noise and narrowed his eyes.

"I'm just going out for a second, they're pissing me off," he said and made to get up.

Fenoglio shook his head. "Drop it, they're going. They're just kids."

At that moment a waiter approached the car and said something, gesticulating towards the interior of the trattoria. The music was turned down and the car drove off.

"What were we saying?" Pellecchia resumed. "Oh, yes. Thinking too much makes people unhappy. It's because people who think too much usually think too much about themselves. They end up like a guy I know."

"Who?"

"This guy's a municipal civil servant. His wife is a colleague of Agnese's, sometimes we all go out together. He makes like he's someone who's figured everything out, namely, that life is shit. Now, I also know that life is pretty shitty, but repeating it every second isn't going to make it any better. If you're on a boat in the middle of the sea and you don't like the boat, because maybe it stinks, or you don't like the people who are with you, you could decide to throw yourself into the sea. But if you don't want to throw yourself into the sea, it's best not to piss off all the people who are in the boat with you. To cut a long story short, a few months ago we were in a pizzeria and the guy starts saying something like: 'Antonio' – the last person who called me that was the nun in catechism class, when

I was nine years old – 'have you ever thought about the time of life we're in?' I say, no, I've never thought about the time of life we're in, and he says I should if I want to understand our situation."

"Whose situation?" Fenoglio asked. He was enjoying himself: Pellecchia had an unexpected talent as a storyteller.

"Us, men in our forties. Not that I understood him. He had to explain."

"So what about men in their forties?"

"Listen to his explanation: 'We've already been through the best part, let's say, between twenty and thirty-five. To be more specific: the average life expectancy of an Italian man is seventy-four. That means we have thirty years left, more or less. Of these thirty, the last will be unpleasant, obviously. But a whole lot of problems start round about now, if they haven't already started. In other words, even if all goes well, we have at most ten good years left. It's no fun living with the knowledge that you have so little time left.'"

"And what did you say?"

"Well, even though I thought he was a dickhead, it made me feel bad. I mean, it's an argument that makes an impression on you. I'm forty-three. When I play football I realize that the guys who are twenty years younger than me, even if they don't know how to kick a ball, run a hell of a lot faster than I do. When I dive, I'm still fine, but I see friends of mine who are a little bit older than me getting into difficulties and starting to feel scared. In other words, that dickhead's argument isn't wrong in itself. I mean, these are facts, right?"

"Yes, they are facts."

"But almost immediately afterwards I started thinking it wasn't right. Okay, I'm a poor son of a bitch, but I think that if you're a man and you're alive you have a right to live every moment."

"You also have a duty, I'd say."

"Yes, you have a duty. You're right. Anyway, I think about this, about having a right to live, and I think that when it comes down to it, his argument is wrong. So I say to him: as far as I'm concerned, the only consequence of thinking like that is to throw yourself into the sea with a big block of concrete around your neck. That's the only thing you can do. Turn out the light and leave. But I'm staying, because I like it and because it seems like the right thing to do. Fuck it." Pellecchia broke off all at once, as if embarrassed. "Why are you looking at me like that? Am I talking bullshit?"

Fenoglio smiled. "No, I think you're absolutely right."

They sat there in silence for a few minutes. Then Pellecchia sniffed and called Franco, the Pirate.

"The bill, Franco."

"It's on the house."

"No, it's not," Pellecchia said before Fenoglio could open his mouth. "If I don't pay the bill, it doesn't count."

# 4

The Albino put his head round the door. "Good evening, marshal."

"Vito, come in, sit down."

Fenoglio motioned the Albino to one of the chairs in front of the desk and sat down on the other, leaving his usual seat empty.

"Have you found something?"

"I have three names."

Fenoglio took the sheet of paper the Albino held out to him. "Have you talked to any of them?"

"No. I asked some friends I trust, people who don't ask questions."

"Do you know who they are?"

The Albino cleared his throat and shifted on his chair. He wasn't at his ease here in the station. "No. Next to the names I've written where they're from. The rest is up to you."

"Fair enough."

"But I think it's unlikely they'll tell you anything. When something like that has happened to you, all you want to do is forget. Why should you fuck things up for yourself – pardon the expression – by talking to the Carabinieri?"

Yes, why should you fuck things up for yourself? Fenoglio thought as he dismissed the Albino.

*

The next morning Pellecchia and Fenoglio got to the station at the same time.

"Did the Albino come last night?"

"Yes, he did. He brought me a paper with three names."

"How do you want to proceed?"

"You locate them and then we go and see them together."

Pellecchia took the paper and read it. "Do you think they're going to tell us anything?"

"I don't know. For now let's locate them. One step at a time."

Pellecchia left the room and Fenoglio decided to look at a few reports already available in rough draft and waiting for the captain's signature. He worked for a few hours on old files, listening to music and enjoying the sense of satisfaction, pleasant and slightly mindless, that derives from getting through a not very demanding backlog.

He had just come back from a short walk when the telephone rang.

"Chief, this is Corporal Antonio Pellecchia, remember me?"

"You're hard to forget."

"I've found two. Will you join me?"

"Where?"

Pellecchia was waiting for him outside a bar in Japigia.

"What's this one's name?" Fenoglio asked.

"Patruno. He's a jeweller and, I'll warn you now, he's strange. Two years ago, they took his daughter. He paid and they gave her back after two hours, in one piece. They hadn't done anything to her. They hadn't hit her, they hadn't raped her. She didn't like that."

"Pardon me?"

"Wait till you see her."

The jeweller's shop was a few dozen yards from the bar. The decor was old-fashioned, and there was a smell of wax polish in the air. Behind the counter stood a man and a woman, side by side, as if posing for a photograph. The man might have been anything from fifty to seventy, and was tall, with long, bony arms. His hair was grey and sparse and he had a strangely prominent belly. It was as if the different parts of his body had been stuck together, creating a bizarre, inharmonious ensemble. Even his face showed a kind of programmatic disproportion: too broad, with bulging eyes and a mouth that was too small. The woman was his daughter. A female version, much younger, of the same inharmonious assemblage.

"Signor Patruno says he's willing to talk to us, but he doesn't want to make a statement. The same goes for his daughter. I told him we can accommodate that."

Fenoglio held out his hand. The jeweller's was flaccid and inanimate, like a creature without a backbone.

"Hello, Signor Patruno. I'm Marshal Fenoglio. Is there somewhere quiet we can talk? Maybe an office at the back?"

The jeweller and his daughter looked each other in the eyes. Then he came out from behind the counter and led them down a narrow corridor to a little office.

On the desk and the shelves everything was in perfect, obsessive order. The typewriter, the calculator, the imitation leather document wallet, the pen holder with two well-sharpened pencils.

Patruno sat down in his seat and motioned the two carabinieri to two ugly chairs in front of the desk.

"Corporal Pellecchia has given me a rough idea," Fenoglio began. "I'd be grateful if you could tell us what happened to your daughter."

"I don't know how you found out about it," Patruno said in a neutral, nasal voice.

"In our work we get information from the most varied sources. Often from people belonging to the world of crime."

"My daughter and I want to forget that business. They said that if we talked to anyone they'd come back. They know where we work, where we live. They know everything."

"Don't worry, Signor Patruno. What matters most to us is your safety. I'd like to explain the reason for our interest in what happened to you and your daughter. But first tell me something about yourself. How many are there in your family?"

"Just my daughter and me. My wife died of cancer five years ago. We used to run the shop together. My daughter was studying economics, but she didn't like it much. When her mother died, she decided to take her place. I pay her salary. It's all above board, with a pay sheet and contributions."

"Of course," Fenoglio said with a hint of a smile. "It's obvious you're a careful person who likes things to be straight."

"Yes, I'm a very thorough person."

"We'd like to know what happened to your daughter because it might help us with another case we're working on."

"As I said, marshal, we —"

"Don't worry. You won't be involved."

Patruno looked at Pellecchia.

"It's all right, Patruno. If the marshal says you won't be involved, you can trust him."

The jeweller adjusted his tie and cleared his throat, producing a strange sound, like the cry of a small animal.

"That morning, I had an appointment with the doctor and my daughter had to open the shop. When I got back from the doctor's, I found the shutter down and got worried. As I stood there wondering what might have happened, a young man passed on a scooter and told me to stay by the phone, because someone was going to call me."

"Would you be able to describe this young man?"

"No. I mean, he passed, he said those things to me and he left. I was confused. I didn't even look at his face. He was a normal person."

"Had you ever seen him around?"

"No."

"Did he speak in Italian or in dialect?"

"I'm not sure, but I'd say more dialect than Italian. He was a street kid. Yes, yes, now that I think of it: he spoke in dialect."

"When did they call?"

"Immediately. Less than a minute later."

Someone in the area had been watching him, Fenoglio thought. People from the neighbourhood.

"What did they say?"

"That they'd taken Fiorella, and that if I wanted her back I had to give them thirty million in cash by the afternoon, or they'd kill her."

"Did they speak in Italian or in dialect?"

"Dialect. I mean, a mixture, dialect and Italian. But they were from Bari, I'm sure of that."

"And then?"

"I asked who they were, and the man told me that if I asked him any more questions, they'd cut off one of my daughter's fingers and send it to me. Then I told him I didn't have thirty million in cash and he told me to go to the bank and get it out."

In recounting these events, Patruno came to life a little, as if recalling such a fearful episode lessened the inertia of his face.

"And did you have that money in the bank?"

Patruno paused for quite a long time, as if suddenly realizing that what he was saying might be used against him.

"Signor Patruno, don't worry. We're not the Finance Police, we're not interested in whether you pay your taxes or anything like that. We just want to understand how these people work. Did you get hold of the thirty million?"

"Yes. I have two accounts. I withdrew twenty million from one and ten from the other, then came back here."

"Did they call you immediately this time, too?"

"Immediately, as soon as I got in. They ordered me to wrap the money in a newspaper, put everything in a shopping bag and go to the Bar Biancorosso, which is two blocks from here. Outside it, I would find a young man next to a Fiat Panda. He would open the boot for me and I would put the bag in it. Then I had to walk away without turning around. If I did as they said, Fiorella would be sent straight back to the shop."

"Did you follow the instructions?"

"Yes."

"The young man who opened the boot for you …"

"I don't even remember what he looked like. I probably wouldn't have remembered if you'd asked me half an hour later, because I really didn't want to look him in the face, I didn't want to run the risk of recognizing him."

Fenoglio didn't insist. "I don't suppose you glanced at the car's number plate?"

"I did look at it, accidentally. It was covered with a cloth."

Banal, simple and effective. No real need to do complicated things.

"What happened after you delivered the payment?"

"I continued doing what they'd told me: I went back to the shop without turning around. Half an hour later my daughter arrived."

"How was she?"

"Quite well. The biggest fright had been when they grabbed her: she thought they wanted to rape her" – Fenoglio had to make an effort to avoid Pellecchia's eyes – "but in fact they didn't do anything to her."

Patruno kept his hands on the table, with the backs upward; a kind of expectant position. Pellecchia stood up, walked around the desk and placed a hand on the jeweller's shoulder. The gesture was meant to be friendly, but it seemed like a threat.

"Listen, Patruno, we appreciate your help. But we have to ask you another favour. We have to talk to your daughter."

Patruno looked at Pellecchia, then at Fenoglio. Then he searched for a space in that small room where his eyes could move without meeting the others'. An escape route.

"We'll only ask her a few questions to get her point of view on the story, and then we'll go," Fenoglio said, leaning across the desk a little.

Patruno got up and went to call his daughter, who appeared in the office soon afterwards. Fenoglio motioned her to sit down and she did so, with stiff composure, like a badly built automaton. Looking at her like this, defenceless and mechanical, a diminished human creature, Fenoglio had a sense of sadness, almost of anguish. He could only vaguely imagine the existence of this ugly, solitary girl who lived with her father and worked with her father and would spend her days, one after the other, with her father as she got older, defending the wretched well-being of that life and that work: jewellers on the outskirts of town, sellers of little rings, little necklaces, earrings of poor-quality gold, tiny diamonds; small tax evasions, maybe a bit of fencing. Looking into people's lives was starting to weigh on him, he told himself.

"Signora Fiorella —"

"Signorina."

"I'm sorry, Signorina Fiorella. Your father has already told us about the unpleasant business in which you were involved. But we need a few more details, which only you can supply."

"Go on."

"How did the kidnapping happen? I'm referring to when they took you."

"I'd driven to the shop in the car. I had to open up that day because my father had an appointment —"

"With the doctor, right?"

"Precisely. I parked the car and was about to close the steering lock when a young man got in on the other side —"

"You mean in front, on the passenger side?"

"Yes. He just opened the door and sat down. He had a knife. He held it to my neck and said that I mustn't look him in the face or he would cut my throat."

"But you'd already seen him when he got in the car?"

"A little. He had a big plaster on his nose. The only thing I remember is the plaster."

An old technique, but always effective. If you're in a stressful situation and you see someone with a big plaster on his face, ninety-nine times out of a hundred all you remember is the plaster.

"What happened then?"

"I was told to start the engine again and drive on. I drove out into the country between Torre a Mare and Noicattaro. After a while, on a country lane, he told me to get out of the car, take two steps forward and not turn around. I obeyed and someone else put a hood over my head from behind. They took me somewhere indoors and made me sit down; I stayed there for maybe an hour. Then we got back in the car – they made me lie down on the back seat – and left. A quarter of an hour later we stopped, and the man who'd got into the car and was the only one who said anything told me to count to a hundred. Then I could get up and return home."

"Did they leave the keys in the ignition?"

"Yes."

"Where had they stopped the car?"

"Here in Japigia, at the end of Via Caldarola, in a side street I'd never been down, behind the petrol station."

Professional criminals, calm, sure of themselves. In all probability, that kidnapping hadn't been the first and, considering how composed they had been, they must have been people with experience of robberies.

"When did this happen?"

"The twenty-sixth of April, 1990."

"We've almost finished. Could you describe the voices of the two kidnappers for me?"

"As I said, the only one I heard was the first one."

"Didn't they talk to each other at all?"

"No."

"And how was this voice?"

"I really couldn't say."

"Let me give you some adjectives and see if any of them are appropriate to describe it. High or low?"

The woman seemed to concentrate. "It definitely wasn't high. It was like when someone smokes a lot ..."

"Husky?"

"Yes, husky."

"Is there any other reason you referred to smoking?"

"Now that I come to think of it, he stank of cigarettes. You know when someone smokes a lot and has that smell ..."

"Of course, the kind that stays on their clothes. Do you remember anything else?"

She shook her head. She seemed surprised to have remembered that detail.

"Let's go back to how he spoke. Dialect or Italian?"

"A mixture, but more dialect."

"So, to sum up: he had a low, husky voice, he was a heavy smoker and he spoke mainly in dialect. What about his physical appearance? His build, his height?"

She shook her head again. "It's hard to say. He was ... average. He didn't seem particularly tall or short. He definitely wasn't fat."

"If you had to guess, just guess, without giving any reason: how old would you say he was?"

"About thirty, maybe more. He wasn't a boy."

"Did you by any chance, in the months that followed, ever have the impression you encountered this person? Even if it was just an impression. Maybe you passed someone in the street and heard that voice, or else smelled the same smell of cigarettes."

"No."

Fenoglio was silent for a minute or two to see if any further memories emerged. But nothing came.

"All right, Signorina Fiorella, if you remember anything else, please call me. I'm writing down my office number. I'm Marshal Fenoglio. If you don't find me, leave a message and I'll call you back."

"My father and I just want to forget all about this business."

# 5

The man was about forty, he was wearing a well-cut grey suit, and there was something evasive in his manner.

They were sitting around a table in an anonymously furnished reception room. The apartment was on the top floor of a modern building on Corso Vittorio Emanuele: from the windows there was a spectacular view of the old city.

"How did you find out?"

Fenoglio made the same speech he'd given a few hours earlier, with the necessary variations. He wasn't to worry, the information was only needed for an investigation into another kidnapping, they wouldn't take a statement and the conversation would remain confidential. The important thing was that he tell them everything that had happened on the occasion of his kidnapping.

"But it wasn't me they kidnapped."

"Who was it?"

The man contracted his jaw and there was a suspicious gleam in his eyes. "My father."

"Ah. And what does your father do?"

"He was the owner of this building company. But he's dead now."

"I'm sorry, Signor Angiuli. Did his death have anything to do with the kidnapping?"

"Who knows? Six months after it happened, they discovered he had cancer, and six months after that he was dead. They say cancer is sometimes caused by stress."

"When did it happen, Signor Angiuli?"

"February of last year."

The man recounted what his father had told him. He had just left home when a fellow with a beard, moustache and long hair had approached him, introduced himself as a police officer and told him to follow him in order to check something. He had asked the reason and the man had punched him twice in the face, knocking him out. He had come to a few minutes later, in a van. He was blindfolded and handcuffed. Soon afterwards they had phoned the son, demanding eighty million in cash. They had been told that it was impossible to get hold of a sum like that in such a short time, and in the end they had agreed to fifty. The money was left under a dustbin in Valenzano. The father had been freed in Bari, near the cemetery. From there, he had called and the son had gone to pick him up. From the kidnapping to the release, it had all taken five hours.

"The man with the beard said he was a police officer?"

"Apparently, yes. It must have been to trick him."

"And were those your father's exact words: blindfolded and handcuffed?"

"Yes, I think so …"

"Blindfolded or with a hood over his head?"

"Blindfolded. He never said anything about a hood."

"All right. And he did say 'handcuffs', like the things we use?"

"I'm really not sure now. He said something like: they handcuffed me, but —"

"Try to make an effort. It may be important. Try to hear your father's voice in your head, his voice more than his words."

"He said … they handcuffed me … and then that when they let him go they used shears …"

"So they'd tied him up?"

"He didn't say 'tied'. I remember that very well. He said 'handcuffed'."

Pellecchia intervened in a strangely low voice and a grim tone that was unlike him. "Single-use plastic handcuffs."

"Yes. Is there anything else you remember from your father's account?" Fenoglio asked.

"He said they'd struck him as … bad people. I know that sounds like a childish thing to say, but it's the expression he used. He came back terrified. It's obvious that anyone would be frightened after something like that, but he was *more* frightened. I don't know if I'm making sense."

"You're making perfect sense. He'd been aware of a very intense threat that went beyond the situation he was in, serious as that was. Have I understood correctly?"

"I think so."

"Did he tell you anything about the way the two men spoke? In Italian or in dialect?"

Angiuli thought this over. He put his elbow on the table and his chin on his closed fist. "I don't remember."

"But you talked to them on the phone."

"Yes, although the first two calls were taken by the secretary we had then."

"Doesn't she work here any more?"

"No, she lives in Milan."

"How was the voice of the person you spoke to? If it was the same."

"Yes, it was always the same. It was a normal voice."

"Italian or dialect?"

"Italian."

"Calm or agitated?"

"Very calm. And very cold. The voice of someone without any emotion. Strange, I never thought of it before in those terms. He gave orders. He had the tone of someone who gives orders."

"In what sense?"

"I really don't know. It wasn't that he was threatening. It was as if the threat was taken for granted, as if there was no need. I had to obey and that was it."

Fenoglio looked at Pellecchia, who seemed lost in thought.

"Maybe I'm imagining things ..."

"On the contrary, you're providing us with some very useful leads. Do you remember any particular expressions used on the telephone by this man?"

"In what sense?"

"He gave you instructions about how to hand over the money and in general about how to behave: was there anything unusual about the way he expressed himself?"

Angiuli shook his head.

As they were taking their leave, Fenoglio told him to call him if he remembered anything else. He thought it unlikely he would do so. There was something about the man, even though he had cooperated and provided them with useful information, which didn't convince him. Something untrustworthy, hidden and somehow dangerous.

They went back on foot, as they had arrived: the station was a quarter of an hour's walk from Angiuli's office.

"What did you think of him?" Fenoglio asked as they turned onto the seafront. The wind had risen and the sky was an absolute, almost tragic blue.

"A son of a bitch. I don't know why, but he's a son of a bitch."

"I had the same impression. Anyway, it wasn't the same people as with the Patrunos."

Pellecchia replied with a kind of grunt which was hard to interpret. It might mean yes; it might mean that he had to think about it.

"The pathologist said the boy had rope marks on his wrists. That would be one element in common."

Another grunt, identical to the previous one.

"You're verbose today."

"Verbose. That means someone who talks a lot, right?"

"Right. What can you tell me about the third name the Albino gave us?"

"That we should ask him to check things better."

"Meaning what?"

"Meaning that in the register office in Bitonto – the paper said that was where he was from – that name doesn't exist. I asked my colleagues at the station if, apart from the records, they knew anyone of that name, and they said no. I also tried someone at the police station, a very bright guy, a friend of mine. Zilch."

# 6

Fenoglio walked the two miles home. As he went in, he had to suppress the usual wave of anguish he felt on seeing the apartment without Serena, although in the last few days the situation seemed to have improved a little: the shock was less violent, the sense of dizziness less intense.

He took a shower, changed and put his dirty clothes in the laundry basket. If you let yourself go, you're done for. You start to shave badly, you wear the same shirt for three days, talking to yourself becomes a habit. They say it's like a disease, when someone leaves you. There's an acute phase, then there's the convalescence. He didn't want to be in a really terrible state by the time he was cured. And to be cured, the last thing he must do was dismiss the thought of Serena. Dismissing it was like taking a painkiller whose effect only lasts a few minutes. Afterwards, the pain returns, stronger than before. When the thought comes, you just have to leave it alone, not try to stop it or control it. The problem is that we like to control everything: a stupid, pointless, unhealthy idea. We need to have the opposite attitude, accept the fact that nobody really has any control over his or her own life: that was what the barman Nicola, from the Caffè Bohème, had said to him once. He had been an alcoholic, and one evening, at closing time, he had told Fenoglio how he had got out of it by going to meetings of Alcoholics Anonymous and following their twelve-step programme. One day at a time. He had also added that it's a good rule not to take anything personally. We think that everything revolves around us: both what other people do and what they *don't* do. It's almost never true. Things happen and that's it; most other people are uninterested in us, for good or ill. Right, Fenoglio had replied, standing up and saluting him to the strains of the Intermezzo from *Manon Lescaut*.

It was Saturday. The air was warm. The perfect evening for going out, having a nice pizza and seeing a film in an open-air cinema.

Alone.

All right, alone. For a few moments, he thought of calling Pellecchia. Hi, Tonino, I decided to accept your offer, can you please ask your girlfriend to bring along a friend?

He felt like crying, which didn't happen often. Luckily, he was alone. The last time anyone had seen him cry was when his father had died. He had that strange, stupid conviction that crying wasn't dignified. A question of vanity, when it came down to it.

I could call D'Angelo. Maybe she's also alone, maybe she'll be pleased. The idea lasted only a few seconds longer.

Go and have a pizza, catch a film, then home to bed. Tomorrow, you can think. One day at a time, as the barman Nicola says.

That was what he did. He went to a pizzeria in the centre of town, near the railway station, and had a pizza and a couple of beers. Then he moved a few hundred yards to see what was showing at the Arena. It was *Robin Hood: Prince of Thieves*, with Kevin Costner. A film from the previous year, which strangely he'd missed. Strangely, because Robin

Hood was one of his favourite characters. He bought the ticket; after a moment's hesitation – Serena would have disapproved – he bought another cold beer and immersed himself in the unreal, timeless atmosphere of the old arena. The film was good, Kevin Costner was fine, even though nobody would ever be able to play Robin Hood better than Errol Flynn, but the best character was the one played by Morgan Freeman. Great actor, Fenoglio thought, sooner or later he'd win an Oscar.

By the time he got home, he was almost in a good mood. He cleaned his teeth, carefully folded his trousers on a chair and went to bed. Before falling asleep, he told himself that Serena would have liked that. If she came back, she wouldn't find him looking like a tramp.

The following morning he woke late, which was unusual for him. He liked it. One of the unpleasant aspects of waking early, when it isn't yet light, is that you're confronted with your own anguish. Usually, it wins, at least as long as you stay in bed. If you wake up and discover that it's half past nine, for example, that means you've escaped the tentacles of the night, and you can even allow yourself to laze about a bit longer. So he switched on the radio and stayed in bed for another half hour, gliding, with less effort than the past few weeks, over the waves of anxiety that spread from the empty side of the bed.

At last he got up, had a shower and made himself breakfast. After eating, he tidied everything up and decided not to run away to escape the solitude. First of all, he wouldn't go to the office, as he had done almost every Sunday in that early part of summer. He would read, listen to music, watch the television news, have lunch and go out for a walk in the afternoon. During the walk, he would try to reorganize his ideas about the Grimaldi kidnapping. Though maybe *reorganize* wasn't the right word. There weren't that many ideas in the first place. It was rather a question of reaching some kind of working hypothesis – something he had failed to do so far.

He listened twice to Beethoven's *Emperor* concerto and read a little of Moravia's *Time of Desecration*, finding it very boring. In the end he gave up and switched to a book by Bertrand Russell – *Religion and Science* – which was a much more pleasant read. He underlined a number of sentences and one passage in particular he marked with an exclamation mark in the margin: "towards the end of the sixteenth century Flade, Rector of the University of Trèves, and Chief Judge of the Electoral Court, after condemning countless witches, began to think that perhaps their confessions were due to the desire to escape from the tortures of the rack, with the result that he showed unwillingness to convict. He was accused of having sold himself to Satan, and was subjected to the same tortures as he had inflicted upon others. Like them, he confessed his guilt, and in 1589 he was strangled and then burnt."

At one o'clock, he stopped reading, switched off the stereo and transferred to the kitchen, where he made himself a potato omelette; he ate it, watched the television news, had a coffee and cleaned up, leaving everything in perfect order. For a moment, he thought in all seriousness that if Serena came back without warning she wouldn't find the sink full of dirty dishes and cutlery. Then he remembered that she was in Pesaro for the school-leaving exams – she had phoned him a few days earlier to tell him, and he hadn't known what to make of the hesitant tone of her voice, the hint of something unexpressed.

He went out. The weather was unsettled. It didn't seem like July; the air had the ambiguous coolness of September.

He had never liked the harsh colours, the sharp contrasts, the absence of doubt and the sadness of high summer. But he had always liked September, ever since he was a little boy. It was an elusive, unclassifiable month. In that old game – if you were a train, what kind of train would you be? if you were an animal …? if you were a flower …? – when the question was: if you were a month …? he always replied September.

September is the month of new responsibilities, someone had said. It seemed an accurate definition, and *responsibility* was a word he liked. He had often thought about it: he hated the idea of a sense of guilt and loved the idea of a sense of responsibility.

He passed an apartment building on Via De Ruggiero. One of those beautiful municipal blocks from the 1920s: big apartments with high ceilings, large windows, well-lit staircases. There was a couple in their sixties who had lived there for thirty-five years. They'd had two daughters who had married and moved away. A normal couple, as far as the neighbours knew, although very reserved – they weren't on familiar terms with anyone. One morning, the woman had turned up at the Carabinieri station on Viale Unità d'Italia, wearing a bloodstained dressing gown. I've killed my husband, she had said, putting down a hammer, also bloodstained, on the desk of an astonished sergeant. At that time, Fenoglio had only just joined the department. It was he, with two colleagues and the woman, who entered the apartment and found the husband sitting in his vest in an armchair in front of the television, which was still on. At first sight, he seemed to be asleep, with a coffee cup and an ashtray full of cigarette butts beside him. Going closer, you could see his smashed skull. There was a look of infinite surprise in his wide-open eyes.

The woman was calm, didn't say anything. When they asked her why she had done it she stood up, lifted her blouse and showed them the marks of the lashes. Then the marks of the cigarette burns. And she told them about her life with this man she had hammered to death a few hours earlier. I didn't want all these things any more, she said. I woke up and I thought I didn't want him to do these things to me any more. So I took the hammer and when he finished his coffee I did what I did. She was serene. The strangest thing was that she exuded serenity. As if her gesture had cleaned up part of the world.

They were things that had happened a long time ago. Or maybe not, maybe not so long ago. Time – long or short – depends on how you measure it.

Whatever, it had been a very easy investigation. In fact, when you got down to it, it wasn't even an investigation, given that the case had already been solved the moment the woman had turned up at the station.

In a hypothetical scale of investigative difficulty, that murder was a one, the death of young Grimaldi a ten. Was what they had learned about the Patruno and Angiuli kidnappings going to be of any use? The Japigia episode really seemed like something else. Locals, almost certainly. Individuals who moved about the streets of the neighbourhood like predators in their territory. It was very unlikely – as he had already said to Pellecchia – that people from Japigia would have moved into the northern districts to kidnap the son of the boss who ruled that part of the city.

The case of the builder, on the other hand, seemed less easily related to something territorial. The perpetrators had been harder, less scatterbrained; they didn't speak in dialect; they were violent, even more so than was necessary; they had taken care to keep the kidnap victim under control with ropes or plastic handcuffs and blindfolds, whereas they hadn't taken too many precautions in grabbing the ransom money. These two things were contradictory in a way: greater caution in controlling the victim, less caution during an extremely delicate phase like the retrieval of the money. The opposite modus operandi from the Japigia kidnappers, who had been less concerned with controlling the victim but had paid more attention to the retrieval.

What did this difference mean? Assuming it meant anything at all. As Lopez had told them, lightning kidnappings had become a widespread activity, convenient and of little risk. So thinking about what these differences meant might turn out to be a pointless exercise.

He remembered the story of the drunk who has lost his house keys and looks for them in the street, under a lamp post. He looks for them but doesn't find them. After a while, a passer-by asks him what he's doing, and he replies that he's lost his keys and is looking for them. Did you lose them under this lamp post? the passer-by asks. No, I lost them in that alleyway, the drunk replies. So why are you looking for them here? Because it's light here, whereas in there it's dark and you can't see anything. A clever little joke that explains what we often do, without realizing it, when we try to solve a problem without the right coordinates. We look where it's light, even though that's exactly how *not* to solve the problem.

Fenoglio had reached Corso Cavour. The sky was overcast now and the wind had turned colder. The *maestrale*'s coming, he told himself, putting on the jacket he'd been carrying over his shoulder.

He heard someone calling him.

"Marshal!" The voice was so heavily accented as to seem a caricature. He turned and recognized Francesco Albanese, the clumsy robber.

"Good afternoon, marshal."

Fenoglio smiled. "You still haven't got rid of that Bolzano accent."

The young man looked at him for a few moments, puzzled. Then he got the joke and returned the smile.

"So you're out, I see?"

"Yes, Marshal, I plea-bargained, like you told me. They gave me a year, but as I didn't have a record they released me straight away."

Fenoglio looked at him for a few moments. "And what are you doing now?"

"No more robberies, I swear. I do cigarettes, sometimes a little pot."

"What about a normal job?"

"A normal job? Would you hire me? I'm also a car park attendant."

"Unlicensed."

"All right, unlicensed, yes. But I behave myself. First of all, I don't ask for any money. If they want to give me something, fine. If not, I don't say anything, I don't threaten them. Nothing. If they leave me the keys, I just use them to park the car when it's double-parked, so that they don't have to pay a fine. I'm honest."

"Would you like a coffee, Albanese?" That at least was a quality that Fenoglio possessed: he never forgot a face or a name, or a face coupled with a name. It was a spontaneous thing with him, a thing that helps in many jobs – particularly in that of a law enforcement officer, for a variety of reasons. Some obvious, some much less obvious.

Albanese smiled, surprised. "Thanks, marshal. I never refuse a coffee."

They went into the Saicaf coffee bar. The young man greeted everyone like a regular customer and they all greeted him warmly.

"I guess they know you here," Fenoglio said.

"They know me, and they know they can trust me. If for example someone has their engine stolen, they ask me, and sometimes I can help them find it."

"Just like that, out of friendship, right?"

"Well, maybe they give me a little something."

"Yes, and sooner or later you get arrested as an accessory to extortion."

"What's extortion got to do with it? I'm just doing a few favours."

Fenoglio decided to drop it. Now was not the time to get involved in legal niceties on the concept of accessory to extortion on the part of a go-between. When they left the coffee bar, Albanese resumed speaking.

"You say I'm unlicensed. All right, I'm unlicensed. But you know what the guys in the proper car parks do, all above board, with the permission of the municipal council? The ones at the railway station or down by the harbour?"

"What do they do?"

"They get people to leave them their keys if the car park is full. It seems like they're doing them a favour, because they're licensed by the council, they even have uniforms, right?" He paused, as if expecting a confirmation from Fenoglio that they were indeed licensed by the council, or perhaps something else.

"And then?"

"And then they let their criminal friends take the cars when they have something to do. A delivery, a robbery, whatever. That way they have a clean car, and if anyone gets the licence number it's down to you, I mean, to the owner. Maybe you've gone away somewhere, you're on a train or a ship, you think your car's in a safe place, instead of which it's become an underworld taxi."

Fenoglio was interested now. "And they do this at the station and the harbour?"

"Yes, they always do it. The licensed car park attendants with the council uniforms, you know what I mean. Because people think that if you have a uniform you're an honest person and they can trust you, and if you don't have one – like me – you're a criminal. You have no idea of the dirty tricks those guys in uniforms get up to. When I was in the army, those lousy officers – no offence to you, obviously – stole petrol, stole food, even stole blankets …"

The young man continued his speech, but Fenoglio had stopped listening.

Soon afterwards, they parted. Fenoglio could have repeated word for word what the young man had said up to a certain point, but nothing of the last part of the conversation.

Because hearing about criminals in uniform had given him an idea. One of those ideas where it's pointless thinking it's Sunday and you can go home and watch TV or continue with your stroll, maybe go to the cinema again, whatever.

Thinking these things, he had already turned into Via Imbriani, heading in the direction of the station. He had a few things to check. And he had to do it this afternoon. No question of putting it off till tomorrow.

# 7

The next morning he went looking for Pellecchia and found him in the courtyard, chatting in a friendly manner with a handcuffed young man. The scene had its own grotesque normality.

"Let's go upstairs, we need to talk."

"What's up?"

"An idea. So absurd that right now I don't feel like talking about it with our superiors or the prosecutor. As we've been doing this little investigation together, I can only talk about it with you."

"I don't know what the fuck you're talking about, but all right."

They got to Fenoglio's office. He closed the door and sat down on the desk.

"Well?"

"What if the kidnapping of the Grimaldi boy was carried out by police officers or carabinieri?"

Pellecchia didn't reply immediately, and didn't display any surprise. He went and sat down, as if he needed to, and lit a cigar without asking for permission. "What made you think of that?"

Fenoglio didn't reply immediately either. Pellecchia's reaction had been strange. It had a strange *slowness* about it. He tried to figure it out and couldn't.

"It first crossed my mind when Angiuli mentioned handcuffs, I mean, when he said that his father had been handcuffed. An obvious association: you hear handcuffs and you think police or Carabinieri. What's more, those people had said they were from the police. When it was clear they were plastic handcuffs, I dropped the idea. Anyone can buy plastic straps from a hardware store."

Pellecchia sniffed, then passed his hand over his chin. He nodded, pursing his lips. It was almost as if he already knew what Fenoglio was about to say.

"Yesterday, I ran into a guy I arrested for attempted robbery a couple of months ago, the same day we found out about the kidnapping of the Grimaldi boy and there was that shoot-out in Enziteto. We stopped and had a chat, and after a while he said something that brought the idea back in my head. So I decided to do a check."

"What kind of check?"

"I checked the records of the kidnap victims and their families."

"Damn right," Pellecchia said after thinking for a moment. "Did anything come out?"

"The jeweller has never even been stopped for driving without a licence."

"And the other guy?"

"Officially, Angiuli doesn't have a record either. But by consulting the databank and making a few phone calls, I discovered that the Prosecutor's Department in Naples and the Finance Police here have both looked into him; I've just got back from talking to a friend of mine, an anti-drug marshal in the Finance Police. They're convinced he's involved in shifting large quantities of cocaine from Venezuela to Italy by way of Spain. At least that's their hypothesis. His wife's Venezuelan, and according to the Finance Police her family are involved in trafficking over there. They investigated him for months."

"What did they come up with?"

"Nothing. They're pretty sure he and his wife are the driving force behind the traffic and that the building company is just a money-laundering operation. But they haven't been able to pin anything on him."

Pellecchia's face, which up until then had been devoid of expression, seemed to come back to life. "A trafficker. I knew there was something not quite right about him."

"Okay. So let's assume for a moment that my hypothesis is correct. Let's assume that among the people responsible for the kidnapping of Angiuli's father and the kidnapping of the boy there was a carabiniere or a police officer. Someone who has access to confidential information, or at least someone who knows who the criminals are, who knows which people have money but would be highly unlikely to report a kidnapping to the authorities."

"Actually, *none* of the victims of these lightning kidnappings ever reported it."

"Correct. So let's suppose you and I decide to go into the kidnapping business. We want to maximize our earnings and reduce our risks to the absolute minimum. If we're really determined, intelligent, unscrupulous sons of bitches, who do we choose as victims? People who have instant access to large amounts of cash and absolutely no desire for the authorities to know about it. Since we're detectives, we have access to confidential information, and since we're crooked detectives we have the balls – maybe it turns us on – to grab the son of a boss like Grimaldi in the middle of a Mafia war and make everyone think his rivals are responsible for the kidnapping."

Pellecchia didn't reply. He went over to the window that overlooked the courtyard and looked out, half closing his eyes. As if he didn't recognize what he was seeing, or as if all at once, at that exact moment, he had noticed something he had never seen before.

"Are you all right?" Fenoglio asked.

Pellecchia turned, as if only now realizing he wasn't alone in the room. "Do you mind if we take a walk?"

Fenoglio stared at him for a long time. "All right," he said at last.

No sooner were they outside than a huge cloud covered the sky. Pellecchia put his hands in his pockets. As he walked, he looked around as if lost. It occurred to Fenoglio that he had never seen him with his hands in his pockets. Distortions. Shifting sands. Regularities that suddenly lose their rhythm and form a different alignment.

"Let's go over to the seafront." He crossed the road without waiting for Fenoglio's reply. "I like the water. I like the sea. I like going in it, swimming, sailing. I like looking at it. It makes me feel clean. It's a nice feeling."

"Feeling clean?"

"Yes, a nice feeling. When it happens." He stopped by a cast-iron lamp post and looked out at the horizon. Finally, he shook his head. "I once heard you say that you became a carabiniere by chance."

"More or less, yes."

"I don't understand how you can become a carabiniere by chance."

Fenoglio shrugged. The clouds were moving rapidly because of the wind. The air had a salty tang. There was something dramatic and yet sweet in that backdrop.

"We do almost everything by chance," Fenoglio said, "even if we're not conscious of it most of the time." He immediately regretted his words, thinking them banal.

"Sometimes I don't understand the things you say," Pellecchia replied. "Anyway, I *wanted* to be a carabiniere."

"Why?"

"Because I wasn't good enough to play football."

"How do you mean?"

"I used to play. I even tried out for first-division teams, but it was immediately obvious that I'd never get beyond the interregional championships and would never earn a living from it. As a boy, whenever they asked me what I wanted to be when I grew up, I'd say: a football player or a carabiniere. Having ruled out football player, which was dream number one, I chose carabiniere, which was number two. But apart from my boyhood ambitions, you know why I became a carabiniere?"

"Why?"

"Because I didn't like criminals. Because they scared me, although I would never have admitted it. I wanted to be on one side, I wanted things to be clear. The good guys and the bad guys. The bastards and the others, us. The rules. Those who obey them and those who don't. I joined when I was eighteen, and soon enough I realized things weren't clear at all."

"It isn't easy to establish who are the good guys and who are the bad guys."

"Precisely."

Precisely, Fenoglio thought. And the question of the rules is even more complicated. It's wrong to break them systematically, but it's also impossible to always respect them. Sometimes you let someone go who you should arrest. Sometimes you put the screws on someone and lock him up even though you don't have anything to go on. There's no way of living in this world if you don't handle the rules in a flexible manner. Rules exist, and they should usually be respected, but you have to be ready to set them aside, at least every now and again, otherwise it's better not to do certain jobs. Black and white are abstract concepts. There is a broad grey area in which you have to move with caution, because the maps are inaccurate.

"Let's suppose I've done things that were … wrong," Pellecchia said. "And let's suppose I tell you about them. What would you do with that information?"

Fenoglio caught himself sniffing, just as Pellecchia did. "That depends."

"On what?"

"On what you tell me. And on the reasons why you're telling me."

"Crimes. Committed by me."

The clouds were still moving rapidly, making the sun appear and disappear. "If there are no good reasons, maybe it's best you don't tell me anything else."

Pellecchia took a puff at his cigar and blew out the smoke. "And what if it's useful to the investigation?"

"Which one?"

"The Grimaldi kidnapping."

Fenoglio looked at him. He looked at him as he had probably never done before. He made what amounted to an inventory of his features, one that was even more thorough than if he'd had to register them and then describe them as accurately as possible. The slightly crooked nose; the skin made leathery by unprotected exposure to the sun; the long lashes; the grey eyes that were green in the sunlight; the short, thick, greying hair. It was true, he did look like Robert De Niro. Strange, Fenoglio thought, he'd never noticed it before.

"Maybe it doesn't have a damn thing to do with it. Or maybe it's important. I don't know."

"Let me see if I'm following you. Are you saying there are things you've done, or things you've been involved in, that might help us with our investigation into the Grimaldi kidnapping?"

"Yes."

"Things that happened recently?"

"No, in the past ..." He made an exasperated gesture with his hands. Exasperated and angry. "Fuck it, enough of this shilly-shallying. I'll tell you everything, then you do what you want to. You decide, but right now I can't keep this stuff to myself."

Fenoglio was about to repeat that he couldn't guarantee anything. But he didn't say it: there was no point. They were in the middle of the grey area. Black and white are abstract concepts.

"Do you mind if we stay here by the sea and talk? I don't feel like going inside."

"Of course, let's stay here."

"Do you remember when we went to the medium?"

"Yes?"

"I told you I was ashamed. You thought I was ashamed of myself in general. Partly, I am, but at that moment I was thinking of a specific thing, something I've never been able to forgive myself for." There was an awareness in Pellecchia's expression that was rare for him. "Do you know Guglielmo Savicchio?"

"The fellow at the command unit, who works with the colonel?"

"That's the one. Do you know anything about him?"

"I barely know him, I've never worked there."

"Some years ago, before you came to Bari, we worked together in the criminal investigation unit."

"Wait, wait. Was he the one who killed a young guy in a shoot-out?"

"Yes." Then, after a long pause: "We were together that time. I'd had a reliable report about a guy who was supposed to be transporting half a kilo of cocaine on behalf of certain people in the Libertà area. We waited for him near the garage where he was meant to be depositing the stuff. He noticed us as he drove up on his motorbike; we tried to stop him and he swerved in this crazy way and managed to get away from us. Savicchio already had his gun in his hand. He took aim and fired. Five shots. The bike skidded and the guy fell off. We went to him and he was dying. Savicchio took another gun from his pouch, a small one, and fired two shots in the direction of where we'd been standing. Both of them hit the side of our car. I can still remember the noise. The noise is the thing I remember best about that evening. The five shots from his service pistol, the two shots from the 6.35, like branches snapping. He cleaned that fucking dummy pistol with his shirt, to remove his prints, and put it in the guy's hand."

It took Fenoglio a while to realize that he was holding his breath.

"I asked him what the fuck he was doing. He was very calm. He said I shouldn't worry, he'd see to it – the duty report and all the rest. I'd fallen on the ground and hadn't seen what had happened. I just had to confirm that I'd heard the guy shooting."

"What are you saying?"

"I think you know what I'm saying."

For a few moments, Fenoglio was enveloped in an unbearable, suffocating sense of unreality. "Did the 6.35 have an erased serial number?"

"Of course."

"Did you know he had it?"

"No."

"You confirmed his version."

"Yes. I signed the duty report, and when the examining magistrate questioned me I repeated the same things."

"Why?"

"I didn't know what to do, I felt trapped. Everything happened too quickly. When the others arrived, that was the story he told them. Then they asked me and I confirmed it. You know when things happen to you and you realize you can't control them?"

"Damn."

"But it wasn't only that. I was scared. We'd done things together." Pellecchia seemed to be all psyched up, and he couldn't stop now. "Illegal things. Things that happen when you're working in narcotics for a long time."

"Go on."

Pellecchia sniffed, rubbed his eyes and went on. "Sometimes when we confiscated coke, we kept back part of it. We used it for our informants." He shook himself as if an unpleasant idea had suddenly occurred to him and he had to express it immediately. "I never put a sachet in someone's pocket to frame them, though. I swear that. I used it only as gifts for the junkies who gave me tip-offs."

"And maybe you did some yourselves."

Pellecchia nodded without even attempting to deny it. "It helped with girls he knew, girls who wanted to have fun. If you had coke, everything was much easier."

"What else did you do?"

"Nothing. Just the drugs."

The words hung in the air for a few minutes. The smell of the sea had become more intense.

"Savicchio did other things."

"Such as?"

"More than once he suggested robberies. He said we should rob a gambling den or steal from one of the whores. I told him I didn't agree with that, and anyway it was too dangerous. He'd say I didn't understand a damned thing, we wouldn't be doing anything wrong, we wouldn't be taking money from respectable people, but from criminals. Nobody would ever report it, and anyway it was perfectly safe, because we were carabinieri. We could wear balaclavas and drive a service car but with stolen number plates. Immediately afterwards, we could take off the balaclavas, put the number plates back and continue on our rounds. Maybe we could even make an arrest immediately afterwards."

"Do you think he went ahead with these robberies?"

"Yes."

"Who with?"

"I don't know."

"With another …" – Fenoglio realized he couldn't use the word "colleague" – "… with another carabiniere?"

"It's possible. It's just as possible that he worked with a professional criminal. He's crazy. Anyway, after that business with the young guy, I asked to change departments. They put me on robbery, and a couple of years later I went to organized crime."

"With that shooting, did they accept it as self-defence?"

"Yes."

"What has this got to do with the Grimaldi case?"

Pellecchia screwed up his eyes. Whenever the sun managed to break through the clouds, it was blinding.

"Savicchio was always talking about how to make easy money. It was an obsession with him. Once, he said we should kidnap the wife of some big trafficker and demand a ransom. I didn't know whether to tell you about this, because if I did I'd have to tell you about myself as well. I couldn't make up my mind, but when we heard about the plastic handcuffs – and you told me the boy had that kind of mark on his wrists – I didn't think I could keep quiet any more."

"Why?"

"Because Savicchio was obsessed with these cops' gadgets from American films. Plastic handcuffs, pepper spray, stun batons. Actually, he had all kinds of obsessions. For example, he was obsessed with cleanliness. If he shook anyone's hand, he'd immediately run and wash himself, to get rid of germs, he said. He even shaved his armpits. And he was crazy about anagrams, or reading words backwards. Sometimes he called me Oninot."

"Why?"

"It's Tonino backwards. He was always doing that, sometimes whole sentences backwards, sometimes anagrams."

Fenoglio tapped his temple with his index and middle fingers. "Crazy."

"Crazy. It's my fault that I didn't realize it straight away."

"How come something as important as this – the fact that Savicchio was thinking about kidnappings – only occurred to you now?"

"Savicchio said all kinds of things, often just for the pleasure of talking big. He talked about robbing a bank, he talked about getting a consignment of coke from Peru. Once he said that it would be amusing to rape a girl from the flying squad. We could screw a policewoman, he would say. Who would ever think it was carabinieri? He needed to impress: I'm the baddest, I'm the most dangerous. I'm the Antichrist, he sometimes said. You remember when you told me what a psychopath is?"

"Yes."

"When you said that, it struck me that if I'd ever known a real psychopath, it was him. Anyway, what he said about kidnapping the wife of a trafficker I remembered just a few days ago, when I was in the Tremiti Islands."

Fenoglio processed this answer. It was a plausible explanation. There was no reason to think that Pellecchia was lying.

"Is there anything else you haven't told me? Do you have any other reasons to think it was him?"

"No, and I don't have any evidence that it was. But think about it: if it was him, everything would fit."

It would fit, yes.

"What do you think I should do now?" Fenoglio said.

"If you decide to put in writing what I've told you, I won't deny it. Anyway, I have an idea about what we could do."

Fenoglio walked away until he was about thirty feet from Pellecchia. He had the sea at his side and in front of him, and on the horizon the clouds met the water. It struck him as meaningful, some kind of metaphor. He stood there looking at that combination of colours – white and blue and green – for a few minutes. Finally, he turned and walked back.

"Tell me about your idea."

# 8

They had gone to a café with tables out on the pavement. There were no other customers, so they could talk without being disturbed and without anyone listening in.

"You could call him a high-class fence. Though maybe 'fence' isn't quite accurate. If you need to buy something – whatever it is – he can get it for you. If you need to sell something, he can find you a buyer. We're not just talking about Bari, this guy does business all over Italy and even abroad."

"What's his name?"

"Luigi Ambrosini."

"Never heard of him."

"He's invisible. Never been sentenced, never been tried, never been searched. He's like Mandrake the Magician. I don't know how he's managed to stay under the radar for so long."

"How come nobody knows him if he's so well connected?"

"I told you, he's a magician. Maybe the only case I've seen of someone who's a professional criminal without being known to the police or the Carabinieri."

"What's his cover?"

"A toyshop."

"And you've never mentioned him at the station?"

"No. Every now and again, he gives me a tip-off. When he wants to, when he has some reason connected with his business."

"A grown-up criminal," Fenoglio said, as if talking to himself.

"What?"

"A grown-up criminal. I make a distinction between criminals who are grown-ups – and there aren't many – and those who are children, the vast majority."

"What do you mean?"

"When children behave badly, they almost always do it because they want to attract their parents' attention, because their parents represent authority. They have an ambivalent attitude towards breaking the rules. They don't want to be punished, but they want to be found out. Most criminals behave the same way; they reproduce the identical model of behaviour in a different situation. They want to be noticed by the authorities, even at the risk of being punished."

"Is that why they always boast about what they've done, so in the end we catch them?"

"Exactly. They talk to someone who talks to someone else and so on until someone talks to us. That's why, as you say, in the end we catch them, one way or another. Except for the grown-up ones."

"And who are the grown-up ones?"

"Those who commit crimes just to obtain an advantage, like shopkeepers, like entrepreneurs. They don't feel the need to make themselves noticed – which means they don't boast. They act out of purely utilitarian motives. They want to gain an advantage and they *don't* want to be caught. Very often, they succeed. They're grown-ups pursuing rational objectives, not children looking for attention."

Pellecchia sniffed. "Shit. Sometimes I wonder ..." He let the sentence hang. As if he didn't know what to say, or as if what he had to say embarrassed him.

Fenoglio let a few seconds go by before returning to the matter in hand. "Where is Ambrosini's shop?"

"In Via Bovio, behind the Garibaldi School. He also has a warehouse nearby, and other premises, but I don't know where they are."

"Why do you think he might help us?"

"He was on very good terms with Savicchio. Savicchio introduced us; we'd go to see him, he'd offer us coffee and give us some information. My impression was that the two of them met often, not just when we went to see him together. Sometimes they went off into a corner and talked between themselves. Sometimes when they said goodbye, they'd say things like: I'll give you a call. I think they were doing some kind of business together."

"Okay, so we can say they're friends. Let's assume, although it's pure conjecture at the moment, that Savicchio has something to do with the kidnappings in general and the Grimaldi kidnapping in particular. Why should Ambrosini know anything about it?"

"I have no idea. But I think it's worth a try. Savicchio talks a lot, and Ambrosini's a very intelligent man. If the relationship between them is what it used to be and if Savicchio is mixed up in the kidnappings, I'm almost sure that Ambrosini knows something about it."

"And why should he help us?"

"Because we need to make him shit himself. Let's do a 41 on him, just the two of us. We don't need to wait for a warrant from the Prosecutor's Department that way.

He won't be expecting a search, he's too sure of himself. Let's put pressure on him. He has to understand that if he doesn't help us he's not going to be left in peace any more. We don't have a fucking thing, so why not try it?"

It was a flawless argument. They had no clues, no suspects, not even a working hypothesis. They didn't have a fucking thing, as Pellecchia had put it. So they might as well go and see what this Ambrosini was like. Worst-case scenario, they would gather more material for his incoherent criminological deliberations, Fenoglio told himself, concluding his mental soliloquy.

"All right. When?"

"I think we should go when the shop opens this afternoon. As soon as he arrives, we go in with him and make him close up again. That way nobody will bother us and we can start working on him."

"Is he the only one in the shop?"

"There used to be an assistant sometimes. But not always. If she or anyone else comes to open up, we put it off. There's no point unless he's alone."

"All right," Fenoglio said, getting to his feet. "The shops open at five. Let's meet at the corner of Via Bovio and the Garibaldi School at 4.45."

"Pietro …"

Fenoglio made a gesture with his hand, as if to say: I don't want to hear another word. "Pay the bill," he said. Then he shook his head, turned and walked away.

# 9

As he crossed Piazza Risorgimento, he looked absently at the Garibaldi School. The two large buildings at the opposite ends of Via Putignani – the Garibaldi School, with its vaguely colonial appearance, and the Teatro Petruzzelli – had, just a few years earlier, been the backdrop for a Hollywood epic about the life of Toscanini. The female lead had been Elizabeth Taylor, playing the soprano Nadina Bulichoff.

Now the school and the theatre were both closed and unusable. The first due to the wear and tear of years, the second because of the fire that had destroyed it.

Fenoglio suppressed the impulse to look for a meaning in this symmetry. The problem is always the same: we look for meanings, even where there are none.

Investigations, too, are an attempt to construct order, to find a meaning. The risk, though, is that the need to be rational makes us lose sight of the most common characteristic of many crimes: their *lack* of meaning, their dizzying, inscrutable banality.

He reached the back of the school, where Via Bovio begins, and saw some little boys running after each other. An apparently harmless game, but Fenoglio seemed to perceive a latent violence, something almost feral, in it.

Pellecchia was already where they had agreed to meet. The toyshop was a few dozen yards further along the street.

Ambrosini arrived at five on the dot. He was short and incongruously dressed in jacket and tie even though it was July; he wore round glasses in light frames. He looked like a provincial pharmacist.

"Good afternoon, Signor Ambrosini, Carabinieri," Fenoglio said, slowly raising his badge. There was no need. The man had seen Pellecchia and recognized him. The two of them didn't greet each other.

"Good afternoon, marshal, has something happened?" Ambrosini said.

"Do you mind if we come in?"

"No, not at all."

"Please close up again when we're inside. We don't want to be disturbed for a while."

"But I have to open the shop —"

"Close up, please. You can't open the shop, we have to conduct a search."

"A search? Why?"

"Let's go in."

"But do you have a warrant?"

Fenoglio smiled without any warmth.

"Go in, Ambrosini, and don't mess us about," Pellecchia said and shoved him by the shoulder.

"We're here to conduct a search as allowed by Article 41 of the Unified Code of Public Safety, Signor Ambrosini. Do you know what that is?"

"No."

In an overly kindly tone Fenoglio recited by heart: "Article 41 of the Unified Code of Public Safety allows law enforcement officers who have information regarding the

270

existence, in any public or private premises or any dwelling, of arms, ammunition or explosives kept without authorization, to conduct an immediate search and confiscate said items. Even without a warrant."

"What does that mean?"

"It means we've had a tip-off that there's an illegal cache of arms here. We thought it only right to come straight here and check. As you can well understand, there was no time to request a warrant. Haven't you ever been subjected to a search?"

Another icy smile, while Pellecchia pulled down the shutter from the inside.

"Sorry, Ambrosini," Pellecchia said. "Switch the light on. With this shutter down, we can't see a damn thing."

Ambrosini pressed an old light switch. The place lit up, showing a line of shelves reaching up to the ceiling, overflowing with cardboard boxes, stuffed animals, dolls, plastic rifles, bags of confetti, packets of streamers, robots, snakes and ladders, party tricks, water pistols.

"Am I allowed to call my lawyer?" Ambrosini asked.

"Why do you want a lawyer, got something to hide?" Pellecchia said, stroking the man's face. It was a highly intimidating gesture, much more so than a slap would have been.

"Signor Ambrosini is right. If he wants a lawyer, he can call one. If he thinks it's a good idea. Do you think it's a good idea, *signore*? You know, we can be quite flexible or very strict, depending on the circumstances. If a lawyer comes, we can't afford to look bad. So we'll have to search every corner very, very carefully. We might even have to turn everything upside down until we find something. If we don't find anything, they'll say we're conducting arbitrary searches without a warrant and on the basis of unreliable information. When lawyers are involved, we always have to be careful. Are you following me?"

Ambrosini barely moved his head, to say, yes, he was following. Pellecchia kept one hand on his shoulder.

"If, on the other hand, you're less formal about it, then we won't be forced to be too finicky. Let's suppose you have something interesting to tell us. Then the search would be – how can I put it? – much less invasive. Maybe you have nothing to fear, maybe you're not keeping anything illegal, and then you could just say: do what you have to do, I have no problem with it. I'd appreciate that, I like people who have nothing to hide. If the opposite is the case, then a little friendly chat might be a good idea. Because if we do find something illegal, that sets a whole mechanism in motion that's difficult to stop. Confiscation, arrest, trial. You don't have a criminal record, do you?"

"No."

Pellecchia moved his hand up to Ambrosini's neck and started massaging it.

"What do you want to know?" Ambrosini said.

"We're working on the kidnapping of Nicola Grimaldi's son."

Ambrosini started moving his head from side to side. A slap from Pellecchia put a stop to the movement at its birth. "Don't be a fool, Ambrosini. If you force us to go ahead and search, we're bound to find something. And if things are the way I think they are, we'll find something that'll be sufficient for us to arrest you. And even if we find nothing, which we may only discover after several hours, from now on making you unhappy is going to be one of our top priorities. You know how you've worked in peace for all these years? Not any more. Game over." Pellecchia took his chin in one hand and forced him to look him in the eyes. "You are following me, aren't you?"

"Yes."

"Is there anywhere we can sit, Signor Ambrosini?" Fenoglio said.

"There's my office."

"Good, let's go there, if you don't mind."

They walked along a narrow, high-ceilinged corridor, at the end of which was the room Ambrosini called his office. Here, too, there were boxes and plastic containers of all kinds with toy soldiers, cars, tanks, little plastic animals, boxes of building blocks, train sets. There were even a few original boxes of Meccano, which had been Fenoglio's favourite toy when he was a child. In among the toys was a desk cluttered with folders, registers and other papers.

"Do you have three chairs, Ambrosini?" Pellecchia asked.

Behind the desk was a torn fake leather armchair. Ambrosini plunged into the stacks of merchandise and came out with two folding stools.

"Mind if I smoke?" Pellecchia asked, lighting his cigar.

"Signor Ambrosini, we don't want to waste your time and we don't want to waste ours either. We have reason to believe that you can help us in some way with the investigation I just mentioned."

Ambrosini looked at them. "If I do happen to know something and I tell you, what'll happen then?"

"Let's put it this way: if it's something very interesting, we might be able to go away immediately and check it out. Which means we won't have time to search and we won't have time to take a statement. It'll be as if we'd never even been here."

"And what if I tell you about things I've done myself?"

"Then you're an idiot, Ambrosini," Pellecchia said. "You're making me look bad in front of the marshal. I told him you were an intelligent man, someone with his head screwed on. Instead of which, you're asking stupid questions,"

"Just tell us," Fenoglio cut in. "We'll find a way to use your information without involving you. I know that in the past Corporal Pellecchia has seen you with Savicchio. The corporal is fully part of this investigation, you don't have to worry about a thing."

Ambrosini seemed to ponder this for a few seconds. Then he said only: "All right."

"First of all, tell us about Savicchio and your relationship with him."

"We've known each other for many years. He's often brought me merchandise for sale."

"What kind of merchandise?"

"He was part of a group of carabinieri and police officers who stole from shops that had been broken into."

"Can you be a bit clearer about that?"

"Suppose there's a break-in at night in a shop. Clothes, electronics, sometimes even jewellery. The police or the Carabinieri are called, a patrol car arrives on the scene and finds the shutter off its hinges. The cars are filled with merchandise before the owner of the shop arrives, and it looks as if everything was stolen by the robbers."

"So this happened when Savicchio was in uniform and was working the patrol cars?"

"Yes, several years ago. But he continued to bring merchandise even after he transferred to plain clothes."

"Did he sell it only to you?"

"I think so, but I'm not sure."

"How many carabinieri and how many police officers were involved?"

"I don't know. Quite a few, I think. He mentioned a group, who were all in agreement. He never mentioned any names. But he liked to say that *they* were the real masters of the city and that he was untouchable."

"Did you ever see him with anybody else? Apart from the corporal here."

"Someone started coming with him a couple of years ago."

"Do you know his name?"

"Ruotolo, Antonio Ruotolo. He's also a carabiniere."

Fenoglio looked at Pellecchia, who nodded, lips pursed. He knew him.

"All right, let's continue. Do you remember the first time he came with this Ruotolo?"

"I was supposed to be delivering some jewels to Perugia. They came from a big robbery in a villa in Trani."

"Why Perugia?"

"Because there's a jeweller there who's happy to buy things of great value and pays good prices for them."

"How much was the merchandise worth?"

"The man in Perugia was going to pay 500 million. To transport something like that, I needed an escort. So I asked Savicchio."

"Had he provided a service like that before?"

"Yes."

"Why specifically a carabiniere?"

"Being escorted by a carabiniere or a police officer means you're unlikely to be stopped. Or robbed. Anyway, this time he came with this other fellow. He introduced him to me as a colleague, a partner and a real friend. Those were his exact words."

"So you delivered the jewels and everything went fine, I assume. How much did you pay them?"

"The usual fee was twenty million. This time, he said he wanted more because there were two of them. In the end we agreed on twenty-five. I gave him the whole amount. I don't know how they divided it, but I don't think it was fifty–fifty."

"And after that?"

"We saw a lot of each other. This other fellow was nice, a really great guy. On the journey to Perugia and back we became quite friendly. Sometimes he'd drop by for no particular reason. We'd have coffee and chat. He always needed money."

"Why?"

"He was separated, or maybe divorced, and paid a lot of money to his ex-wife. And he was with a girl, a model, who cost him a lot of money."

"What's the name of this girl?"

"I only know her first name: Marina. He showed me some photos. Quite a looker."

"Did Ruotolo talk to you about what he and Savicchio did together?"

"No. He mainly talked about Savicchio. He said he was brilliant, but that he was also crazy and capable of anything. All of which I already knew."

"Apart from these encounters, these chats, did you do other business together?"

"They both provided an escort for me on other occasions."

Fenoglio was on the verge of asking for further information on these escort services. Then he told himself that this wasn't the reason they were here, that he had to focus on the objective. "Is it fair to say that of the two of them, Savicchio is the leader?"

"No doubt about it. Ruotolo is an athletic young man,

a martial arts champion, someone who can take care of himself. But the leader is Savicchio."

"All right, Ambrosini, let's get to the point," Pellecchia said, after stubbing out his cigar butt on the floor. "Do you know anything that could link them to the kidnapping of the Grimaldi boy?"

Ambrosini closed his eyes, moved his glasses up and massaged the bridge of his nose with two fingers.

"One day when they were here, they started talking about these lightning kidnappings. Savicchio said it was a brilliant idea, kidnapping the wife or child of some criminal who was rolling in money. Someone who could pay immediately and would never report it because they couldn't explain to the law how come they had that much money. He said it was something we should do ourselves."

"Who did he mean by 'we'?"

"He said it had to be the two of them and me. I would select the people to be kidnapped. Maybe people I'd done business with and who had large amounts of cash at their disposal. They would see to the rest of it. I didn't like the idea, for various reasons, but I didn't go into detail. I just said I thought it was too dangerous and that it wasn't worth it."

"And what did they say?"

"Ruotolo kept quiet. When Savicchio was around, he almost never said a word. But Savicchio insisted. He said that if he was involved, we were untouchable. He'd been in some pretty crazy situations before, and had always come out of them as pure as the driven snow."

"Is that how he put it?"

"His very words. I told him again that I wasn't interested. It was a good idea, I was sure they'd pull it off brilliantly, but I preferred to stay out of it."

"Do you think they went ahead and did it?"

"Yes. We met again months later and Savicchio boasted that they'd already done two jobs."

"Did he tell you the names of the people they'd kidnapped?"

"No."

"This was before the kidnapping of the Grimaldi boy, right?"

"Yes, several months earlier."

"Did you see them after the Grimaldi kidnapping?"

"No." He paused for a few seconds, as if bracing himself to say the most important thing. "But I think it was them."

"Why?"

"For two years, they came to see me at least two or three times a month. The last time was about ten days before the news about the Grimaldi boy came out. Since then, nothing. I don't believe in coincidence. Do you believe in coincidence, marshal?"

"In coincidence? I don't know. Didn't you even talk on the phone?"

"No. A few weeks later, I thought I might need them for something and I realized that I hadn't seen them or heard from them in quite a while. At that moment, I assumed they might have had something to do with the kidnapping of the boy. It wasn't a very clear thought, it just suddenly occurred to me. And I haven't called them since."

"Why?"

"If it was them, I didn't want them to tell me anything about it. With some things, the less you know, the better."

Fenoglio got to his feet and took a few steps, measuring the room between the desk and the boxes. "And have you seen them again?"

"I ran into Ruotolo by chance a few days ago."

"Did you talk?"

"He told me he hadn't been well and that he'd taken a few days off sick. He actually did look ill. He'd got thinner, and had circles under his eyes."

"Did he tell you anything?" Pellecchia asked, a tone of urgency in his voice.

"No."

"Did you ask him about Savicchio?"

"No, but he told me they hadn't seen each other in a while."

They were silent for a few minutes. As motionless as figures in a painting. Ambrosini behind the desk, Pellecchia on the other side, Fenoglio on his feet, near a tower of boxes.

"How do you think we could persuade Ruotolo to cooperate?"

"I don't know. He's like a zombie, maybe he needs to break free. If you try to pressure him ..."

"To break free," Pellecchia said, "he'd have to confess things that'd lose him his job and land him in prison. If he thinks about it, he might prefer to keep feeling guilty and hold on to his job and his salary."

Ambrosini shrugged. When it came down to it, getting Ruotolo to talk wasn't his problem.

"Of course, if you agreed to wear a wire and have a little chat with Ruotolo —" Pellecchia started to say.

Ambrosini interrupted him. "You can't ask me to do that. They'd all find out, I'd be known as a snitch and I wouldn't be able to work in this city any more. Or rather, I wouldn't be able to *live* in this city any more. You promised —"

"Okay, okay, you're right," Fenoglio said. "Forget about the wire. What if we tried bugging him?"

"Meaning what?"

"We place a bug somewhere where the two of you meet. We'll need a court order to do it. The result is the same, but nobody will be able to say you cooperated."

"Marshal, I'm sorry, but let's not fool ourselves. If there's a bug and I start asking strange questions about what he's done or hasn't done – assuming he answers me – everyone will know I was in cahoots with you when they read the transcript. Not to mention that if we start talking about crimes we're bound to end up mentioning something we did together. And, correct me if I'm wrong, but what's in a transcript gets to a judge, and then your promise to keep me out of it goes down the tubes."

Fenoglio sighed. "I can't argue with that."

"Marshal, I've done what you asked me. I've told you all I know. Maybe you think it was because I was afraid you'd search the place. But it wasn't. You can search as much as you like, the only thing you'll find here is toys. This kidnapping business has been going around in my head for a long time, and I've been wanting to tell someone about it. And then today you showed up. That wasn't coincidence either. Think how easy it was to persuade me, apart from that little bit of a scene I made. I *wanted* to help you, and I have helped you, but don't ask me to do things that would land me in the shit."

"You're right," Fenoglio said, exchanging glances with Pellecchia.

"Try to do what I suggested. Try to put pressure on Ruotolo. I think it's quite feasible that he'll break down."

"What kind of education did you have, Ambrosini?"

"Why do you ask?"

"You're quite well spoken."

"For a fence, you mean?"

Fenoglio shook his head, although it was clear that was precisely what he meant.

"I qualified as an accountant. My school was close to your station."

"The Vivante?"

"That's right. Then I studied law. I took fourteen exams, including criminal law. I still had seven to go. I'd have liked to have been a magistrate. Then I started working. If you work and earn money, it's difficult to stay focused on your studies."

Fenoglio and Pellecchia looked at him closely, searching for any hint of irony. They didn't find any. Ambrosini was serious. He merely added that often you don't do what you would have liked to do in life, but that what you'd like to do isn't necessarily what you would be good at doing.

Which, needless to say, is true.

# 10

"Well, what do we do now?" Pellecchia asked when they were some distance from Ambrosini's shop.

"The first question is whether we should go straight to the captain with all this or wait."

"If we tell the captain, two minutes later he'll talk to the colonel and —"

"I know. Savicchio works at the command unit, in the office next to the colonel's, he's an intelligent son of a bitch and we have no guarantee he won't guess something's up if the news starts to circulate."

"Precisely. Let's wait a few days, Pietro. We'll do a few checks, then decide when to tell the captain. I'm sure you'll find a way to tell him."

"I don't know this Ruotolo fellow. Where does he work?"

"He's in the prosecutor's detective team on the seafront. He was on radio patrol for many years, then on the detective unit in Bari Central. He's quite free with his hands, as far as I remember. Like Ambrosini said, he was a champion at some oriental crap, karate, judo, something like that. They call him Bruce Lee."

Pellecchia calling someone "free with his hands" was really quite strange, Fenoglio thought fleetingly.

"Anyway, Ambrosini's right," Pellecchia continued. "If we go after anyone, it has to be Bruce Lee."

"He said the same things about Savicchio as you did. The image of a psychopath."

"He must have got worse since I had dealings with him."

"The problem is, even assuming Ruotolo's as fragile as Ambrosini says, we don't have anything concrete on him. Nothing to charge him with, nothing we can use to put pressure on him. What do we do, go to him and say: listen, Ruotolo, we think you were involved in the kidnapping of the Grimaldi boy? How about spilling the beans and throwing away your career, your freedom, everything in fact?"

"We have to work on him a little. Find something to throw in his face."

"The problem is that without telling the captain we can't report it to the Prosecutor's Department. And without authorization from a magistrate we can't acquire anything. No phone records, no bank statements. Not to mention bugs: no magistrate would authorize that on the basis of a tip-off. And right now that's all we have."

"Give me half a day to ask around. I'll see if I can find anything and then we'll talk again. I'll make sure I'm free tomorrow morning, all right?"

Fenoglio said yes, it was all right, and felt a strange sense of relief.

Pellecchia reappeared early in the afternoon of the following day. Fenoglio had just got back from lunch and found him waiting outside his office.

"Can we talk?"

They went in and Fenoglio closed the door.

"Well?"

"First: Ruotolo has been off sick since May. The medical reports say: cluster headaches. You know what they are?"

"A particularly painful kind of headache, I think."

"Precisely. I looked it up: they call it 'suicide headache'. The problem is that there's no objective way to verify it. In practice, the doctor takes the patient's word for it. Anyway, the first certificate was issued six days after the boy's body was found."

"That's quite a coincidence."

"I agree. Secondly: Savicchio and Ruotolo both have mobile phones. But not like mine, which I only use to receive calls. Savicchio and Ruotolo spend a whole lot of money on theirs, up to 400,000 lire a month. They're constantly on the phone, at all hours of the day and night."

"You have a mobile phone?"

"Don't look at me like that. I told you I only use it to receive calls. The thing that costs you an arm and a leg is making calls. You should get one. That way they can call you from the station and piss you off even when you're out."

"I'll think about it," Fenoglio replied, dismissing the subject. "How did you get this information about the phone bills?"

"A friend at the phone company owed me a favour."

Fenoglio omitted to point out that this favour amounted to an offence. It wasn't the first and it wouldn't be the last in this investigation. They were deep inside the grey area.

"You know the most interesting thing?" Pellecchia went on.

"What?"

"Before, the two of them spoke on the phone five times a day. After the kidnapping of the boy, the calls became less frequent until they almost stopped completely. Since then, there've been just nine calls between them, always from Savicchio's phone. And all very short, less than a minute."

"Did you find anything else?"

"Ambrosini gave us a good description of Ruotolo. People who saw him a few days ago say he's going around like a tramp. He never used to be like that. A bit of a pain in the arse, but a good-looking guy, always well dressed, sometimes in expensive things."

"Which —"

"Wait, now comes the most interesting part. You know what a colleague from his team told me?"

"What?"

"Ruotolo has been seen in the cemetery several times in the last few weeks."

Fenoglio took a few seconds to process the information. "The cemetery where the Grimaldi boy is buried?"

"That's right."

"How did this colleague find out?"

"From the police."

"The police?"

"The flying squad has the cemetery under surveillance because of a gang of guys who deal there. They saw Ruotolo there several times, and as some of them knew him they wondered what he was doing there. And I mean, several times. An inspector from the flying squad talked to a marshal from Ruotolo's team … Are you following me?"

"Yes."

"Anyway, they asked how come this Ruotolo was going to the cemetery so often. They wanted to know if his team were doing an investigation and if that was why he was there. They were worried that some of the dealers would notice him and that would ruin their work, or worse, that it would all end up with a shoot-out, like two years ago."

Fenoglio remembered that episode well. The police and the Carabinieri had both managed to track down the perpetrators of an attempted extortion. The problem was that neither body knew of the other's investigation. And they had all taken up position, ready to catch the criminals red-handed just as the money was being handed over. There was a shoot-out; one of the criminals and one of the carabinieri were wounded and only narrowly escaped death.

"The marshal in charge of the team called Ruotolo, and asked him if he'd had a bereavement. He told him that showing his face in the cemetery was causing problems."

"And what did Ruotolo say?"

"He stammered something about someone close to him who'd died recently and assured him that he was going to stop these visits anyway."

"Someone close to him who'd died recently," Fenoglio repeated.

"That's right."

"Isn't it possible it's some relative of his?"

"Ruotolo is from the province of Avellino. He doesn't have any relatives in the cemetery in Bari."

"You've already checked?"

"Yes."

From the courtyard a siren sounded briefly, two notes and that was it. As if someone had pressed a button by mistake.

"It was them, Pietro."

"It was them."

"Let's go and get him and turn the screws on him."

Fenoglio stood up, grabbed his jacket and went to the door.

"What are you doing?" Pellecchia said.

"I have to think. See you later."

# 11

At least three or four times a year, Fenoglio was in the habit of visiting the City Art Gallery. As far as he was concerned, the place was one of the mysteries of Bari: a museum full of beautiful works by great artists, where there was never anybody around. Every time he went there, he counted the number of visitors. The most he had ever counted was eight.

It was something he couldn't understand, something that made him angry. It seemed absurd to him that such riches should be somehow hidden, wasted. On the other hand, with the passing of time, he had started thinking of the gallery as a kind of private collection of his own and enjoying the privilege of these solitary visits. It was only three minutes on foot, at an unhurried pace, from the station. He went there when he was tired, when he wanted to think in peace, or even just to take another look at one of the works he liked most.

That afternoon the gallery was quite crowded, by its usual standards. There was a man in his fifties observing the works of the Apulian masters through a magnifying glass and scribbling in a notebook, and a small group of five German tourists moving from one room to another, somewhat incredulous at the privilege of having a museum all to themselves.

Fenoglio did a quick tour of his favourite works from the nineteenth and twentieth centuries, lingering as usual over a small oil by Silvestro Lega – *Reading* – which had always seemed to him a perfect painting. Then he went and sat down in front of a painting by Felice Casorati – a girl in an armchair – which was a minor obsession of his.

Who was this adolescent with the precocious circles under her eyes? What was she looking at outside the painting, behind the painter? What had she understood, young as she was, that gave her that melancholy awareness?

As he did during every visit, Fenoglio wondered what kind of job he would have to do – oil tycoon, film producer, industrialist? – to afford a collection like this. But when it came down to it, he often told himself, what is a collector's greatest pleasure? Having his works within easy reach and being able to look at them over and over, whenever he likes. In other words, the same thing he was doing now, but for the small price of an entrance ticket.

After studying Casorati's girl for about ten minutes without solving the mystery, he decided that the moment had come to get his head back to questions of work.

Had it really been those two? Probably, yes. It was hard to see what had emerged so far as merely an accumulation of coincidences. In any case, it didn't look as if there was any alternative to the simple plan of trying to put Ruotolo on the spot and urging him to cooperate. Simple and risky. If Ruotolo didn't break down – or if he had nothing to do with the affair, which was unlikely but not impossible – he and Pellecchia would be in serious trouble. In the last few days they had conducted an investigation against fellow carabinieri without informing their superiors and without putting anything in writing.

If Ruotolo were to confess, all these irregularities would fade into the background, nobody would notice, and nobody would ask for an explanation. But if he didn't, they would have to provide a lot of explanations, and in all probability they wouldn't be enough. Picking up Ruotolo, taking him somewhere – but where? – and giving him the third degree, without a lawyer present and without any legal guarantees, would involve at least three or four serious offences, from kidnapping to abuse of office.

He thought, almost inadvertently, that he would have liked to discuss this with Serena. They had almost never talked about his investigations, but whenever they had, she'd always had a few ideas, mostly just thrown out as casual observations. For a moment, he felt something like a sense of breathlessness at the awareness of his loss.

In investigations, there are rules of various kinds. There are legal rules, rules of investigative method and rules of opportunity. The most important, though, have to do with awareness, which, if you think about it, are valid for any activity.

Not lying to yourself (lying to others is inevitable), not making it personal (the very concept expressed by the barman Nicola), not getting too fond of your own conjectures, not abusing your own power. These are rules of behaviour, and in order to respect them you have to be aware of a fundamental truth: sooner or later, you will break all of them. You're always walking a thin line, where balance is precarious. You always have to be on to avoid slipping and falling on the wrong side.

None of this concerns you if all you do is stamp reports and check that the statistics are up to date.

In fact, there's another rule – Fenoglio would not have said it out loud for fear of appearing rhetorical – which is the most important of all: you always have to do your best. He remembered a quotation – who was it by? He couldn't remember – that Serena had liked very much: if one is forever cautious, can one remain a human being?

His reflections finished with that phrase.

He left the gallery about an hour after going in. He felt serene, like someone who has made a decision and now just needs to put it into effect. The most difficult part was over. Before going home, he would call an old friend and ask for a favour, so that he could proceed in comparative tranquillity. The next day, he and Pellecchia would pick up Ruotolo and do what needed to be done.

That was all.

He told himself that Serena would approve of his incautious plan, and the thought made him absurdly cheerful.

# 12

Ruotolo was a tall young man with an athletic build. He was walking with his head down, dragging his feet; he wore cotton trousers that were too big for him and an unironed polo shirt.

He saw Fenoglio and Pellecchia when he was about twenty yards from his front door, where they were waiting for him. He stopped and for a few moments appeared about to turn and walk away. Then he must have thought that wouldn't be a good idea.

"Hi, Ruotolo, what are you doing around here?" Pellecchia said in a cheerful tone.

"I live here," Ruotolo replied cautiously. There was something weak and evasive in his features. His lips quivered, a sign that Fenoglio had learned to associate with those who are inclined to bully the weak and be submissive towards the strong.

"Imagine that. There was me thinking: that's my colleague Ruotolo, he's on foot, we have a car, let's give him a lift."

"Thanks, but I live here." He made a move towards the door. Pellecchia blocked his way.

"What are you doing at home at this hour, Ruotolo? Aren't you on duty?"

"I'm convalescing."

"Oh, sorry to hear that. Have you been ill?"

Ruotolo nodded without conviction. Then he looked around, as if to size up the situation.

"It's true, you don't look too good. Sorry to be nosey, but what exactly's the matter?"

"Headaches. I get these really bad headaches."

"Right. Isn't an aspirin enough? I don't know, whenever I get a headache I take an aspirin or an ibuprofen and after a while it goes."

"These aren't normal headaches."

"Come on, don't make that face, we're not the tax people. What's this kind of headache called? A cluster headache?"

"How did you know —"

"Hey, Ruotolo, don't get excited. What's our job? We're carabinieri, aren't we? We like to be informed about everything, you should know that. You know a lot of things, too, I bet. Anyway, I hope you're feeling better now. Have you been out for a walk?"

"Yes, I —"

"Have you been to the cemetery by any chance?"

"The cemetery? Why —"

"Just a guess. You look to me like someone who goes to the cemetery."

Ruotolo said nothing.

"I'm sorry, Ruotolo, I don't remember your first name."

"Antonio."

"Oh, yes, of course. Look, why don't we go for a nice ride? We'll have a coffee, you can relax a bit. Maybe we'll also have a bit of a chat."

"No, thanks. I have to get home."

Pellecchia went closer to him. He was smiling, but his eyes were half closed and motionless. He took one of Ruotolo's arms, just above the elbow, and squeezed it. Ruotolo made an attempt to break free, but Pellecchia squeezed harder. This was the first, delicate phase. Fenoglio held himself ready, in case Ruotolo retaliated. Nobody would want to come to blows with Pellecchia – you just had to look at him – but Ruotolo was a martial arts expert.

It wasn't necessary to intervene.

"Come with us," Pellecchia said, and led him towards the car, still holding him by the arm.

Fenoglio walked with them, placing himself on the other side of Ruotolo. Anyone seeing them would have thought they were arresting him.

Getting out of the car, Fenoglio grabbed the copy of the Penal Code he had brought with him. Outside the main entrance, they found the station's commanding officer waiting for them. They were in the middle of the Murge, at a height of thirteen hundred feet. It was warmer here than in Bari.

"Hi, Michele."

"Hi, Pietro."

Marshal Michele Iannantuono was of medium height, very sturdy, his shaved head attached directly to his shoulders without the mediation of a neck, his blue eyes somewhat Slav. He was a good carabiniere, a fine person, and a dog lover: in his free time, he trained Alsatians.

He and Fenoglio had attended officers' school together and they had remained friends ever since. When his old classmate had called to ask if he could use a room in his station – a large building, recently built – for something connected with a private investigation, he hadn't asked any questions.

He led them down deserted corridors to a window-less room used for records. Apart from metal shelving filled with folders, there were a desk with an ordinary looking armchair and a few wooden chairs against the wall. Fenoglio placed the code well in view on a clear surface.

Iannantuono asked him if he needed anything. He said, no, thank you, Michele, he was fine like this. Michele gave an imperceptible bow and withdrew.

"Sit down, Tonio," Pellecchia said. "They do call you Tonio, don't they?"

"No."

"What do they call you, then?"

Ruotolo didn't reply.

"I think they call you Tony. Tony Ruotolo. A nice name, like a Neapolitan singer. I can just see the posters. An evening with the great Tony Ruotolo presenting his latest autobiographical album: *Underworld Boy.*" Pellecchia burst out laughing. It was scary.

"Sit down," Fenoglio said, pushing a chair towards him. Ruotolo sat down and Fenoglio did the same. Pellecchia remained standing.

"So, do you want to tell us anything, Tony?" Pellecchia put the emphasis on the name – *Tony* – and uttered it in a tone of condescension, of fake benevolence, as if it were an insult.

"I don't know what —"

The slap was launched, neither too fast nor too slow. It described a precise, geometric trajectory, from high to low, because Pellecchia was on his feet and Ruotolo sitting. It landed full on Ruotolo's face, covering it completely, from the chin to the ear. A pianist stretching to a full octave, Fenoglio thought, unable to control the thought.

"Sorry, I couldn't help it." Then, to Fenoglio: "Maybe I ought to worry now, because this guy's a martial arts champion. What if he loses his temper?"

Ruotolo tried to stand. Pellecchia pushed him back down onto his chair.

"Stay in your seat, Ruotolo," Fenoglio said. "Do you have any idea why we're here?"

Ruotolo shook his head, avoiding his gaze. If body language were admissible as evidence, that gesture alone would be a confession.

"We hear you've been going to the cemetery quite a lot in the last few weeks. Have we been given the wrong information?"

"Is it forbidden to go to the cemetery?"

"No, of course it isn't forbidden. Maybe you'd like to tell us whose grave you went to see? Because unless I'm mistaken you come from the province of Avellino. Do you have any loved ones in the cemetery in Bari?"

Ruotolo searched for something to say, but nothing came.

"Let me ask you the question again," Pellecchia said. "Do you want to tell us anything? For example: how you kidnapped that boy, how he died, what you and your friend did with the money."

"You can't do this. You're illegally detaining an officer of the Carabinieri. You laid your hands on me. You're going to be in real trouble, I'll see to that."

Pellecchia turned to Fenoglio. "You see, chief? We have a real tough guy here. You kept saying: I'm sure that poor son of a bitch is sorry for kidnapping and murdering a ten-year-old boy. We'll just have to ask him and he'll help us, because he wants to clear his conscience. But I kept saying: no, no. Ruotolo is a tough guy. And now you see:

he said he'll make sure we get in trouble. We even laid our hands on him. Which isn't done, is it, Ruotolo? You've never lifted a finger to anybody, have you? Never touched some poor bastard of a junkie, have you?"

Before Ruotolo could even think of an answer, the next slap hit him, followed by a backhander. Both much stronger than before. The image remained motionless, suspended for a few seconds. It occurred to Fenoglio that they were hitting a carabiniere. Not stopping it, while having the power to do so, is equivalent to inflicting the blow. *The two of them* were hitting him, even if Fenoglio hadn't raised a finger.

"That's enough now," he said. "Go and smoke a cigar."

Pellecchia let out a whistle, letting the air pass through a crack between his upper incisors and his lower lip. He turned and left the room.

Fenoglio moved his chair closer to Ruotolo. The marks left by the slaps were quite visible. It crossed his mind that he would have liked to slap him, too. Not to make him talk. To vent his anger. Because this man was a carabiniere and had done what he had done.

"What are you thinking?" he said. "Do you think we're playing good cop, bad cop?" Saying this, he placed a hand on his shoulder. "You think that Pellecchia's the bad cop and I'm the good one. I know you think that, but it isn't so. He gave you a few slaps, but I'm the one who's really going to destroy you."

Ruotolo made to open his mouth; Fenoglio interrupted him before he could begin.

"Shut up and listen to me. You say we don't have a damned thing. That isn't true. We know that up until the kidnapping of the boy, you and Savicchio talked constantly on the phone; after it, for reasons you'll have to explain, almost never. We know what your standard of living was – mobile phone bills of 400,000 lire a month inclusive. You'll have to explain that. Just as you'll have to explain this strange business of the medical certificates. While you try to explain, we'll continue to investigate you. We'll question all those you've been involved with in the last few years and, as you well know, many of them aren't exactly good people. Something will come out, you can be sure of that."

He waited about ten seconds, to let the message sink in. Then he resumed:

"I want to give you an opportunity. I won't beat about the bush. We both know why you're here. As I see it, there are three possibilities. The first is this: at the end of our encounter you persist in saying that you don't know what we're talking about and therefore have no intention of cooperating. We continue the work we're already doing and maybe, I say maybe, we manage to find sufficient evidence to arrest you and have you sentenced. I'm sure you already know it, but Article 630 of the Penal Code – kidnapping – is punishable by thirty years in prison if the kidnapping results, *for whatever reason*, in the death of the person kidnapped. In other words, the sentence applies even if you didn't deliberately kill the victim. Otherwise, it's life imprisonment."

Ruotolo's face was a corpse-like grey.

"Of course, it's possible we won't find any evidence and you'll escape arrest and trial. That's the second hypothesis. In which case I think Grimaldi's friends will come after you – both of you – and they're not too bothered about legal niceties like clues, evidence, trials. Let's put it this way: as soon as word gets out that it was you who took the boy and killed him, whatever the result of these proceedings, you and your friend are dead men walking."

His words hung in the air. The room stank of ink and dusty paper. Silence emphasizes smells, for those able to perceive them.

"What's the third?" Ruotolo asked in a very low voice.

Fenoglio stood up, went and took the code and opened it. "Article 630 of the Penal Code, which I was talking about, also allows for extenuating circumstances. In particular for 'the perpetrator who, dissociating himself from his accomplices, makes an effort to prevent a criminal activity being taken any further or else in concrete terms helps the law enforcement agencies or the legal authorities in the gathering of evidence crucial to the identification or capture of said accomplices'. The meaning is clear, I don't have to explain it to you, do I?"

Ruotolo moved his head slightly: no, there was no need to explain.

Pellecchia came back in without saying anything. He leaned his back against the wall furthest from Ruotolo and remained there.

"Without dragging this out and without making precise calculations now: if you cooperate, what with the extenuating circumstances as laid down in Article 630, the general extenuating circumstances and the reduction of sentence if we go for a short-form trial, you could get away with six years. Not to mention the possibility of entering witness protection and all the rest of it. That's the way things stand, so now think about what suits you."

He, too, thought it over. He thought about the unreal silence of the station, to start with. Then about the man he had in front of him and his broken life – broken however things went. He thought about what Tonino Pellecchia had told him, about why he had wanted to be a carabiniere. Had Sergeant Antonio Ruotolo also dreamed of being a carabiniere when he was a boy because he wanted to be on the right side of the fence? The problem, it goes without saying, is that the fence is full of gaps, some so well hidden that you don't notice them until you've gone through them and found yourself somewhere else, doing something else.

"Could I have some water?" Ruotolo asked, suddenly breaking the silence.

Fenoglio turned to Pellecchia without a word. Pellecchia nodded, left the room and a few minutes later came back with a bottle of mineral water and some plastic cups.

"Can I smoke?" Ruotolo asked once he had drunk. He had got a bit of colour back into his cheeks.

"Of course." Fenoglio looked around. "There are no ashtrays, throw it in the cup."

Ruotolo took out a packet of Multifilters, took one and lit it with an expensive-looking lighter. He coughed a few times.

"Maybe it's better this way."

"Yes, it is," Fenoglio said.

"How did you do it?"

Fenoglio shrugged. What did it matter? "Tell us everything, Ruotolo. Then we'll call a lawyer and decide together what to put in the statement. If you help us, we'll help you, as far as we possibly can."

Ruotolo took a couple of drags on his cigarette and started telling his story.

# 13

They hadn't met at work, but in a disco where Ruotolo moonlighted as a bouncer.

One evening, there had been a problem with some drunken youths. Savicchio was there as a customer, with a woman.

"He helped us sort out the mess and get rid of them. Some of them managed to get away, others we collared and ID'd. I remember we were in the back of the disco, and these guys were on their knees with their faces against the wall and their hands behind their heads. Savicchio went from one to the other, taking their wallets, looking at their documents, writing down their particulars in a notebook and saying to each of them: now I know where you live. I can find you whenever I like. Then he put the documents back, took the money and put it in his pocket."

"Did any of them object?"

"Just one. He got beaten up, and his friends had to carry him out on their backs."

"Did Savicchio give you part of the money?"

"No, he kept it all for himself."

"Okay, go on."

"After finishing with these guys, we went back into the disco and had a drink in the private room – one of the owners offered Savicchio a bottle of champagne to thank him. We stayed there chatting and drinking until late, and after a while Guglielmo asked me how much I earned as a bouncer. I was getting 300,000 an evening, and he said that was loose change. He asked me if I wanted to make real money, if I considered myself a man of action. I said yes, and he told me he'd be in touch. A few days later he called me and said that if I wanted I could help him."

"Help him with what?"

"Debt collecting."

"For loan sharks?"

"We did sometimes work for loan sharks later, but that time it was for a regular businessman, someone who sold building materials. There was a customer who hadn't paid for a large supply of concrete or bricks, I can't remember which. I don't know for what reason, but this guy, the creditor, instead of going to his lawyer, had called in Savicchio. I think it was a habit."

"So what did you do?"

"We went to the guy, Savicchio talked to him, told him that if he didn't pay he might be in serious trouble and in the end, to cut a long story short, the guy paid the debt."

"Why did Savicchio involve you in this?"

"He said he needed an assistant, because of all the work he was doing. He wasn't satisfied with the ones he'd had before. I'd made a good impression on him, he thought I was reliable."

Fenoglio felt a sense of unease. For a few seconds he lost contact with his surroundings. He had the sensation he had already heard these replies and couldn't understand why. Then he realized. A similar story, almost word for word, had been told by Lopez two months earlier, talking about how he'd met Grimaldi.

"We provided an escort for transporting things of value. Sometimes they were jewels, stolen jewels. Once, even a valuable painting."

Ruotolo went back over three years of criminal activity in uniform. Fenoglio let him talk almost without interrupting him or asking him any questions. At last, they got to the kidnappings.

"One day, Mino – Savicchio – came to me and said we should get involved in something new, a way to really make a lot of easy money. I asked him what he was talking about and he asked me if I'd ever heard of lightning kidnappings. I didn't know anything about them, so he explained. They were something that had started in Cerignola, but now people were doing it around here, too. He said it could be a goldmine and we had to figure out a way to get in on it. I didn't agree. It was one thing providing an escort for transporting stolen goods, collecting debts or robbing prostitutes. This was something else entirely, a really serious thing that would involve people who had nothing to do with the underworld."

Here it was, that self-absolving tone that crops up, to a greater or lesser degree, in all confessions. I want to make it clear that I didn't mean to hurt anybody. I may have failed in my duty, but I have principles. It's one thing to rob whores, quite another to kidnap respectable people.

"Anyway, I told him that I didn't feel up to it, that it sounded like a bad idea, but he told me to let him finish. He wasn't planning to kidnap respectable people; his brilliant idea was to kidnap the relatives of underworld figures. He said: think of a drug trafficker who's just sold a consignment; he has hundreds of millions in cash. We grab his wife, we call half an hour later and we ask him for

303

a hundred million if he doesn't want to get her back dead. The guy pays immediately, nobody gets hurt, and for half a day's work we pick up two years' salary."

"Did he say how you would choose the victims?"

"Simple: they had to have easy access to dirty money. To select the people, we'd use both information we had in records and our contacts in the underworld."

"How many did you do?"

"Three in all."

"The Grimaldi boy, Angiuli, and who was the third?"

"How do you know about Angiuli?"

Fenoglio again had the impulse to slap him. "Listen to me, Ruotolo, don't concern yourself about what we know and how we found out. Just concentrate on telling us everything, from start to finish. The benefits I mentioned before are cancelled if you tell us any lies or leave anything out. Got that?"

Ruotolo nodded. He told them about the third kidnapping, which had actually been the first chronologically: they'd abducted the wife of a big loan shark and had come away with forty million.

They'd used cars – in one case a van – borrowed from dealers who were friends of Savicchio's; the number plates had been replaced with others stolen recently and were later put back.

"Tell me one thing, Tony," Pellecchia said. "Is it true you told Angiuli you were police?"

"The woman, too. It was an idea of Mino's. He said that if it came out that the kidnappers had disguised themselves as police officers, it would be even more unlikely that anybody would think it was true. But you know something?"

"What?"

"I think he liked committing a crime and saying he was police. He thought it was ... funny."

"Very funny. Now let's talk about the boy. Before anything else: how did the plan come about?"

"One day, at the beginning of May, he told me that the war going on in the city was internal to the Grimaldi clan: a small group had rebelled against the boss. Savicchio thought it was the perfect moment to kidnap Grimaldi's son. Everyone would think it was the rebel group. Grimaldi, who obviously had lots of cash, would immediately pay up to save the boy. Then he would launch a manhunt for the others and make sure they were killed, one way or another. We would be like bullfighters."

"Like bullfighters?"

"Yes, that's the kind of bullshit he comes out with. He meant we'd get into a dangerous position, the way a bullfighter does with the bull, and then get out of it unscathed, with our pockets full of money."

"But the bullfighter can also get the bull's horns up his arse," Pellecchia cut in.

"That's what I told him, the very same words," Ruotolo said. For a moment a smile escaped him. "He replied that he was starting to get pissed off, that for every idea he came up with I cast doubt on it and that maybe he'd been wrong to think I was the ideal partner for him. If I wasn't interested, I should tell him and we'd stop working together. If I wasn't interested in making two hundred million, split fifty–fifty, we could say goodbye there and then. He would find someone else."

"And you decided you were interested in two hundred million after all," Pellecchia said. "Am I right?"

Ruotolo lit a cigarette. "I was an idiot. I had a feeling it'd go wrong."

"How did you go about it?"

"He had it all planned. He knew what school the boy attended, what route he took, what time he left home and where was the best place to grab him."

"Had he found all this out for himself, or had someone else provided him with the information?"

"I don't know. He didn't tell me. There were some things he was always evasive about. He implied that he was able to find out everything he wanted, both in criminal circles, and in … ours. He used to say that working at the command unit he had access to everything. Nothing ever happened that he didn't find out about. He's a megalomaniac. But it's true, one way or another he manages to find out a whole lot of things."

"Did he ever talk about any other carabinieri or police officers who worked with him?"

"He said he'd worked with others in the past." Fenoglio avoided looking at Pellecchia. "But right now I was his only partner."

"Do you think that was true?"

Ruotolo shrugged. "Yes, I think so. We were always together. I don't see where he would have found the time … I mean, to do that kind of thing with other people, too. But then you're never sure of anything with Mino Savicchio."

"Let's get back to the Grimaldi incident," Fenoglio said.

Incident. For a moment, Fenoglio thought about the disciplined way he was respecting the rules of interrogation. The choice of words is vital to obtaining results. You have to choose expressions that are as neutral as possible – event, incident, episode, and so on – and avoid words like rape, murder, death, crime. Expressions like these, laden with emotion, remind the suspect of the seriousness of what he's done, evoke vague, fearsome consequences, reduce the chances of a confession.

"We approached the boy a few hundred yards from the school, where it was most unlikely anyone would see us. We had a BMW estate car with blacked-out windows, which as usual Savicchio had borrowed from one of his car dealer friends. We'd replaced the number plates with others that we'd stolen from a garage a little while earlier."

"Why from a garage?"

"Savicchio kept his eye on the cars in his garage – the one where he left his own car – which were never used. We'd take the plates from those, because it was more unlikely that the owners would notice the theft."

Fenoglio nodded and signalled to Ruotolo to continue.

"I was driving. Savicchio got out of the car and told the boy we were friends of his father's and that we had to take him back home because something had happened. The boy asked what it was, and Savicchio said his mother had been shot. I don't know where he got these ideas from. At that point, anyway, the boy got into the car without making a fuss."

"Were your faces uncovered?"

"We were wearing wigs and false moustaches. Savicchio sat in the back seat with the boy. When the boy realized we weren't going to his house, he started getting agitated. Savicchio gave him a couple of slaps and told him not to make any fuss, but he didn't calm down, he started yelling that his father would kill us and things like that, and Savicchio grabbed him, put a hood over his head and tied his hands and feet with plastic straps. Then we stopped and put him in the boot."

The account continued, monotonous and banal. Like almost all confessions of terrible deeds.

They went and phoned the family, still with the boy in the boot – it was spacious, there was no problem, they thought. Then they made the second and third phone calls, moving from village to village. No, there was no criterion, no particular reason for the choice of the places from which to call: the idea was just to move around at random to avoid providing any clues in a possible investigation. Once they had obtained the father's consent to the payment – they had asked for 200 million – they had to wait a few hours for the cash to be collected. So they decided to go to an abandoned quarry near Trani, where they would take the boy out and wait.

When they opened the boot, the boy didn't move. They pulled him out, took off his hood, freed his hands and tried to revive him.

"I said we had to take him to accident and emergency right away, and Savicchio told me I was crazy. He said the boy was dead, and if I wanted to go to the hospital, I might as well go straight to prison. I broke down at this point and started crying, and he slapped me to make me stop. Then he said that we had to get rid of the body immediately, without wasting another minute. We drove to the country-side near Casamassima, where there was a well, and we …"

He couldn't find the word. He didn't want to say: we threw him in, a verb that makes you think of a bag of rubbish.

"We put him in," he said at last.

"Are you sure he was dead?"

"Yes, I'm sure. There was no pulse; we held the blade of a penknife under his nostrils, but it didn't steam up even a little. We also tried pinching him to see if there was any reaction. He was dead, I swear it to you. If he hadn't been dead, I'd have taken him to hospital. But that bastard was right: if we'd gone to hospital, we wouldn't have saved the boy and we would have signed our own death sentences."

"Why the countryside near Casamassima?"

"There was no why."

"Sorry?"

"That's what Savicchio said. Let's take him to a place that has nothing to do with us, he said. They'll look for a meaning, they'll come up with every kind of hypothesis – local perverts, for example – and they'll be quite wrong because there's no meaning to discover. Like a puzzle that has no solution."

"That's what he said?"

"Yes. He's crazy about puzzles. He likes rebuses, ana-grams, he reads words backwards. I'm like the Antichrist, he says."

"Son of a bitch," Pellecchia growled.

"After putting the boy in the well, what did you do?" Fenoglio asked.

"Savicchio said we had to carry on with the ransom. Not so much for the money, but because it would help us to stall for time. If we didn't call them, anything might happen. Grimaldi might even bring in the police or the Carabinieri, who would start making searches and inquiries and might find witnesses. It could all get very dangerous. We had to make them give us the money, collect it as carefully as we could and disappear."

Ruotolo lit another cigarette, rubbed his face, looked somewhere into space between Pellecchia and Fenoglio. He moved his head as if in time to a sentence he didn't utter. His eyes were watery.

"I told him I'd had enough. He could do what he wanted, but I'd had enough. I had him drop me in the city and told him I didn't want to hear from him again, didn't want anything more to do with it. He asked me if I was planning to do anything stupid, if I was sure I wouldn't immediately start squealing. I told him I was perfectly well aware that if I squealed I was done for. I just wanted to be left alone, I'd had enough." He rubbed his eyes. "He took the money, didn't he?"

"Don't you know?" Pellecchia asked, incredulous.

"No. I mean, I assume he did, but he never told me straight out."

"Have you seen each other since that day?"

"No. We spoke on the phone a few days after it happened. He asked me if we could meet. He said he had something of mine that he needed to give back. I thought it was my share of the ransom money. I replied that I didn't feel up to meeting him. I think the reason for the phone call was to ask me if I'd been the one who'd tipped you off about the whereabouts of the boy, but he was very careful not to say anything compromising."

"It was you who made that call, wasn't it?"

"Yes. I didn't like the idea that the boy was down there and wouldn't be buried, or that he'd be found … you know, the way bodies are when a lot of time has passed."

"Have there been other phone calls since that one?"

"He's been calling me every ten days or so. He'd say he wanted to know how I was. Or he'd say something like: 'Whenever you want to come and get that thing …' and leave the sentence hanging."

"You think he meant the money?"

"I think so, although he's never mentioned it specifically. What he was really calling about was to find out if I was cracking up and if there was any risk I'd talk to someone."

"When was the last time he called you?"

"About three weeks ago. I told him not to worry, there was no problem, that if he was afraid of anything he could forget about it. I just needed to be on my own for a while."

"And what did he say?"

"That if I needed anything I just had to call him."

# 14

The captain seemed not to understand at first. Why this sudden development of the investigation – one that had come about *by chance*, Fenoglio had said – and above all, were carabinieri really involved?

Yes, sir, unfortunately yes, carabinieri are involved. Two of them. Yes, the officer decided to collaborate of his own free will – he heard the sound of his own voice as he uttered these words: a lie. No, I'd avoid bringing him here, I think it's best to keep the matter confidential for as long as possible. Also to avoid the risk of the other officer guessing something's up. Yes, we thought it was best to choose an isolated place for the encounter. I think the best thing we can do now is to take him straight to Dottoressa D'Angelo. All right, sir, I'll inform her. If you'll allow me, we need to advise the colonel, with all due respect, to exercise maximum caution. Savicchio works in the command unit; the problem is his physical proximity to the colonel's office and the ease with which he can gain access to all important reports. If you agree, I'd avoid any written communication for the moment. Of course, I'll let you know when we go to the Prosecutor's Department and you can join us there.

Fenoglio was in Marshal Iannantuono's office. Grasping how serious the matter was, Iannantuono hadn't asked any questions and had let his colleague use his office so that he could talk freely on the phone, ordering his men not to disturb him for any reason.

Once his call to the captain was over, Fenoglio sat there for a long time with his hand on the keypad of the telephone. He wasn't thinking about anything. The strangest thing, he realized later, was that he didn't feel any satisfaction about the way the investigation had developed. Only tiredness, and an autistic interest in a few small cracks on the wall in front of him. The station's new, God knows how come there are cracks, he thought just before dialling D'Angelo's number.

There were four rings at the other end. He was about to put the phone down when he heard the assistant prosecutor's voice.

"Dottoressa, hello, Fenoglio here."

"Marshal, hello."

"Are you busy?"

"Why?"

"We need to take a statement. It's rather urgent."

"Who is it?"

"One of the people responsible for the Grimaldi kidnapping. He's here with us now and wants to make a statement."

"Who is he?"

"A carabiniere," Fenoglio said.

"What?"

"It was two carabinieri."

"Where are you?"

"We can join you in an hour. With this individual."

"Does he have a lawyer?"

"I took the liberty of telling him you'd find a lawyer who was immediately available and wouldn't be anyone who's had contacts with organized crime."

"All right, I'll see to it. I'll wait for you in my office. Before starting the interview, I hope you'll tell me what happened."

They met with the captain at the entrance to the courthouse.

Fenoglio didn't know what reaction to expect from Valente. What had happened was clearly the result of an investigation that had been conducted without his knowledge, and he would be perfectly within his rights not to take it well.

"Does this sergeant really want to confess to the Grimaldi kidnapping in front of the assistant prosecutor?" the captain asked.

"Yes, sir."

"I assume it wasn't a decision he made of his own free will."

"No, sir," Fenoglio replied, undecided as to how to continue and wondering how he would answer further questions about this unorthodox investigation. But there were no further questions.

"You've done an excellent job."

"Most of the credit goes to Corporal Pellecchia," Fenoglio said, unable to decipher the captain's expression.

"Before we go up to the assistant prosecutor's office, tell me what I need to know, so that I don't look like someone who just happened to be passing." The tone was friendly, almost conspiratorial.

Fifteen minutes later, they walked into Dottoressa D'Angelo's office. The captain told her everything – omitting the parts that might have caused embarrassment to a magistrate – in a sober and concise way, as if he had been kept informed of the investigation as it developed, but without taking any credit for himself. It struck Fenoglio that he had underestimated the man.

When D'Angelo said that there was enough information to proceed with an interview, Ruotolo and the court-appointed lawyer, who had been waiting with Pellecchia in the administration office, were admitted. There followed three hours of interrogation. When this was over, D'Angelo pushed a dozen sheets of paper across the desk towards the suspect.

"Read it, and tell me if there's anything to be corrected, if there are any points where I've distorted what you said."

Ruotolo shook his head and made a gesture with his open hand. "I don't need to read it. Just give me a pen and —"

"*Please* read it. It's not a matter of trust. Check that everything corresponds to your account and your thoughts. At the end of the statement, there are the words: 'Read, confirmed and signed.' So read it, confirm it – or rectify it, if there's anything to rectify – and *then* sign." D'Angelo's tone only appeared neutral. "You read it, too, please, Avvocato," she concluded.

The two looked through the statement together, corrected a few inaccuracies in pen and finally both signed, page by page.

"When does your period of convalescence end, Ruotolo?"

"I have two more weeks, dottoressa."

"Get a new certificate from your doctor. Another month, then we'll see. Goodbye, Avvocato, thank you."

"How do we proceed now, dottoressa?" the captain asked when Ruotolo and the lawyer had left the room. D'Angelo did not reply. She looked around as if she didn't recognize her own office. She went to the window and opened it, as if seeking comfort in the noise of the traffic. She took a cigarette and lit it, leaning against the window. Outside, it was dark.

It was summer, but it didn't feel like it.

# 15

The captain's question was rhetorical. What needed to be done was clear and, from a conceptual point of view, simple: to find corroboration for Ruotolo's statement so that it could be used against Savicchio. Just as with Lopez. Without corroboration, there was no arrest and no sentence.

D'Angelo wrote a detailed and meticulous proxy requesting:

1) that they identify the car dealer who had lent the car used in the kidnapping and obtain his statement in order to verify if he confirmed the circumstances reported by Ruotolo;

2) that they obtain statements from all the inhabitants of the apartment buildings and the owners of the commercial premises in the vicinity of the place where, according to Ruotolo's account, the kidnapping had taken place;

3) that they investigate Savicchio's assets – property, motor vehicles, bank statements;

4) that they acquire both Savicchio's and Ruotolo's mobile phone records;

5) that they tap Savicchio's mobile phone, house phone and office phone and install bugs in his residence and the interior of his car.

Attached were warrants for acquiring the phone records and for the tapping and bugging. The proxy concluded with a recommendation for maximum confidentiality and a request to supply the Prosecutor's Department with the names of those law enforcement officers either involved in the investigation or with knowledge of it.

They got to work, starting with the search for eye-witnesses who could confirm Ruotolo's account of how the kidnapping had been carried out. It was immediately clear that knowing precisely where the boy had been kidnapped did not greatly change the situation recorded during the initial investigation. Or rather, it didn't change it at all. Nobody had seen anything, and many of those questioned were not even aware that such a serious incident had happened so close to their own homes.

The problem – Fenoglio told himself after two days spent pointlessly pressing entryphone buttons, going in and out of apartments of all kinds, talking to old men and young boys, petty crooks and clerical workers, housewives and prostitutes – was that there was no way of knowing anything for sure.

It might even be true that nobody had seen anything. There are many things that happen right in front of our eyes which we don't notice. Genuine tragedies or even historical events sometimes brush past us and we're totally unaware of them.

Common sense tells us that if we find ourselves in the vicinity of a dramatic incident, we can't help but notice it. That, at least, is the belief. The truth is that usually people mind their own business; that attention and perception are subjective; that the ability to catch changes in the ordinary rhythm of things depends on predisposition and opportunity. In short, it is not at all unusual for extremely important events to occur in front of everyone's eyes without anybody noticing.

Then, of course, there's the whole question of *omertà*, which depends on fear or, worse still, on the deliberate decision to mind one's own business: to act any differently causes nothing but trouble. In any case, whatever the reason, talking to all the tenants and all the shopkeepers in the block where the kidnapping had taken place added nothing to the case file.

What came out of the phone records was what they already knew – but for obvious reasons had not been able to tell the assistant prosecutor – thanks to Pellecchia's informal investigation. A small corroboration of Ruotolo's statement, but nothing more.

Savicchio's telephone conversations – both mobile and landline – were completely useless from an investigative point of view. Brief service calls, in the tone of someone who doesn't have time to waste and who anyway, out of ingrained habit, talks as if his phones are always tapped. Nor did the bugging of the apartment yield any results, other than a poor-quality recording of hours and hours of heavy metal music.

Ruotolo had said that Savicchio borrowed the cars from friends of his who were dealers. One of these had his showroom on the outskirts of Bari, near the industrial zone; about the others they knew nothing.

The carabinieri located the dealer and questioned him.

The man admitted that he knew Savicchio, that he had sold him a car years before, and had lent him others; in spite of the officers' insistence, however, he denied that any had been lent in the last few months.

He seemed genuine, Fenoglio thought. So they questioned Ruotolo again, to identify some of the other dealers who were friends of Savicchio's, but the sergeant merely confirmed what he had already said in his first statement: he knew just one dealer, he was aware there were others, but didn't know who they were.

Financial investigations, especially into bank accounts, take time. From the first inquiries it emerged that Savicchio was the owner of his own bachelor apartment, that he paid a mortgage and that the instalments were completely compatible with the salary of a marshal in the Carabinieri. It also emerged that he had two cars and a current account – the one into which his salary was paid – without any suspicious movements of money. His standard of living was certainly a little higher than that of a normal non-commissioned officer in the Carabinieri and they would have to wait for the outcome of the other financial checks – accounts and shares in every bank in the country – but after ten days in search of corroborating evidence, the Carabinieri and the assistant prosecutor had to acknowledge an unpleasant truth. Almost nothing of what Ruotolo had told them had been confirmed by the investigations.

# 16

If someone accuses you of having committed a crime with him, his statement is not enough by itself to have you arrested, let alone sentenced, even if it appears highly credible and there is no reason to suspect that it is slander. The Prosecutor's Department and the investigating body need to find corroborating evidence – in other words, evidence that confirms the validity of the co-defendant's accusations.

In the course of their meeting to take stock of the investigation, these were the things that D'Angelo told the captain and Fenoglio. Outside, stubborn, almost autumnal rain was falling.

The one concrete piece of evidence was the phone records, which had now been formally acquired. Ruotolo and Savicchio had spoken on the phone very regularly up to and including almost the whole of the first half of May. On some days there had been as many as ten calls. From 14 May, the day after the kidnapping, the phone traffic had abruptly dwindled. This was one element that confirmed Ruotolo's statement, but in itself it was not unequivocal. There might be a number of reasons why their contacts had decreased; alone, the circumstance was not sufficient to justify custody.

On this basis, D'Angelo repeated, it was completely pointless and even counterproductive to request an arrest warrant. The judge at the preliminary hearing would not grant it; and if, making a grave mistake, he did so, the appeal court would release Savicchio. At that point, the investigation would be seriously, perhaps irredeemably, compromised.

"Do you know the most annoying thing, marshal?" D'Angelo said, lighting another cigarette.

"What?"

"As things stand, Ruotolo could be found guilty of kidnapping because his own statement, in other words, his full confession, is sufficient to justify a sentence. But on that same basis, Savicchio could get away scot-free."

They were silent for a long time. D'Angelo smoked her cigarette with grim determination.

"Dottoressa, we're working on it slowly but surely. However long it takes, we'll find something."

"We can't afford to work slowly but surely. In a few days Ruotolo will have to be transferred and then suspended."

"And then everyone will know."

"Precisely. There's no way of keeping it secret. When Savicchio finds out that Ruotolo has been transferred, the first thing he'll do is get rid of any remaining evidence. Assuming there is any remaining evidence. Assuming there ever was."

Fenoglio tried to process this. In reality, there wasn't much to process: the investigation had led almost nowhere, and as soon as Savicchio found out about it, its inadequacy would be consolidated. And D'Angelo was right: he would get away scot-free. It made you want to break something.

"What if we tried sending Ruotolo to him with a wire? He provokes him in some way, catches him unawares,

Savicchio admits to some things and we have our corroborating evidence."

D'Angelo thought this over for about ten seconds. Then, even before replying, she started shaking her head, her lips pursed. "It can't be done for two opposite and convergent reasons. Firstly, Ruotolo is still a law enforcement officer until he's formally suspended. To all intents and purposes, he would be a law enforcement officer soliciting a suspect's confession illicitly and without any legal guarantees."

"But Ruotolo is also a suspect."

"Precisely, that's the second reason. He's a suspect himself, we can't force him to do anything outside the framework of another statement made in the presence of his defence lawyer. What do we do, send him to talk to Savicchio in the presence of a lawyer?"

"But what if he goes to him of his own free will? He's been released, he decides to go and talk to his accomplice to clear his conscience, manages to record some useful admissions and brings them to us. We don't find out about it until that moment, and we arrest the son of a bitch. Pardon my language."

"Oh, 'son of a bitch' seems the least we could say. How long do you think Ruotolo would last under cross-examination by a good lawyer? Who would buy the story that this was his own idea? And, above all, do you think that Savicchio would fall for it? Do you think that if Ruotolo shows up suddenly after two months of silence, he wouldn't suspect anything and would start to confess his sins word for word, blow by blow, into a microphone?"

*We could shoot him.*

Or rather, we could *have him shot*. We could spread the rumour in criminal circles so that everybody found out about it. They would deal with it, people from Grimaldi's organization who were still at large, or members of another clan. Someone. They would compete with each other. No wasting time on evidence and legal proceedings. You killed a child, this is your payment. *Bang bang*.

These thoughts crossed Fenoglio's brain as complete sentences, almost as if written down. Statements that dissolved his frustration into an idea of perfect, elementary justice. To hell with corroboration, legal guarantees, all the various taboos. To hell with them.

"Let's go and search his place," Fenoglio said, re-emerging with difficulty from that poisonous flurry of thoughts.

"You mean it's worth a try?"

"I don't know. Of course, he may have put the money anywhere, but I don't think he'll have spent it all. Obviously, he'll be very careful about what he keeps at home. But yes, it's worth a try. Maybe we'll come across something, a document that leads us to his bank accounts or a figurehead. Or maybe something that leads us to a place where he keeps something else. All right, yes, it's worth a try," he concluded with a gesture of annoyance. As sometimes happened to him in such situations, he heard his voice from a point outside him, as if it was someone else's, someone speaking nothing but bullshit. The search was pointless.

"All right," D'Angelo said.

"All right what?" Fenoglio asked, shaking his head like someone who has been woken abruptly.

"The search. Let's try it. Given that we have no other options right now. Only the financial investigations are still pending, but in that case there's no risk he'll get rid of the evidence. So let's go and see what he has at home. I'll go with you."

# 17

Article 247 of the Code of Penal Procedure is entitled "Cases and rules of searches" and provides, down to the last comma, for "legal authorities to proceed personally or arrange for the act to be carried out by law enforcement officers delegated with the same warrant".

The expression "legal authorities" indicates the totality of those who hold judicial office – not a person, therefore unable to do anything *personally*, Fenoglio had thought when he had studied the new code. Whoever had written that article had a somewhat weak knowledge of grammar and concepts. The badly written rule means that the public prosecutor or the judge – who are physical people – can proceed *personally* or can delegate the procedure to the law enforcement bodies.

In fact, magistrates almost never carry out searches personally. For many reasons, the usual practice is that these are delegated to the relevant law enforcement body, and prosecutors decide to intervene only in rare and exceptional cases. When they don't trust the law enforcement body, for example: or else, on the contrary, when they want to assume direct responsibility for a delicate operation.

The search of Savicchio's apartment and office, they all knew, had little probability of success. It was very unlikely that someone like him would keep compromising material at home or in his office. Going there personally, as D'Angelo proposed to do, meant one specific thing: if something goes wrong, if we don't find anything and the investigation leads to a dead end, as is very likely, then I'm the one responsible, not the carabinieri who are working with me.

The truth about people can be seen in the nuances of their actions. It struck Fenoglio that he had never before respected a magistrate as much.

# 18

The previous evening Pellecchia had asked Fenoglio if he could participate in the search.

"Let me come, Pietro, please."

Fenoglio shook his head.

"Please," Pellecchia repeated. "I have a score to settle with that son of a bitch. You know that, you're the only one who does."

Fenoglio shook his head again. "You can't, Tonino. Precisely because you have that score to settle. We can't allow it. It's unlikely, but what if he were to say something about … about what you did together, in the presence of the captain and the assistant prosecutor. Leave it to us."

Pellecchia had cleared his throat, as if to reply, but had remained silent. After a while, he had simply nodded quietly, pursing his lips, as if with painful but unavoidable awareness. "All right. Will you call me if you find anything? Have you got my mobile number?"

Fenoglio had said yes, he had put the number in his pocket diary and would call him immediately.

If he found anything.

A hypothesis in which, if anyone had asked him, he would have replied that he had very little belief.

*

They decided to carry out the search starting with the office and continuing with the apartment, getting Savicchio to come with them. That seemed the most effective strategy when dealing with someone like him. Hearing a knock at the door early in the morning, he would guess what was happening and, if there was anything compromising in the apartment, he would try to get rid of it. If it was drugs he could throw them in the toilet, if it was documents he could tear them up and burn them. At least there was no risk of this if they went into the apartment with him.

The colonel remembered an outside engagement that day. He would never have admitted it, but the idea that his officer – the command unit was *his* office – should be searched by a magistrate made him very uncomfortable, as if it were a kind of personal affront.

"Good morning, Savicchio," Fenoglio said, walking into the room.

Savicchio turned and was about to reply when he saw D'Angelo and Captain Valente come in immediately after Fenoglio. He almost leapt to his feet.

"Good morning, dottoressa. Sir."

"We need to conduct a search, Marshal Savicchio," D'Angelo said, handing him a copy of the warrant. He took it and looked at it for a few minutes, calmly and attentively.

"You're entitled to have a lawyer present," said D'Angelo. "Do you want to call one?"

"No, thank you, dottoressa. I'm fine, I have the greatest trust in your conduct. Besides, I've read what this warrant is based on …" He said these last words with a contrite expression and a calculated hint of indulgence.

"What do you mean?"

"Ruotolo. He was a good man, but unfortunately, because of various personal problems of his, he's been gradually losing it. He's seriously unbalanced. I'm sorry to say it, but he shouldn't be a carabiniere. We were friends, I tried to help him for years, but his situation just kept getting worse every day. He was being treated by a neurologist, did you know that? After a while, I had to break off relations with him, he kept saying stranger and stranger things, he said he'd committed sins he had to atone for, he had some kind of hallucinations. I don't like saying these things, but unfortunately it's all true. You can put it on record if you like."

D'Angelo looked him in the eyes for a long time. He returned her gaze. "All right, if you don't need a lawyer, let's start. After this, we'll move to your home."

It didn't take them long to search the office. As was to be expected, they found nothing, apart from two .38 calibre bullets at the back of a desk drawer.

"What are these?" Fenoglio asked, picking up the bullets.

"Two .38 wadcutters. I go shooting with friends at the rifle range, we do target practice."

"Do you have any guns other than your service pistol?"

"No. I use my friends' guns. Just at the range, of course."

"And how come you have these?"

Savicchio shrugged and gave a slightly mocking smile. "You know how it is, Fenoglio. When you finish shooting you always end up with something in your jacket pockets. Rather than throw them away on the street you take them to the office and leave them there, to use the next time."

"Obviously they haven't been reported." As he uttered these words, Fenoglio felt pathetic. The unreported possession of ammunition for common firearms is a minor offence, and may at most lead to a small fine. Savicchio's smile became more openly mocking. It would take a lot more than this to worry him. It was at that moment that

Fenoglio had a distinct and unpleasant sensation of futility. Savicchio was too calm. They wouldn't find anything, the investigation would grind to a halt and he would get away scot-free.

"All right, let's go to the apartment," D'Angelo said after a few minutes, when it was clear that there was nothing to look for in the office and nothing to find.

Savicchio lived in Poggiofranco. It was a neighbourhood that had been the dream of the upwardly mobile middle classes of Bari in the 1970s. A place you moved to when you were comfortably off but still insecure and needing confirmation of your social status.

The block was in a complex of four buildings around a shared garden. There was a children's playground with a slide and a small roundabout. A pretty little blonde girl was playing on the slide, gliding down, climbing back up and going down again. Gravely, methodically, almost as if performing a task she had been assigned.

Apart from the captain and Fenoglio, D'Angelo was accompanied by Grandolfo and Montemurro.

The apartment was a penthouse with a view over much of the city. It consisted of a living room, a kitchen-diner and a bedroom. Well furnished, tidy, with an expensive television, an expensive stereo (the one from which the heavy metal music had come, Fenoglio thought) and good-quality furniture. On the walls of the living room, framed posters of action movies, westerns, thrillers. There was a bookcase with an encyclopaedia, a few legal codes, and a few Book Club volumes. The overall impression was a cut above the normal lifestyle of a marshal of the Carabinieri, but not in a startling way, not enough to constitute evidence of unspecified offences.

"Is there a safe?" Fenoglio asked.

"Yes, of course," Savicchio replied.

"Can we see it?"

Savicchio went up to one of the posters: *The French Connection*, Gene Hackman aiming his .38 at someone, looking very pissed off. He took it off the nail, revealing a safe embedded in the wall. He fiddled with the knobs to dial the combination; there was the typical click of gears falling into place, and the door opened.

Inside were a million lire in 50,000-lire notes; jewels and some gold sterling coins – they were his mother's, he said; a savings account book with a few million and a couple of cheque books. Nothing significant, nothing incompatible with the normal life of a bachelor with a decent salary and no particular family expenses.

"Would you mind taking down the other posters?" Fenoglio asked, having closed the safe.

"No problem," Savicchio replied.

He took down the posters one by one: *GoodFellas*, *The Wild Bunch*, *Magnum Force*, *The Godfather*, *Escape from New York*, *A Fistful of Dollars*. By the end, the walls were bare and white, the outlines of the frames just visible. Behind these posters there was nothing.

At this point, to give the search some kind of order, they moved the mirrors and fittings in all the rooms. There were no other safes, no hiding places. So they started searching in the furniture, starting with the living room, where the most interesting discoveries were a collection of video cassettes of thrillers, westerns and action movies and another of imported porn films. Judging from the titles of the porn films and the images on the cassette boxes Savicchio seemed to have a certain predilection for games with whips, handcuffs and rubber masks.

The kitchen was typical of a bachelor who doesn't eat in very much. The refrigerator contained beer, wine, champagne, mineral water, Coca-Cola, a few yogurts, cheese and cured ham. In the pantry were boxes of crackers, packets of crisps, cartons of juice, jars of tomato sauce. In the kitchen cupboard, pots and plates that gave every indication of not being used much. Savicchio was at his ease, and it was clear that he wasn't in the least worried by this search. Nobody spoke. Fenoglio felt an unbearable sense of growing frustration and could already imagine the moment when they would leave, having filled in a pointless negative search report.

The bedroom had black, lacquered fittings, halfway between the tacky and the louche, and a large mirror on the ceiling. That and the collection of porn films told them something of the tastes of Savicchio the man, but unfortunately nothing useful about Savicchio the suspect.

They rummaged through shirts, T-shirts, underwear, socks, ties, towels, sheets and designer suits, only to discover that there was nothing hidden in them. They shifted the bed in a pointless search for trapdoors or other devices. They searched everywhere in the bathroom, where they discovered Savicchio's predilection for expensive scents, anti-wrinkle creams, body oils – generally, for the kinds of cosmetics you wouldn't expect to find in a carabiniere's bathroom. Once again, useful pointers to the man's character, but of no use at all for the investigation.

There's nothing, Fenoglio thought as Montemurro and Grandolfo flung medicines, cosmetics, scents and aftershaves back into the bathroom cabinets. There's nothing in the whole damned place. Or in the remote likelihood that there is something, it's too well hidden to find. We've screwed up with this search, and now the investigation is over. He remembered Pellecchia, who must be waiting on tenterhooks. He thought it only right to tell him immediately how things were going.

"Can I use your phone, Savicchio?"

"Of course," Savicchio said with a politeness that was excessive and tinged with sarcasm, pointing to a cordless phone on the bedside table.

Fenoglio took it, moved out onto the shadowy balcony and called. Pellecchia replied after a single ring.

"Yes?"

"Pietro here."

"What have you found?"

"Nothing."

"Shit. What's the apartment like?"

"Haven't you ever been here?"

"I've never been to his place and he's never been to mine. It may seem odd to you, but we weren't *friends*."

"The apartment is quite normal, all things considered. He has a collection of S&M porn films, money and jewellery in a safe, but nothing significant."

"No trapdoors, no secret drawers?"

"If he has them, we haven't found them."

"Cellars, letter boxes, parking spaces?"

"We're checking now, but I have to tell you something. Even if he has them, I don't think we're going to find anything. He's too calm, too sure of himself. It's almost as if he's enjoying himself."

From the other end came a long sigh of frustration. Fenoglio imagined Pellecchia half closing his eyes and trying to keep his anger at bay.

"Let me come there and have a look. Just a quick look. I might get a few ideas. If I don't, I'll leave immediately without saying a word, without causing a fuss."

Fenoglio was about to say no again, that it wasn't appropriate and that there was nothing he could do that they hadn't already done. Then something held him back. When it came down to it, Pellecchia could drop in while they were writing up the report. At that point, the risk of accidents was almost nil.

"All right, come, but promise me you won't touch anything. Have a look around and then we'll leave together. How long will it take you to get here?"

"Five minutes."

"Five minutes? Where are you?"

"At the Bar Moderno, just round the corner."

# 19

The two men greeted each other with a nod. For the first time since the search had started, Savicchio seemed uncertain as to how to behave. Up until that moment, he'd had everything under control: he had a clear sense of what was happening and didn't perceive any danger. The arrival of Pellecchia, almost at the end of everything, didn't fit into the pattern.

"Did you ask if there are cellars or parking spaces?" Pellecchia asked Fenoglio as he came into the living room.

"He says there aren't. But as soon as we're finished here we'll take a look downstairs, just to be on the safe side."

Grandolfo and Montemurro were putting the posters back. The captain had left a little while earlier. D'Angelo had told him it wasn't necessary for him to stay any longer. It was an investigative activity supervised directly by her; three carabinieri were more than enough to assist her, given that it was just a matter of drawing up and signing a report that the search had yielded nothing.

"Good morning, dottoressa," Pellecchia said.

She looked up from her paper. "Good morning, corporal. I'd been wondering how come you weren't here, too."

"I had a little problem, I came as soon as I could."

"A bit late, I fear. We're just finishing."

Pellecchia looked around, as if to get his bearings. Suddenly he froze, and stood there for a few very long moments, with his head turned to his right: he was staring at one of the posters on the wall. Then he abruptly turned away.

"Can we talk?" he said to Fenoglio, a sudden frenzy in his eyes.

"Let's go on the balcony."

"Did you look behind that poster, the one for *The Wild Bunch*?"

"We looked behind *all* the posters, the mirrors and the furniture. There's nothing. Why do you ask about that one in particular?"

Pellecchia sniffed. "It's his name."

"What?"

"*The Wild Bunch*. Italian title: *Il Mucchio selvaggio*. It's an anagram of Guglielmo Savicchio. I told you, don't you remember? The bastard's obsessed with anagrams and words read backwards."

"I remember."

"He loved the fact that the title of that fucking film was an anagram of his name, although I can't remember why."

"You think the wall's thick enough for a hiding place?"

"Yes, it's the outside wall. At a guess, I'd say it's at least a foot thick."

"We have to look behind there again," Fenoglio said, speaking slowly, articulating the words as if to compensate for the fact that his heart was beating faster.

They went back inside. There was a strange, almost metaphysical stillness about the scene. D'Angelo was sitting at the table in the living room. Savicchio was standing with his hands behind his back, looking as if he were handcuffed. Grandolfo and Montemurro were just finishing putting back the last poster, almost motionless, in a suspended gesture.

"How come you have this?" Fenoglio said, approaching the wall on which the poster for *The Wild Bunch* hung.

"I like the film. It's an original poster, I found it in a second-hand shop."

Fenoglio thought he caught a flash of fear in the man's eyes, an imperceptible crack in his voice. Maybe it was only his imagination. Or maybe not. Maybe one of those moments was about to arrive, so rare in investigations, in which a clutter of useless, chaotic material all at once starts to move in unison, like a perfect machine.

He took the poster, placed it on the sofa and started rapping with his knuckles on the wall. D'Angelo stopped writing, and the other carabinieri turned to look. Savicchio was motionless, as if petrified. After four or five blows the wall gave back a hollow noise, then another and another still, right in the centre of the space that had been occupied by the poster.

"What's in there?" D'Angelo asked.

"It sounds like a small, very well-hidden glory hole," Fenoglio replied, articulating the words clearly.

She stood up, approached, and also tried knocking. The wall again produced that distinct hollow sound.

"Bring in a pickaxe."

"What are you planning to do?" Savicchio said. The crack in his voice was unmistakable now, like spun glass about to shatter.

"I'm afraid we're going to have to damage your wall, unless there's a less violent way of seeing what's behind here."

"You can't … It's not allowed … You can't knock down a wall. Who's going to pay for the damage?"

D'Angelo stared at him for a few moments, almost as if she wanted to imprint his face in her memory in order not to forget it. When she spoke, there was something fierce and inexorable in the line of her mouth.

"Sue us."

Many things followed, one after the other, like a pre-destined series being performed in an orderly fashion. It does happen sometimes.

Fenoglio ordered Savicchio to hand over his pistol, because, as Lopez had pointed out, it's good to trust people, but better not to. Other carabinieri arrived equipped with a pickaxe, hammers and bradawls. The captain came back at the same time. A few well-aimed blows with the pickaxe demolished a plasterboard panel, revealing a small cube-shaped cavity. Inside were three bundles of soft material and a small plastic bag.

They put everything down on the table and checked with torches that there wasn't anything else in the cavity. Each of the three bundles contained a perfectly oiled pistol – a Colt .38, a 9 mm Sig Sauer and a Beretta 6.35 – along with the corresponding box of ammunition.

Savicchio was ashen and his lips had turned blue, like those of a dead man or someone who can't breathe. Which, in all probability, was exactly the case here.

Fenoglio checked the weapons to make sure they weren't loaded. Then he looked for the serial numbers, which, as expected, weren't there: they had been filed off. Illegal possession of clandestine weapons and the corresponding ammunition means automatic arrest. He recited these words mentally, as if they were secret formulas to make sense of the abrupt turn that events had taken.

The small plastic bag contained money – a lot of money – and a transparent sachet of diamonds. D'Angelo, who hadn't said a word since they had started knocking down the wall, took one of the stones between her thumb and middle finger and lifted it to the light to look at it.

"Very well cut, transparent, it must be at least two carats, maybe more," she said in an abstract tone, talking to herself. There was something innocent, almost childlike, in that gesture and in the tone of her voice. The sudden manifestation of a female trait that was unusual in her.

"I think we're going to have to rewrite the report," she said, cautiously putting back the diamond.

"How much is there?" Fenoglio asked, pointing to the money.

Savicchio shook his head, like someone who doesn't understand the language. "It's mine, my savings."

"It's certainly not mine. I'd like to meet your financial adviser. He must be good."

"Maybe it's best if we move to the station," D'Angelo said, rolling up the original report – almost complete and ready to be signed – into a ball.

"Do you have the handcuffs?" Fenoglio asked, turning to Pellecchia. The corporal looked at him as if to be sure he had understood correctly; then he nodded, slowly, and took them from a case hanging from his belt.

"Why do we need handcuffs?" Savicchio said. "We're colleagues."

Colleagues. Fenoglio articulated the word mentally, as if hearing it for the first time.

"Dottoressa, why do we need handcuffs?" Savicchio repeated, in an imploring tone that had something obscene about it.

"The procedures for arrest are the exclusive remit of the arresting officers. I can't give any instructions relating to the question, Signor Savicchio." She said this placing the emphasis on the word "signor". Signor Savicchio, not Marshal Savicchio. Not any more.

Pellecchia approached. "Put your hands behind your back," was all he said.

# 20

A few hours later, an Alfetta left the station and set off for Gaeta Military Prison. They had told Savicchio that he could choose – it was expressly allowed by the law – between that and an ordinary prison. He hadn't hesitated. In a common penitentiary – in Bari or elsewhere – it would only have been a matter of time before someone plunged a sharpened spoon handle in between his shoulder blades or cut his throat with the lid from a can of peeled tomatoes.

The assistant prosecutor, the captain and the other carabinieri who had been present at the search and the arrest had left after completing the paperwork. The seizure report stated that in a "cavity carved out of an outside wall and concealed behind a plasterboard panel, the following were found: 57,300,000 lire in banknotes of 50,000 and 100,000; 11 diamonds with an overall weight of 26 carats and an approximate value of a hundred million lire", as well as the three pistols and 150 bullets of various calibres.

Fenoglio and Pellecchia had remained alone. On the desk were the remains of a lunch of not very good sandwiches, pizza by the slice, and canned beer.

"What now?" Pellecchia asked. "Do we have enough to get him for the kidnapping, too? What did Dottoressa D'Angelo say?"

Fenoglio noticed a different tone in the way the corporal referred to the assistant prosecutor. A lot of things seemed to have changed.

"Right now, he's inside for illegal possession of unauthorized weapons. Dottoressa D'Angelo says he'll be committed for trial and there's no danger he'll get out. Apart from anything he actually did, the judges won't like the circumstances of the discovery – the hiding place, the money, the diamonds. After which – she said – we have to take stock of the evidence on the kidnapping. Or rather, the kidnappings, given that Ruotolo also talked about those other two episodes. What with the discovery of the money and the diamonds, and the mobile phone records, we may already have enough corroborating evidence to keep him in custody. Then we'll have to dig deeper, find the dealer who lent him the car and continue investigating his bank accounts. But anyway, she seemed quite confident."

Pellecchia checked if there was any beer left in any of the cans, shaking them one by one. They were all empty. He seemed to be brooding about something. "So he's not going to be out in a few months?"

"No. He's inside for possession of three unauthorized weapons, which he actually hid in a wall like a criminal on the run. For that alone he'll get at least six or seven years. Then there's the money and the precious stones, which can't be justified in any way. Let's put it this way: we can be certain he's going to be in prison for quite a while and that he'll definitely be thrown out of the Carabinieri. As far as the rest is concerned, we can take our time. Even Al Capone was nabbed for tax evasion."

"He died of syphilis in prison, I think?"

"Right."

"Sometimes I think justice is strange."

"You can say that again."

"I'm going out in the dinghy tomorrow to do some fishing."

"Good idea."

"Maybe you'd like to come with me? The dinghy, a few hours of sea and fishing, and then a nice plate of spaghetti with clams and a bottle of chilled white wine."

"Another time, maybe. On Sundays I like to take it easy. Laze around a little, go for a walk, read quietly."

"All right. What do we do now? Shall we go?"

"I'd say it's time."

They threw the remains of their lunch in the wastepaper basket. Fenoglio closed the window and they left the room.

"Pietro?"

"Yes?"

"Thank you."

# Epilogue

You achieve results you've been obsessing about for weeks, for months. It's natural you should think about relaxing, reading in peace, listening to music. Sleeping for a long time without putting the alarm clock on.

It didn't work out that way. After taking a walk, having dinner and reading for an hour, Fenoglio switched on the light and tried to get to sleep. He couldn't. He tossed and turned for at least two hours: he was hot, even though it wasn't. He pulled up the blinds to let the night air in and again tried to get to sleep. He couldn't. So he got up, switched the TV on and saw part of an old black-and-white film with William Powell and Myrna Loy. He went back to bed, switched off the light and tried once again to fall asleep. He couldn't. He lay there, wide awake, until the light of day entered with gentle determination through the half-open window.

He felt rested, even though he hadn't slept a wink all night. It was 19 July, a Sunday, and he told himself that maybe the moment had arrived to go for his first swim of the season. So he got up when the radio alarm clock showed 5.58, made himself coffee and grabbed a pair of swimming trunks and a beach towel from the summer wardrobe, trying to ignore all those things of Serena's that were still there. At 6.40 he started the car, and by 7.25 he was taking off his shoes on the very long, deserted beach at Capitolo. The sand was cool, the sea calm and transparent, the sky cornflower blue. On the foreshore, a few people were walking and some dogs were running. Nobody was swimming yet, and the horizon was dotted with motionless little boats.

Fenoglio spread the towel near the sea, undressed and looked at his own shadow, thinking, God alone knew why, that there was something both alien and friendly about it. He entered the water and walked, breathing in the breeze, looking at the schools of fish darting between his feet in perfect synchronicity. Then he dived in and swam for a long time, perhaps half an hour, perhaps more, alone, the private owner of that sea.

By the time he came out, the sun was starting to warm the air. He went and sat down on the towel and observed the beach, which was filling up: young families with small children; elderly couples, equipped with deckchairs, beach umbrellas and iceboxes; the first young men – those who hadn't spent the night in a disco – with balls, rackets and radios.

He left before the place became something else and before the July sun started to eat at his skin. He stopped in Monopoli, where he took a walk and bought a bag of freshly made, still warm mozzarellas in a dairy. He drove back to Bari along the semi-deserted road while in the other direction the cars were lining up on the way to the beaches. In a total inversion of the rhythms of the day, he arrived home when the city was silent and unpopulated. Peace.

As he ate, he watched the television news, which was full of banal items. There was nothing about the arrest of Savicchio: the press conference was scheduled for Monday morning. A good reason to keep away from the station the next day.

The sleepless night, the long swim, the two cold beers he'd had with lunch started to make themselves felt. He decided to throw himself on the bed for half an hour. Half an hour, no more than that, otherwise tonight we'll be back where we started, he said to himself, speaking out loud.

He woke up at 6.30, dazed, bathed in sweat and with that unpleasant sensation of anxiety and even of guilt that sometimes follows waking up in the afternoon. He was still lying on the bed when the phone rang. Something must have happened: they were calling from the station to ask him to go back. He was tempted not to answer. Then he cleared his throat, still thick from sleep, reached out his hand to the bedside table and picked up the receiver.

"Hello."

"Pietro ..."

He jerked upright and sat down on the edge of the bed.

"Serena." He almost hadn't recognized her voice.

"Have you seen the news on TV?"

"The news on TV?" He thought there had been a leak and that they had talked about the arrest of Savicchio and everything else on television.

But why was Serena calling him about that? And why in a voice that sounded like glass about to shatter?

"They've killed Borsellino, too."

"Borsellino? What are you talking about?"

"They blew him up along with his bodyguards, outside his mother's place."

As a child Fenoglio had often gone to the parish cinema. They had shown old films in terrible condition and, almost always, there had been an accident. The soundtrack of the film would all at once be replaced by the frantic noise of the projector jamming; the image would distort until it melted; the machine would stop and all that remained on the screen would be a large hole with burnt edges. That sequence appeared in its entirety in his head, as if from the effects of a hallucinogenic drug.

"It's hopeless," Serena murmured.

But then the projectionist would switch the light on, sort things out – he was very fast – and the film would resume. It always resumed.

"No," Fenoglio replied. "That's not true."

They talked for a long time. She told him about the exams, and her colleagues, and the children. He listened, mainly. It was the thing he did best. In the bedroom, there was quiet and semi-darkness, and their words now were light.

"Will you wait for me?" Serena asked finally.

Yes, he said, he would wait for her.

# NOTE

The article by Italo Calvino, *L'antilingua*, quoted in Act Two, Chapter 7, was first published in *Il Giorno*, 3 February 1965, then in *The Uses of Literature* (Harcourt Publishers, 1987).

The quotation in Act Three, Chapter 1, is from Carlo Emilio Gadda, *That Awful Mess on the Via Merulana* (New York Review of Books, 2006).

The quotation in Act Three, Chapter 6, is from Bertrand Russell, *Religion and Science* (Oxford University Press, 1961).

For the record, the police officers killed on 23 May 1992 with Giovanni Falcone and Francesca Morvillo in the Capaci attack were Vito Schifani, Rocco Dicillo and Antonio Montinaro. The police officers killed on 19 July 1992 with Judge Paolo Borsellino in the Via D'Amelio attack in Palermo were Agostino Catalano, Emanuela Loi, Vincenzo Li Muli, Walter Eddie Cosina and Claudio Traina.